ORCUS FLED

THE ARNATH CHRONICLES

BOOK 1

CASSIE GREUTMAN

CHAPTER ONE

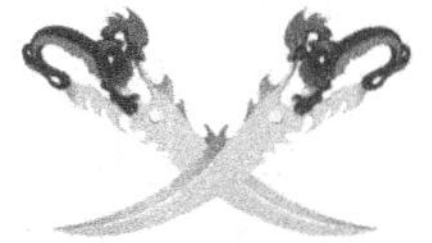

Pain. Pain woke her. The normal aches of sleeping on the frozen ground barely registered. This was a different kind of pain.

Senara clenched her eyes closed even tighter. Maybe no one would see she was awake. Maybe she could have this moment of peace before the day started, before the pain began anew.

But no. Why would she even allow herself to think that was a possibility? The sound of heavy boots stalking her way across the hard earth was enough to make her cringe. *Stop at someone else. Anyone else,* she begged whichever guard was coming in this direction. And it was a no again, of course.

"Get up, girl." The voice was low, the accent slightly different from the ones she was used to hearing. The sergeant. Most officers had their underlings do all the dirty work. Not this one. "I know you're awake," he hissed. "The men will be wanting breakfast soon. Get a move on it."

Pain exploded through her side, stars dancing on the back of her closed eyelids. The kick hadn't been a hard one, but it was well placed. Right where the beating had gone the night before. Senara rolled onto her side to protect her ribs and flung an arm out in the man's direction. He laughed and moved away from her, not bothering to be quiet while the rest of the slaves slept, but not waking any of them to help her either. Apparently she was to make the entire morning meal by herself. Good. Best not to spend time with anyone here anyway.

Once he was far enough away that she didn't have to worry about being knocked to the ground, Senara rolled to her back, biting her lip to keep a groan from escaping. Agonizingly slow, she got to her feet and picked her way toward the cooking tent through the dark. No one here could have slept through the sergeant rousing her. They were all awake, but pretending otherwise. They had the time. The sun hadn't even peeked over the horizon yet.

The rest had blankets, but she had none to worry about getting back to the quartermaster. She rubbed at her arms, trying to build up some warmth. Thanks to her big mouth and bad attitude, she hadn't been lucky enough to be allowed one the night before. Almost surprising, really. The Empire needed to be at its best tomorrow when the troops arrived at Tarsh Vannen. The sergeant was out of line. If one of the commanders found out what had been done to her, one of their most prized fighters, there would be blood. But so far no one she could appeal to had visited the Orcus.

The quartermaster was waiting for her in the food tent. He gave her a grunt and nodded toward a pot. Gruel. Again. She set to work, first going to fill the pot with water under the quartermaster's less than watchful eye. She was no threat as long as this cursed bracelet was on her arm. She sent a little shiver of magic down toward her side, just a small healing spell. The zap on her bicep made her bite her lip. It was more of a warning than a punishment, but uncomfortable none-the-less. Every morning she felt the need to test the bracelet. Every morning held the same result.

Though the amount of food she had to make was staggering, it didn't take long since all there was left was gruel and some dried fruit. The soldiers would be angry, but it would be her and the other Orcus who would get that. Orcus couldn't practice at optimal force when their nutrition was lacking, so they received anything extra while the regular troops would only get gruel.

Soon the soldiers had the other Orcus filing into the small cooking area. They came through in order of power, the first a small, old woman named Wanha. Senara carefully averted her gaze. One did not become old as an Orcus unless one was willing to do things most people would not.

Today, as cook, she would be last. She waited until the children went through and then followed, filling her plate with an extra portion of fruit. No one tried to stop her. The sergeant who had gotten rough with her the night before was new, and a fool. He should have asked around before he had chosen her to bear the brunt of his need to exert authority.

The table stayed almost impossibly quiet. With the amount of people lining the benches, it seemed out of place. No doubt everyone's thoughts were on the battle tomorrow. She forced down a piece of fruit, the pain in her side nearly causing it to come straight back up. Once she managed to get some privacy, as much as she could anyway, she would have to check and see the extent of the injury. But, for now, she had to swallow as much of this meal down as she could. If she was to survive the trek today, she would need all the energy she could muster. And, always there, in the back of her mind, was the hope that somehow, someday, she would find a way to run. The hope was fading. After years of fighting for the Empire, it was nearly extinguished. But she wouldn't see a chance come and let it pass by because she was too weak.

Senara eyed her handler, who had a seat at the next table with the rest of them. His dark eyes flashed to hers, but he went right back to his meal. He would have something to say about the beating she took, if he knew. But talk between Orcus and their handlers was forbidden, a precaution against the handlers ever seeing the Orcus as Utharians, just as they were. If she were to try to take this to him, it would just start another beating before she even had the chance to speak. And, as long as she wore the bracelet, she couldn't do any magic without his express permission. Just the thought of the control he had over her made her face heat with anger.

The soldiers at the nearby table laughed loudly at some joke shared only between them. The Orcus were not allowed to speak at meals. Heat built up in her face again, driving away the chill of the morning. What gave those men the right to live happy, while the rest of the group had to fight without a choice?

A little hand on her arm brought her attention back. Turner, a child about to see his first battle. He looked her in the eyes, the first eye contact with anyone since her beating the day before. He squeezed her arm and went back to scraping his bowl. The quartermaster noticed and brought over another slop of gruel. At least they were fed well. The leftovers would be given to the regular soldiers. If any of them were hungry enough that they would eat after an Orcus. As if the ability to control the elements was a disease they could catch.

The food disappeared quickly. No one wasted any time. Within moments the whole cooking area was torn down and loaded into carts. Once they were on their way, the speed would be ponderous, but everyone knew their duty when it came to breaking camp.

The caravan started moving all too soon. Covering twenty or so miles today would not be enjoyable with her injuries. The guard would never tell any of the Orcus anything, but she had overheard them talking yesterday, right before the beating. She had gotten disrespectful yesterday, yes, and it would have been smarter to just let the man's taunts go without answer, but even then she hadn't done enough to deserve this.

A jolt went through her and she had to react fast to keep her hand from grabbing her thigh. Another injury, one that hadn't been bothering her until they were moving. But no one would see her weakness. There were a handful of Orcus here, along with their handlers, but only a few guards. At least the fact that most of the normal soldiers feared the Orcus so much left them separated from the rest of the army, traveling on the outskirts.

She eyed the other Orcus walking beside her in perfect lines. What they could do to their handlers without these accursed bracelets. And not only the handlers, but to go after the Elite who made the laws that allowed this. Even if the Orcus couldn't use magic against their shielded handlers, there were far more ways to take care of things if needed. But the power the bracelet directed at them if they lifted a hand against a handler was devastating. She'd seen it first hand in training, when another initiate had desperately tried to escape.

Not paying attention, Senara tripped on a rock in the path.

Normally it would have been fine, but today she was slow. She fell, unable to hold back a hiss of pain as the bracelet jarred into her arm.

"Get up." The sergeant, of course. Had he been waiting for her to make a mistake today? He toed her robe. "I said, get up."

"Do we have a problem here?" Senara's eyes closed in relief. Her handler. He was not a kind man by any means, but each handler received rank and honor based on how well their Orcus did in combat. Her handler far outranked the sergeant. If he knew what had been done to her the night before, the sergeant would be the one on the ground. But there was time enough for that later.

"No problem." The sergeant turned and spat on the ground. "Other than this wench is slowing everyone down." As if anyone would have waited for her. The other Orcus flowed around her as if she wasn't there.

"Good. You know what's happening tomorrow. We need everyone in perfect shape." Her handler looked at her, his eyes cold. He gestured for her to get up but didn't lend a hand. Orcus and handlers couldn't ever touch, on pain of death. Not that it was forbidden, but the spells binding them together could not stand contact.

Senara pushed herself to her feet, wincing when something creaked inside. She would not show any sign of pain. They wouldn't risk losing an Orcus if she wasn't at full readiness, and if she missed this fight, she would lose her place in the Orcus rankings. She had fought hard for that spot, and wouldn't give it up easily.

Just as she was straightening, the twang of an arrow leaving a bow sent her straight back to the ground. A soldier beside her dropped.

A hail of arrows came after the first one, raining down on the fighters. Senara scrambled behind a boulder beside the road. Somehow the enemy must have learned they were coming and had come to take them out before they could rule the battlefield.

By the time she was in enough cover to look for her handler, he had shielded himself behind a nearby tree. He nodded to her and mouthed 'fight.'

The bracelet heated for a second, and the intense feeling of her magic returning to her flooded her body with heat and numbed all the pain she had been in. Senara jumped out from around the boulder and screamed her war cry, twirling her hand to whip wind around her, creating a shield of twisting rage.

The glint of light off a helmet on the rock-face above betrayed where one of her opponents was stationed. Sending a bolt of lightning his way with one hand, she threw up a wave of ice in front of Turner with her other. The Elite were sending kids out here far too young. But the war had been going on for years, and the Orcus were dwindling. Some day, when she went down, there may be none to take her place. The kid reminded her... no. Not going there while in the middle of a skirmish.

Turner was wise enough not to waste time acknowledging what she'd done. He sent a spray of ice shards toward the mountain. Not bad, but not very effective.

More arrows were released, and more of the less experienced Orcus fell. Senara threw another bolt of lightning in the general direction the arrows were coming from, but didn't see anything to truly aim at.

"Shield me!" Wanha yelled from somewhere to her left. Blindly, she threw up a rock wall, barreling in that direction. Wanha moved forward behind it, closed her eyes and lifted her hands. At first, nothing seemed to happen. A fistful of arrows headed toward the old woman. Senara knocked them out of the sky with a blast of air. The battle was continuing around her, but she paid no attention, focusing on keeping the ancient warrior standing.

The intense power it took to protect them both started to overwhelm her. *Whatever you're doing, old woman, hurry it up!*

As if reading her mind, the ground began to rumble. Small pebbles skittered down the face of the cliff. Screams came from above, and a body tumbled down from the heights. Well, that was one way to take care of things.

Turner yelled and she turned to look at him. He lifted his hands and threw a splattering of ice in her direction. Senara jerked around to face the trees and nearly lost her head. Two swordsmen backed up a couple of steps and started circling in opposite directions around her. The archers must have been a distraction.

Three more men ran out from among the trees, headed for Wanha, who was bent over, nearly passed out. That much magic flow always took a toll. How many swordsmen were there? This was a well-planned attack. The enemy would know they needed a large number of troops to best the Orcus Corp.

"Turner!" Senara yelled, not taking her eyes off her new adversaries. He didn't answer, and she didn't turn to see, but she pointed at Wanha. Hopefully he understood what she wanted.

One of the swordsmen lunged at her. She pulled ice from the ground and swiftly formed it into a sword, blocking his thrust. The ice chipped, not having time to fully harden. Curse the handlers for not allowing the Orcus to carry weapons except for straight before a battle.

"Don't kill her," another swordsman shouted. "That's the one!"

Another spray of ice created a dagger in her off hand. At this range, an ice attack would just break against the specially made armor the swordsmen wore. There wasn't enough room for earth to gain enough speed to penetrate either.

Senara threw the dagger, followed quickly by a burst of lightning. The dagger left a dent in his armor, but the lightning just dissipated. Whoever had sent these men had planned for everything, even thick rubber soles no doubt. The soldier kept coming. She blasted him with a gale of wind, but he dug in, only sliding backward a fraction of what she'd intended.

With her attention on his friend, the other swordsman had edged his way closer.

Senara dropped to the ground and twisted back to her feet a short distance away, only just missing a swing meant to cleave her in half. She let her ice sword go and flung a fireball at him. Nothing. Who were these men? Apparently they were warded to avoid flames.

A bloodcurdling shriek sounded behind her. A quick glance showed another Orcus going down. This was not good. These men were here for them. Knew how to fight against them, knew how to protect themselves. Even the place where they'd attacked showed meticulous planning. No real water source for the Orcus to use, not enough room to truly fight with earth or wind.

The blade of a sword shoved through one of the men from behind. A small shimmer of air told her where the blade had come from.

"Senara! Catch!" Her handler. What was he doing here? They were not to get involved at any cost. Too dangerous. If too many handlers were killed, the Orcus might find a way to free themselves. Another sword flew toward her, end over end. Senara used a small blast of air to direct its fall and caught it by the hilt. The weight was good in her hand. She allowed herself a short moment of relief at having a weapon.

Now to see how the swordsman who was left would do against an armed woman. He came at her right away, no doubt trying to keep her off guard.

It didn't work.

She parried a swing, redirecting his blade and letting it slide off hers so she didn't have to absorb as much of the impact. He swooped around and came at her again. She dodged blows, trying not to take any of the massive swings on her blade. The man was just too strong. Black dots crowded her vision and she nearly fell, using her blade to prop herself up. She wasn't going to be able to last much longer. The constant use of elemental magic was exhausting, on top of the fact that she'd started this fight already injured.

The soldier lunged forward. At the last moment he redirected his sword and slammed Senara with his shoulder. She went down, hard, her previous injuries wailing under the pain of new ones. He reached down and grabbed her hair. Her feet scrambled as he pulled her up, sword at her throat.

His first mistake was allowing her to get so close. His second was making her this mad. She reached a hand forward and touched his armor, feeling his sweat underneath and freezing it into small fragments. She closed her eyes and could feel each splinter.

The soldier shook her, but didn't seem to notice what was going on. "The General wants some of you alive. Cooperate and you could be one of them."

"Not likely," Senara said, forming the small ice crystals inside his armor into a knife and driving it into his chest. The man dropped, nicking her neck with his sword and sending warmth seeping down toward her shirt. She didn't have time to deal with that right now.

"Senara, this way, run!"

Leave? Turner was still standing. She shot a blast of wind at a swordsman headed his way. Wanha was down, but still alive. She couldn't just leave! The pull of the bracelet started, urging her to obey her handler. She resisted, nausea threatening to overwhelm her.

"Senara, we're leaving, now!"

"Turner!" she yelled, backing after her handler, Melin, enough to slow the pain the bracelet was radiating through her at her disobedience.

"He is useless. Come. Now." The handler turned and moved into the trees, obviously knowing there was no way she could fight the pull of magic. She sent a shot of lightning, followed by ice, as she backed toward the trees, trying to give Turner any chance he had to slip away. He'd been her second, once.

He was still fighting when she reached the treeline. Once Turner was out of her line of vision, she took off running after Melin.

"Defend me," Melin said.

Senara glared at him, putting all the contempt she felt on her face.

"Someone must warn the rest of the army," Melin snarled, turned and ran. She let him get a few steps ahead, until the bracelet started to heat up, and gave chase.

A man lunged from behind a tree and swung a sword at Melin. Her hand went up automatically and the soldier went down in a rain of sparks. Apparently he was not a part of the forces with special armor. Now they were getting somewhere.

Melin didn't pause to see if she brought down his attacker. He continued forward. She saved him twice more before they came to a small clearing. Melin paused, looking toward the sky. He must have seen something there to figure out which direction they were supposed to be going in, because he started forward again.

Too late. The hiss of an arrow leaving a bow and then Melin was face up on the ground, arrow quivering in his chest. Instantly any magical energy Senara had not depleted melted from her body. She collapsed, muscles in spasms, instant exhaustion nearly causing her to vomit. No, no, not now. Melin could rot for all she cared, but the bracelet blocked all contact with magic unless she had a handler. She crawled along the ground, trying to move out of sight, dragging her sword along behind her. It was her only means of defense now.

Where had the arrow come from? She needed to get away from here. She pulled herself to her feet using a tree and stumbled back toward the battle. Magic was like a drug. She could already feel a light pang of withdrawal creeping through her veins.

Something cracked to her left. Senara flung herself against a tree, fighting to slow her breathing. An enemy. No question about that. Was it the archer? There wasn't much to hide behind this time of year, the trees mostly bare, the bushes dead. Hopefully it was the one who had taken Melin down and there weren't more lurking in the shadows.

Senara moved slowly around the tree, checking the ground each step before putting her foot down, avoiding patches of snow where she would leave prints and anything that would make a noise. She gripped her side tightly. Whatever injuries the sergeant had inflicted last night were being exacerbated by all the intensity of today, especially now when she was cut off from her magic. Hopefully she hadn't broken a rib. Or anything worse.

She needed to get back to the site of the skirmish. Had to find the others, to be assigned a new handler. The fighting had to be over by now. And the Orcus had to have won, even so outnumbered. They always did. She stumbled a little, then eased herself down into a knot of roots. Rest. Only for a moment.

Something cracked, sending her heart nearly through her injured chest, the extra beats pulsing down to her injured side. No animal would be caught this close to so much death unless it was a predator of some type. Unlikely, but that meant it was another type of predator. What had the swordsman meant when he said they were to try to take some of them alive? No Orcus would ever allow themselves to be taken captive.

There. A flash of light off metal. Cursed bracelet was going to get her killed. Senara didn't even have a throwing knife, let alone a bow. One on one combat with a skilled opponent could be difficult under normal circumstances even when she was in full health. One on one combat right now would be a death sentence.

Creeping around the tree, she tried to get a better look at her stalker. Obviously he didn't know where she'd gone, or he would have come at her by now. The fact that she was wanted alive was slightly reassuring. He hadn't put her down beside Melin when he would have had no trouble doing so. The reason they wanted her alive... unknown, so not something to think about at the moment.

Nothing was in her path. That was in view, anyway. She moved forward, slipping from one tree to the next, pausing often to listen.

Finally, she reached the point where she had followed Melin into the woods such a short time ago. She stooped down, making herself as small as possible as she skirted the edge of the treeline, squinting against the white of the snow.

Nothing moved.

Senara sprinted as best she could to a boulder along the road. No sound from the other side. She peeked around the edge. There was Wanha, dead on the ground. She bit her lip to keep from cursing out loud. Wanha? Dead? The woman had seemed indestructible until this moment. In all the battles they'd fought together, she'd never seen her even in great danger before today. How had this happened?

Something moved further up the road and she darted back behind the rock. Soldiers, going through the dead bodies. Was Turner among them?

There was one man on a horse. She hadn't gotten a look at him before she'd hidden. No matter. He was moving in the other direction. A tiny thrill of excitement went through her, the first in years that wasn't caused by a fight of some kind. Her handler was dead. The rest of her Corp were dead. This was it. Her chance to leave all of it behind her. Senara held up her hand, the slight bulge on her upper arm only visible because she knew what was there. To leave would be to give up magic, forever. Unless there was a way to remove this blighted bracelet. No Orcus had ever been able to do it before. It was only a matter of days before the last escapee had come crawling back, needing the flow of magic. No matter. It would not be the same for her. She would control the urges or she would die trying.

She backed away from the giant stone toward the trees. Most of the way there, a shout rang out from the woods, and an arrow fell directly in front of her, sending her sliding to a stop. The archer! She looked down the road. Soldiers were leaving their search of the corpses and running her way.

Back to the woods? No, there was no way of knowing how many men her archer friend had with him. She sprinted down the road in the direction they had traveled from this morning, back toward Arnath. Though she was injured, she still had the advantage over the men all covered in the heavy armor meant to withstand a fight with an Orcus.

A bend in the road and then she was running back through a small pass. Rock face on one side, a sheer fall on the other. Only a few steps in, the sound of hooves ricocheted off of the rock. No, no, no! He was supposed to have gone the other way!

She ran harder, pushing herself far beyond what she would have thought herself capable of. It wasn't enough. The rider was on her in a moment. He kicked out a leg, knocking her from her feet without leaving the saddle. She didn't have time to catch herself as she fell, slamming her face into the frozen ground. He brought his giant grey horse around. It snorted, sending a puff of steam into the cold air, obviously enjoying the chase.

The man dropped to the ground and came to stand over her. Senara waited, hunched over her sword, facedown. Perhaps he would think her unconscious. She held her breath, counting his footsteps. Two more and he would be close enough. One. She swung her sword out from where she'd been hiding it, attempting to strike his legs. He leapt over it and kicked it out of her hand.

"Now, now, is that any way to treat your commanding officer?"

This was her first real look at his face. The sergeant who had beaten her the night before, now wearing the black and sky blue of the enemy. She closed her eyes and dropped her forehead to the ground for a moment. No wonder he had bashed her around the night before with no provocation.

"Traitor." Senara looked up from the ground and spat in his direction.

"To your people, yes." He smiled. "To mine I'll be a hero. We'll finally have one of the legendary Orcus to study, to wield. Even outnumbered fifty to one your people managed to nearly level the field before they were slaughtered. You were the only one we managed to take alive. I will see you bound to me, last of the Orcus."

All of them, dead? Even little Turner? This man was her enemy. She would not believe a word he said until she saw it with her own eyes. She spat in his direction again. "Never. And I am not the last. They will come for you."

He cocked his head, looking down at her. "Do you believe some of your comrades survived? Or are you referring to the children back home?"

Senara nearly recoiled, giving herself away. How did he know about the children?

His smile was sickening. "Trust me. You are the last. With no way of smuggling them out of Arnath, they were just disposed of. Never again will an Orcus stand against Trulathian."

That truly made no difference to her. Uthoria might have need of its Orcus, but it was never kind to them. There was no allegiance here. Still, there was no way she would ever serve this man. If he could be so callous about murdering children, what kinds of things would he force her to do? Years of violence may have hardened her, but not that much. She would die before she allowed herself to be bound to him.

"I apologize for the beating I gave you last night. After watching the Orcus Corp for over a month, you were the one I needed to slow down." He bent down beside her, his words not matching his cold eyes. "You were second only to the old witch, and who knows how long she would have had in this world if I hadn't run my sword through her. No, you were my best choice." He put a hand out to brush a strand of hair off her face. She slapped his hand away. He smiled and stood. "Don't worry. We will become good friends."

He put out a hand as if to help her up.

She slapped it away again.

He laughed.

"Is that any way to treat your future king? I may have brothers before me in line, but even they know it's just a matter of time. Especially when I walk into the throne room with the last Orcus bound to my side."

Future king of Trulathian? Titus, fourth in line for the throne rode a giant grey war horse. And always fought his battles personally. She clenched her hand tightly around some frozen pebbles, keeping herself in the moment. If this truly was Titus, his cruelty to his enemies was legendary.

Someone yelled back in the direction of the skirmish site. He looked that way and she kicked him in the knees with all her remaining strength. He yelled and fell over backward. Senara jumped to her feet and ran at his horse. It shied away snorting, then reared, flailing its front feet in her face. Of course a trained warhorse would let no one but its master ride.

The man struggled to his feet, unbalanced. She must have injured one of his knees. Senara took a second to slice the girth, sending the saddle crashing to the ground. The man may be able to ride without it, but he would have a hard time mounting with the injury she'd just given him.

"Stop!" he yelled. "There is no use fleeing. You will be treated well. I swear it!"

She backed away from the horse, weighing her options.

"Running is futile." Titus straightened to his full height. "I will find you. We can work as partners."

More soldiers came around the bend behind them. They must have been waiting for some type of signal. Senara spat in the prince's direction, turned and sprinted down the pass. Where could she go? What was she doing, running with no way to defend herself? Maybe it would be better to just give in. Would fighting for this man be any worse than fighting for Melin?

Yes. He had killed Turner. And the children back at home. She would not serve such a monster.

Senara pushed forward, the pounding of boots and angry shouts of the soldiers spurring her forward. She made it around another bend in the road and skidded to a stop, nearly within arms distance of a surprised looking group of men. More Trulathians. The man closest to her made a grab for her. She swung wildly out of the way and back-tracked a few steps, lifting her sword and giving the men reason to pause. The calls from behind her were closer. Much closer. The first group closed in. Nowhere to go to her left, only sheer rock face. She leaned a little to look over the edge to her right.

It wasn't a straight drop off, but straight enough she would never be able to keep her balance. Hoofbeats sounded back on the road. She turned. Titus was back on his horse and moving toward her. She could practically see the same look in his eyes as when he beat her the night before. Joy in the fact that he was inflicting pain on another. Her stomach roiled. Becoming his weapon was not an option. Senara ran at the cliff, paused, and then jumped.

CHAPTER TWO

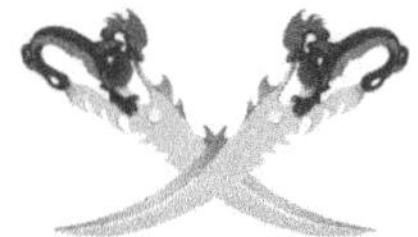

Senara ground her teeth to keep from screeching has she hurtled through the shale down, forever down, in a cloud of dust and small debris. She slid to a stop and couldn't move. Her ears ringing from the sound of falling stone, it took a moment for the voices above to filter through. She groaned. If she could still hear them, she was far too close. She rolled over and checked her sword for damage. Nothing a little time with a stone wouldn't fix.

Another groan would not be contained as she pushed herself to her feet, stumbling before being able to balance. Anything that hadn't hurt before, did now. The light mesh armor she was wearing had protected the skin that was covered, but all of the exposed flesh was now scraped and bleeding. There had to be somewhere nearby where she could hide, could lie down for an hour or so. If there wasn't, that tumble would have been for nothing, because she could not stay ahead of a whole division of soldiers feeling like this.

Wait. Somewhere near here was an old Orcus temple, from back in the days long ago when they were revered instead of enslaved. Janirus, Wanha's illegal mate had told them a few of the stories when the soldiers weren't listening. Even if the temple was abandoned and no good as a place to hide, perhaps there was something there that could remove her bracelet.

Oh, to feel the healing sweep through her body, to reconnect to the magic waiting to be stroked into submission. It had been such a short time since she was cut off, but the pull was there already, the need.

She squinted up at the sky, getting a bearing on where she was. Late morning. The major battle had already begun somewhere close. By now the generals would be screaming at their aides, trying to find the Orcus. There was not much left to find. Having an Uthorian stumble on her held little more appeal than if Titus found her. Her fate would be the same at eithers hand. She was done with that. It was time to decide her own fate.

With the new plan and new hope, Senara headed in the direction the temple should be, pushing aside the pain from the new scrapes and bruises, filing it somewhere to be acknowledged later. One thing at least her teachers in Arnath had been useful for, to teach her to work even while in mind-numbing amounts of pain.

The three mile trek to the temple took far longer than it should have. Twice she had to drop down and cover herself, hiding from soldiers. Thankfully she saw no sign of Titus, or his great warhorse.

The cold began to sink into her body like it never had before. Was the lack of magic flow affecting her, or was there an injury she hadn't felt yet, something sending her into shock? It didn't matter at the moment. The only thing that did was finding the temple. It was one of many spread throughout Uthoria. Only the oldest of the Orcus had stories from their parents of back when the Orcus were not only free, but revered.

Senara moved through the woods, looking for a landmark. The only reason this specific temple had been brought up was that they were going to be near it for this battle. Fortunately for her. The others would never see this place. A tear started down her face, freezing to her cheek. She rarely allowed herself to get close to any of the other Orcus, but their deaths still weighed heavily on her. Was she truly the last?

At least Harington wasn't here to see all of this. No doubt the boy had fought bravely before his death, just as she'd taught him. But he wasn't old enough to die. Just a child, really. He'd been hers to train, but too young to take part in a battle yet.

As if staying behind had done him any good.

Her right hand and shoulder ached from carrying her sword. She switched it to her left and flexed to regain feeling.

There, barely visible in the growing dark. A statue, covered in moss and hardly resembling a person, but manmade none-the-less. A few feet to the left was the remnant of a pedestal. This was it, the path that led to the temple. It had to be.

The ground beneath her feet felt different as she shuffled forward. Harder. She used her toe to kick at it. Pavers of some kind, under the normal forest decay. A tiny tingle of hope went through her.

It wasn't far before the remains of a building showed through the trees. Shrubs grew through cracks in the walls, grass in the courtyard. Now would be a really great time to be able to create a fireball, for light, for heat, and to keep away anything that may have claimed this as their home since the keepers of the temple were driven away by angry peasants and soldiers.

She moved past the outer wall. Inside was another large courtyard. Built to hold petitioners until an Orcus volunteered to go with them and slay a dragon or reroute a river.

The large wood door had been broken open at some point, far in the distant past. Most likely when the temples had been overrun. The second she crossed the threshold, it hit her. The feeling of magic, flowing through her, fighting the magic of the bracelet. She bit back a gasp as angry prickles ran down her arm. Could she overpower the bracelet here? If there was anywhere in the country that she could, it would be one of the temples. Real hope, the first she'd felt in awhile, warmed her. Freedom.

Focusing all her magic into her arm, she pushed, desperately hard, trying to force the bracelet to unlock. Tingling started in her side where the worst of her injuries from the beating the night before still made their presence known, even though it had done some healing during the battle earlier. She was healing. She sent a little trickle of magic in that direction and fell screaming to the floor as searing pain shot through the bracelet and throughout her body.

As soon as she stopped the pain went back to the prickling, which no longer seemed quite as bad. She stayed on the floor for a moment, breath in through her nose, breathe out through her mouth.

She wouldn't be trying that again.

After a bit she was able to stand. It wasn't nearly as painful this time. Somehow she was being healed, even without consciously doing it herself. She made her way over to the wall, picking her way over rocks and wood, looking for something that could remove the bracelet.

After moving closer to the wall, Senara could make out carvings in the dim light. Once beautiful murals chiseled over crudely with depictions of a man, an elemental by the look of the lightning coming off of him. The story went from him side by side with Aranthian soldiers and slowly changed to him killing the ones he had fought with before taking over a throne. Garanath. It had to be. He was the reason for the plight of all Orcus now. He had struck down his comrades to rule many generations ago. And not long after his death the enslavement of the Orcus began.

Senara stepped forward and ran a finger over the man. Had he known when he'd started his attack on his own people how much anguish he would cause? Not only for his generation, but generations after? He had to have known. And yet he hadn't cared. She shivered a little. It would be easy to become like him. To trust only in her power and not care about the consequences.

But now was not the time for pointless self-examination. This bracelet had to come off, one way or another.

Her grip tightened around her sword. One way, or another.

She moved along the room, following the wall. This was still just the first room, where common people were allowed to meet with Orcus and ask for help. The fact that it had been desecrated didn't mean that there wasn't anything useful here, hidden in some vault. But she was going to have to figure out something for light.

She dug around in the growing dark for a couple minutes and found an abandoned torch. She leaned her sword against the wall, tip down, and held the torch out away from her with her left hand.

This is going to hurt. She took a deep breath and started a small flame with her empty hand, letting the warmth of the fire help with the pain the bracelet instantly started sending through her body. Senara held her hand to the torch, but let out a little yelp and had to stop before it lit. Whatever magic was in this place that would allow her to use her magic even with the bracelet was not being very helpful about the consequences. But she shouldn't even be able to manage a flame at all, let alone one big enough to light a torch, so she should be grateful.

Time to try again. Soldiers prowled about outside, looking for her. She needed to find something to remove this bracelet or get out of here. Preferably both.

The torch didn't give off much light. It was probably better that way. If she'd had a choice, she wouldn't have lit one at all. Moving along the wall revealed more of the same type of carvings cut into what would have been beautiful walls. Someone, or many someones, must have been very angry to put this much time into telling their story. Her grip tightened around the torch, the slivered wood biting into her hand. At least the pain in her side was nearly gone. Some type of ambient magic that she didn't have to perform herself apparently, because the bracelet wasn't stopping it.

A few steps later and she almost stumbled over the first of the bodies. The first that she had noticed, anyway. Burned completely, in a way only an elemental could do. So the Orcus had defended the temple. Who had won? Had they fought bravely until death, or were they some of the first to wear the slave bracelets?

There was a small fighting axe lying beneath the next body. Whether the body was the one who had been wielding it or had been passed into eternity by it was hard to tell in the dark. She kicked the handle of the axe. Not her weapon of choice. She could use one, but much preferred daggers.

She held the torch low as she moved along the wall, in case something useful remained.

There, in the grip of another skeleton. A pair of daggers. This place must have been considered haunted or cursed if valuable weapons were still here, lying out in the open a century after they had fallen. Was it the magic that kept looters at bay? Hopefully that was the case, and if any soldiers did pick up her trail it would consider them the same.

The first dagger was nicely weighted, cool in her grip. She propped the torch up beside her sword against the wall and picked up its mate. The blades winked in the torchlight. Strange that the magic would preserve them and not the corpse they belonged to, but that was the only explanation for their condition.

A few slices through the air and already the grips felt nearly melded to her hands. These were not owned by some farm boy angry at the Orcus for Garanath's treachery . These must have belonged to an Orcus long ago. Senara flipped one in the air and caught it by the tip of the blade to examine the grip. A flaming dragon, his wings outspread to form the hilt.

Odd. Dragons were the symbol of Arcasina, in the south. No matter. A good blade was a good blade. She pulled the perfectly intact sheaths from the corpse and belted the daggers to her waist. A little more shuffling found a nice sheath for her sword, which she flung over her back but kept the weapon free. The blade was far inferior in quality to the daggers, but would be much more useful in a fight.

She had picked a little over halfway through the room when something clattered outside, causing her to freeze and raise her sword. She waited for a moment, straining to hear over the roaring of her heart. Animal? Soldier? Predator? A shout sounded, far in the distance, yet far too close. She upped her pace. There had to be something useful here.

Moving forward faster, she nearly missed a slight click. It was quiet, almost quiet enough she could have imagined it. She held the torch up a little higher. There, a crack in the wall. Had that been there before?

There was a grinding noise and the section of the wall with the crack slid back. More magic. It had to be good magic, right? At least good for her? So far the magic had been helpful. Doing some light healing, helping her create a flame. She had to assume this was a good thing.

Sticking the torch through the new doorway revealed a staircase going down into a deep darkness. Unnaturally chilled air rose to meet her. Surely it was safe. She leaned out over the gaping hole. Surely anything here was safe for an Orcus. She kicked a stone over the edge and listened as it bounced its way down.

"Tracks, in the snow!" A voice yelled outside somewhere. Her heart clenched. It had only been a matter of time, but she'd hoped that time would be a little farther in the future. And she would have liked to feel like she had a choice, to descend these stairs or not. But there wasn't much of a choice even if the soldiers weren't gaining on her.

All that mattered now was a way to remove the bracelet. Though it was on her upper arm, it might as well have been a set of shackles.

Senara slipped down the first two steps, catching herself against the wall. The space in the stairway was even more cramped than it had looked from above. She took a breath. The earthy scent that hit her was nearly nauseating. But at least it didn't smell of death.

Another two steps. The grinding noise started behind her. She jerked around in time to see the door start to close.

"I hear something!" A different voice from before. "Coming from inside! Come on, lets-" the door snapped closed, cutting off the man's sentence. Hopefully, they wouldn't be able to see the door from the other side. And, hopefully, it had opened for her because the magic knew she was an Orcus and it wouldn't do the same for them.

Strangely after a few more steps, the atmosphere didn't feel quite as ominous. The air grew warmer and the glow from the torch reflected off the stone walls, making the light reach farther.

It wasn't only the temperature that rose. The level of magic steadily increased as she moved further down. It had been nearly dormant before, compared to what this surge felt like, enveloping her entire body, leaving her upper arm wrapped in the bracelet the only part of her that remained cold.

What did it want? Was it friendly? So far it had felt that way. Would it help her remove her bracelet? Destroy the soldiers? Now she was truly dreaming. What did centuries old magic care for the plight of a young slave.

There. The last step. As soon as her foot hit the floor, sparks flew in the air, bouncing off the rough stone walls and sparkling across the floor. She jumped back onto the stair, dropping the torch to the floor. The sparking stopped. "What in all of Uthoria was that?" she whispered to herself. Senara craned her neck to look back up the twisting staircase, but it was too dark to see anything. The door was probably still closed.

With the torch on the floor, she couldn't see much in the room.

What was this? Was the magic against her after all? The opening door some type of trap? It didn't matter. There was nowhere else to go. She slowly stepped out onto the floor and reached down for the torch. The sparks flew down at her again, this time much stronger. She tried to scramble back up the stairs, but missed the step and nearly went down, slamming into a wall. She threw an arm up to protect her head, clutching the hilt of her sword tightly in one hand. Nothing happened.

When it registered that the sparks hitting her skin didn't cause any pain, she slowly uncovered her head and looked up. The torch was sputtering on the floor, but the sparks, falling like snow, lit the room well. There was nothing here. She stood in a small space, only a couple of strides across in both directions. A dead end. Was the tunnel unfinished? Maybe there was another secret door?

The sparks were still falling, collecting on the floor and piling up. She sloshed through them a step, nearly to the middle of the small space. They intensified, falling so fast she had to close her eyes. It didn't help much; she could still see their bright flashes through her eyelids.

Warmth lapped at her ankles, then her calves. She squinted down. The sparks were melting into a wave of light, lapping at her knees now. She had to get out. Had to get back to the stairs. Soldiers she could handle with her sword and new daggers, but this was a kind of magic she knew nothing about. She couldn't control it, especially not with the bracelet blocking her. She jerked one leg up, trying to take a step, only for it to be pulled back down. The tip of her sword had fallen into the sparks. She jerked on the hilt, but it wouldn't move. She leaned on it as she tried harder to pull her feet free.

Sweat broke out across her skin, the warmth of the room nearly gagging her now. She reached for the wall, clawing at the stone, heart nearly beating out of her chest as she fought to find something to pull herself free with.

Senara shrieked as she fell, the light consuming her until there was only darkness.

CHAPTER THREE

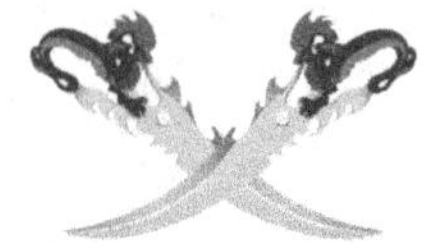

Exams, ugh. Whoever thought up these diabolical things should face some serious jail time. For real, who needed to know what a diphthong was in real life?

Meri sat back in her chair and squinted at the paper in front of her. Like that would actually help. Her gaze wandered to the window and the beautiful Florida sky. An awesome day to jet-ski or head to the lake and wakeboard. But no. She was stuck here, trying to decide between answer A and answer C. C was always supposed to be the one, right?

Normally not knowing the answer would feel like a major disaster. Right now though, she just wanted to get done. To get out of this building and get some sun. Second year English was kicking her butt, no matter how hard she studied, and she didn't like it. What did a history major with a minor in photography need it for anyway? She darkened the little circle for answer A. Someday, when she'd made some big discovery that rocked the world, she'd just turn in her research and have someone else write her articles. She was never going to get this stuff straight.

That was the last of the questions she'd left for the end. She pushed away from her table, bolted for the front and dropped her answers on her professor's desk. He nodded but hardly glanced up from the book he was reading.

She shouldered her bag and gave a little wave to Sandra. Sandra glared and went back to her test. Meri smirked. Her best friend was not going to be happy that Meri had finished first. Especially since Sandra actually was an English major.

Hey, maybe Sandra would be her go-to for publishing, once she started finding things worth publishing about.

A quick stop at her dorm room and she had her books stashed and had grabbed her exploring backpack. She kicked off her flip-flops and put on socks and boots. Today was going to be even better than jet-skiing. The campus was new enough to still be close to the swamp. Today would be the day she found signs of a panther, she could feel it. Something awesome was going to happen.

She passed by the alligator warning signs and jogged to the small canoe shack on the waterfront. It was closed, but the owner left a key for the chain of one of the canoes hidden for her. She fumbled around under the gutter until she found it and ran down to the bank. She unlocked the padlock, took the key back so she wouldn't lose it again, flipped the canoe over, throwing her backpack in the bottom, and shoved it out into the water. If she hung around too long, Tom would be there to open shop. And she really didn't want to deal with seeing her ex today.

Another quick flick of the wrist and the paddle was free too. She hopped in and used the paddle to shove off from the shore.

A few pushes of the paddle through the water and she just let the canoe glide while she grabbed her backpack and pulled out her map of the channels.

The northwest area had been a bust over the last week. Of course she didn't really expect to see a panther at midday, but she just wanted to find a good looking place to set up a camp to watch at dusk some-time. Her paper on the endangered status of different feline species would pack so much more of a punch if she had a picture to go with it.

It only took about twenty minutes to reach the new area she wanted to search. She drifted by a couple of alligators and stopped to watch them laze along. Grabbing her bag, she started to pull out her camera before deciding not to bother. There had to be two hundred pictures of gators on her SD card right now. She paused at the bank before jumping out of the canoe, just to make sure none of those gator's friends were sunning on shore.

A couple good tugs and the canoe slid fully onto shore. She took a red scarf out of her bag and tied it to a nearby tree limb, making it easier to find the canoe in case she got back late and the sun had already started to set.

Slowly she went through the cypress trees, pausing once in a while to study anything interesting. A sleepy coon, a few chipmunks, a soft-shell turtle. Nice to see, but not super exciting. She snapped a couple of pictures of each as they scampered or lumbered by. "Where are you?" she asked the elusive cat. She'd been spending all of her time out here looking, which was why the English class was giving her such a hard time. Wasting all of her study time. None of that mattered if she could just find a trace.

The park rangers in the area had been helpful with ideas, but not too keen on her coming out here by herself. It wasn't dangerous if a person paid attention, but they didn't seem to think most 19 year olds would be watching their surroundings.

Time was so fluid out here. And by the time classes were over, she didn't have much. She hoisted her pack up on her shoulder again and squinted at the sky. Plenty of light still, but that changed fast. It was probably time to head back to the canoe. She retraced her trail, downing some trailmix as she went.

Then there it was. Movement, in a thicker grove of trees. She froze. It was something fairly big. She clamped a hand over her mouth to contain the squeal of excitement and squatted down, checking quickly for snakes even in the middle of a near meltdown. Not in all the time she had spent out here had she ever seen one person. It was possible that whatever it was moving around in there was a deer, but other than that there weren't any large animals out here. Panthers weren't out during the day much, but it wasn't impossible. This could be it.

She focused her camera, using the lens to get a better view. Black. Whatever it was, it was definitely black. And moving in the other direction. Meri scooted around the copse of trees, staying as quiet as she possibly could.

There, it was almost out! But it was... walking. On two legs. She let out a huge sigh of disgust. What was someone else doing this far out? Maybe they were lost.

"Hey, need any help?" Meri called. The figured dropped out of sight. That was weird. A creepy feeling slithered down her back. Hopefully it wasn't some meth cooker or something. One more try. "You okay?"

Slowly the figure rose back up. Meri inched her way forward until she could tell it was a girl in some kind of black robe outfit. Whew. Okay, not so scary. Was there some type of cosplay going on that she hadn't heard about? A LARP group she needed to join? Not fair. It must have been an awesome party if everyone had gone to as much work as this girl had. Though it was kind of hard to tell what fandom she was aiming for. And what she was doing out here. They were probably on some epic quest or something. She had to be about melting right now, with the long sleeves. What was with all the black anyway? Maybe she was trying to be a Sith. Ohh, she totally needed to see how she'd made her lightsaber if she was.

"Are you lost?" Meri tried again.

The girl cocked her head. She narrowed her eyes at Meri for a second, making that skin crawling feeling come right back.

"Yes." Even that one word sounded odd. This girl had LARPing down, for real. Even an awesome accent.

"I have a canoe. Need a ride back to town?"

The girl looked at her a moment again, like she was calculating something. "Is there a blacksmith in your town?"

Okay, that was taking things a little too far, staying in character. "I guess?" There were horses in the area, there had to be whatever a modern day blacksmith was called around, didn't there?

"Then I will go with you." This accent totally rocked. It wasn't like any she'd ever heard before, which make it uber cool.

The girl came forward out of the trees and Meri got her first full look at her. She must have been out here for a while. She was caked in grime, strange colored grime for this part of Florida. What had she gotten into? Her hair was dyed white and when she got close enough, her eyes nearly knocked Meri down with their total awesomeness.

"Where'd you get the contacts?" Purple, but not just one color of purple, but swirls of dark and light. She absolutely had to get a pair. If she could make her student loan payment this month.

Purple Eyes just raised an eyebrow. "You have a map of this place?" she asked.

"Yes?" That wasn't supposed to come out as a question.

"Mark this spot." The girl just stared at her, like she totally just expected to be obeyed. Weird. She fished around in her backpack for a second, pulled out a pen and did exactly what she'd been ordered to do. Also weird.

"What's your name?" Meri asked. She checked her surroundings and then headed for the canoe.

"Senara."

"Nice! My name's Meri. My real name. Where did you come up with yours?"

Another raised eyebrow. She was all for staying in character, but this was kind of extreme.

"Did you lose the rest of your group? I have a radio, I can call the park to send out some rangers to look for them."

Something passed across Senara's face. Then it was gone. "I am alone."

Okay, now things were getting even more weird. She wasn't one of those girls kept in a shack or something and didn't know anything about the world, was she? That would explain the weird name and clothes. Maybe even the accent.

They walked back to the canoe in silence. Afraid to ask any more questions, Meri just kept quiet. And apparently quiet was 'Senara's' default setting.

When they reached the canoe, Meri went over and pulled her red sash loose from the branch. She turned to go back to the canoe and noticed Senara bumping the boat with her toe, an odd look on her face. Had she never seen a canoe before? That seemed unlikely. Maybe she'd never seen plastic.

That slightly freaked out feeling tried to work its way into her stomach again. Meri clamped down on it before it could take hold. "You okay?"

The other girl cocked her head, looking confused. "Yes."

She had to be close to Meri's age. At least she looked like it. But what girl her age didn't like to talk?

"Okay then. Let's get going." The canoe slid easily into the water. Meri motioned for Senara to get in first and move toward the front. She did, but really gingerly. Almost like she was stiff. Was she scared of the canoe, or was something wrong? What was she supposed to do in this situation? Maybe if she knew a little more. "So... you from around here?"

"No."

Okay. Dead end. "Are you visiting from up north?" Senara sat and Meri gave the canoe a shove, jumping into the back as it glided out onto the water.

"No."

Not from around here, but not visiting from the north. Europe maybe. That would explain the accent. A better explanation than a shack anyway. "Do you have family here?"

Senara looked over her shoulder but didn't answer. Well then. Obviously questioning wasn't going to help. They floated along in silence for a couple of minutes while Meri tried to figure out what to say.

A gator popped out of the water to their left. Senara instantly lifted a hand and pointed it in that direction while reaching toward a hilt that Meri hadn't noticed until now at her waist.

"Hey, calm down, you're rocking the canoe!" This girl was wandering the Everglades and she was this afraid of gators? That didn't seem like good planning. Senara's eye narrowed and she stared at the gator, a fierce glare that looked like it could set the poor thing on fire, water or no water.

"Do the swimming dragons not attack your vessels?"

Swimming dragons, for real? "Ahh, no. You don't have to worry about them unless you're in the water." Okay, now she was seriously starting to think this girl was one of those kidnapped people that grew up not knowing anything about the world. What other explanation could there be? She needed to get her to somebody who could help. Maybe one of her professors. And she needed to get that knife or whatever it was away from her too. If it was real, at least.

They made it back to the canoe shack in silence.

She paddled until the front end bumped the shore. Senara jumped out and struggled to tug the nose onto the sand. She seemed to be working a lot harder than she should be. Maybe there wasn't any muscle under those robes, from being locked up too long. That was a thing, right? Her face looked okay though, other than the grime.

The feeling of eyes boring into her followed her as Meri moved out of the canoe and chained it back up. She straightened and brushed the sand from her hands. Whatever was going on, this girl needed help. She should probably take her to the police station, but that just seemed wrong. Unless she was a missing person.

"Town's that way," Meri said, waving down the path that led to the school and then a housing division before turning into a road and hitting some stores.

Senara narrowed her eyes and stared at the path. "Can you show me on your map where the blacksmith shop is located?"

"I would if I could. I don't know where one is." Meri waved Senara along and started up the path. "I can ask around though, if you really want to go. Why do you need one anyway? You have a horse with a problem?"

"No horse. I just need his help repairing something."

Asking a blacksmith to repair something? Seriously, this girl was like two centuries behind.

"Like your phone or something? We can hit the electronics store."

There was the head cocking again. "What is that? Are they able to work with metal?"

Okay, so maybe she legitly needed a blacksmith. Which would be so weird. "No. You can come back to the dorm with me and I'll Google it. My phone died out in the trees. It has an awesome battery, but I forgot to charge it."

Senara stopped. "What killed this phone? One of the water dragons?"

Ummm, so maybe offering to take her to the dorm hadn't been the greatest idea. Maybe she could leave her downstairs and run up and find Sandra. Sandra would know what to do. She always did.

CHAPTER FOUR

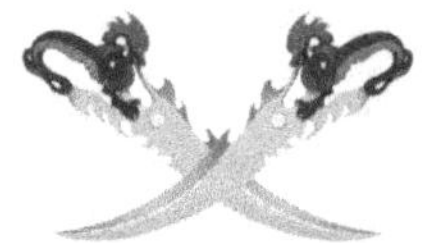

Something was not right with this girl. Her entire body was stiff, emitting an aura of fear. Not that Senara wasn't used to the fear of everyone she came in contact with, but this seemed different. The world here felt... different. In Uthoria she could feel the magic swirling around her, just out of reach, even with the bracelet cutting off access to it.

But here... here was different. The magic felt different. Fragile. Weak. It spoke in whispers to her, instead of the normal shout she had to learn to block out. A wave of nausea hit her. It wasn't the first since she'd come through the portal. The bracelet was calling her back, stronger and stronger already.

She'd lost her sword in the portal somehow. She patted her side. The daggers were still there.

Where was she? The girl was talking about something again. Senara watched her out of the corner of her eye. Why was she speaking in the Swarian dialect? Orcus were forced to study it as a formality since it was considered the language of magic, but no country actually spoke it. Many books on magic had been found in the language, but no one seemed to know its origin. Had she somehow stumbled upon a country where it was still spoken? What had happened at the temple?

The tops of some buildings began to appear over the strange moss-covered trees. Orange half circle shale of some kind. She followed Meri around a corner and her hand went straight to the hilt of one of her new daggers. Other males and females near her age streamed back and forth between large buildings. Buildings made of materials she had never seen. This had to be a school of some sort. Maybe these were their Orcus. Which meant Meri was one of them.

The girl was studying her when she glanced her way. Senara took a step back. "Do one of these know where the blacksmith is?" She had to get this bracelet off. She needed to fully heal. And the feelings the bracelet sent through her body... unpleasant at the very least. Would it get tired of trying and give up?

Unlikely.

Surely in a place where Swarian was actually spoken, even if the accent was wrong, there would be someone she could coerce into removing her bracelet. Perhaps even this girl would be able to aid her. If she spoke Swarian then she must know something about magic.

But it was best not to show the bracelet now, when someone else might see it. Everyone knew exactly what the bracelet meant. Obviously this girl hadn't figured out what she was yet, or she would be cowering in fear or asking some type of favor. It was the life of an Orcus. She didn't need that to deal with right now.

These people dressed strangely, even for Swarians. She had noticed it with the girl, Meri, but had thought it was just the girl who was different. And all of these people seemed to be the same age. How were there this many at one school? It would have been the ideal place to hide from Titus if it wasn't right beside the portal.

Where in all of Arnath was this anyway? She had always been taught that Swarian wasn't spoken anywhere, and yet here she was listening to it, trying to remember how to speak it, only a portal away from Uthoria. No one knew where the Enlightened books came from. Was it here, wherever here was? If so, they were the ones who had first crafted the bracelets. There had to be someone here who could help.

Senara followed Meri along the outside of the building. No one seemed to pay them much extra attention, even though she was dressed so differently. She tugged at her collar as they walked. This abrupt change in temperature did not suit her.

Finally Meri stopped outside one of the buildings. She pointed at a bench. "You can wait here. I'll be right back." She started toward a glass door.

"No." Senara followed right behind her. This girl was the closest thing she had to an ally right now.

Meri looked nervous for a second. Maybe she did understand what Senara was. Maybe this was a trap. Still, better to go with her than be left out here.

"I prefer to stay with you." Senara gentled her tone, trying to soothe the other girl. She really was not good at this. The gentle did not survive long among the Orcus.

Meri shrugged. "Suit yourself." She swiped a card beside the door and a lock clicked.

Magic? And why did she want her to suit herself? Were special clothes necessary here? She followed Meri up three flights of stairs made out of strange materials, passing girls going down in even stranger clothes. Surely a place like this couldn't be hidden from the rest of the world. Senara had never even heard rumors of anything like this. Where exactly had that portal taken her?

There was another door and four flights of stairs. Her mind automatically stored information on their path, in case she needed to leave without Meri. In case this was a trap. She ran a finger along the hilt of one of her daggers, reassuring herself. Even if she couldn't call on the elements right now, she was more than capable of taking care of herself.

A wave of pain worked down her arm from the bracelet.

Normally she was more than capable of taking care of herself.

They passed five doors on either side before Meri ducked into a room on the right, the door held open by a large book. Senara glanced around the room quickly to assess for threats. When none were found, she looked back down at the book. How had the artist made it so perfect, so colorful? She definitely wasn't in Uthoria. She was beginning to doubt she was anywhere in the whole of Arnath. Which could actually be a good thing. Once she found a way to get this bracelet off, she could find somewhere to start a real life. Somewhere far away from the portal she'd somehow fallen through.

"Hey, Sandra," Meri said to a girl sitting over on a bed, leaning up against a pillow. Senara had seen her in her brief look around the room, but had dismissed her as no threat.

"Hey," the girl answered, not looking up.

Meri walked over to a desk by the wall, took something out of her pocket and connected it to a small black cord. She waited a moment and then pushed on the side of it. The front lit up.

Senara leaned closer.

"Just give it a second, my phone needs to charge," Meri said.

Meri glanced back over her shoulder at her, but didn't say anything more. After waiting another moment, a painting of her with a boy came up. It wasn't a painting exactly, but she didn't know what else to call it. After pushing on the screen Meri held it up for Senara to see.

"Looks like the closest thing to a blacksmith is a farrier, and the closest one is fifty miles from here."

"A blacksmith?" The girl on the bed looked up for the first time and did a double take when she saw Senara. "What do you need a blacksmith for?"

Fifty miles? In unknown terrain? That could take days. "Is there a metalsmith of some type closer?" One that also knew something about magic. Otherwise it would be impossible to remove the bracelet. But here, the magic felt different. It was possible, not probable, but at least possible, that it was different enough that the bracelet could not resist and would allow itself to be removed.

The girls glanced at each other, then Meri went back to what she had called her phone. "Nothing comes up."

Senara leaned back against the wall. Now what? She had to find a horse. The blacksmith was the only option. A wave of dizziness hit her and she put more of her weight against the wall.

Meri noticed and took a step forward.

"Are you okay?"

Senara nodded. The portal must have taken more out of her than she had thought.

"Is this blacksmith along the waterway?" If so, fifty miles would still be long, but much easier. And it was less likely a pursuer coming through the portal could find her. If anyone but an Orcus could use the portal.

"No," Meri said, crushing that plan. The girl would be able to keep her boat then. Meri grabbed her arm and tugged her over to a chair. "Sit down, you don't look so good."

Sandra pushed herself off the bed and came over. She leaned in close. Senara shifted her gaze from one set of watchful eyes to the other. If she had been at home she would have slapped both of them for their insolence. No one got this close to an Orcus. If she was at home and she felt better. What was happening to her? She closed her eyes and after a moment the feeling passed, leaving her tired but not as dizzy. Strange.

"When's the last time you ate?" Meri's friend asked. Sandra? Yes, Sandra. She thought for a moment. How long ago had breakfast been?

"It isn't that," she said. She'd gone much longer without eating before. It was these accursed ribs, whatever was wrong with them. She put a hand to her side and let her eyes close. She needed this bracelet off so she could heal herself.

She would betray herself by asking, but she must. There must be other types of magic users that created slavery bracelets, here of all places. All Swarians had some magic, didn't they? By the time anyone found out she was an Orcus, she would be far away. "Where is the closest spell caster?" Even at home there were a few that still used the old Swarian techniques. It was one of them who had forged this bracelet. Surely someone here could remove it.

"Spellcaster? That's taking this a little too far, don't you think?" Sandra asked.

"We don't have any spellcasters here," Meri said, looking concerned.

"None in this city? And no blacksmith? How small is this place?"

"No, not the city. The world. Like, maybe there is someone who thinks they can somewhere in the world, but none that I know."

None in the world? Where was she? Another wave of dizziness hit her. She fought it for a moment and it faded. She needed to sleep. Nowhere was truly safe here, since she knew nothing about this place.

She eyed the two girls in the room. Neither of them were the type that could force themselves to hurt another, even if they wanted to. It was possible they would turn her in, but as long as they didn't figure out what she was, she didn't see that being a problem.

"May I use one of these beds?" she asked.

"Sure." Meri bustled over to the one on the left side of the room and began tossing stuff off it. "You do look tired. Use mine."

Senara nodded her thanks and stumbled over to the bed. She hardly had time to shrug her cloak off before slipping into a welcome, mind-numbingly deep, sleep.

———

Senara blinked, instantly awake. Had she had her fill of sleep, or had something woke her? Without moving her head she glanced around the room, taking everything in. It was easier to notice things now, without the dizziness. What had caused it? She'd been through far worse than the last day over the years, with far greater injuries. Both physical and... not. Other than Turner. Her stomach rolled. Best not to think about that. Or Harington. He was only a boy. The only one of her seconds that she'd allowed to worm their way into her feelings. If she ever ran into Titus again when she regained access to her power...

She squinted at the light in the room. It was completely different than when she'd fallen asleep.

"Ah, you're awake!" Meri said. How did she always sound so cheery? It was getting annoying, and they had barely known each other a day. "I was starting to think I needed to call 911! You slept all night. But you looked okay, so I didn't know what to do. Maybe you were just really tired? I thought maybe you'd be hungry when you got up, so I grabbed you a granola bar." She stood up from behind the desk she'd been seated at and brought something over, holding it out toward Senara

Senara sat up, took it and eyed it warily. This was food? It was so... hard. She lifted it toward her nose. The bracelet buzzed and she closed her eyes to keep from vomiting. Sleeping hadn't helped.

"It's good, I promise," Meri said. She must have misunderstood Senara's grimace.

Good was relative. It couldn't be worse than other things she'd eaten in her life. Senara put it to her mouth.

"Not like that!" Meri said loudly. "You have to open it first!" She snatched it back and demonstrated, pulling a brightly colored layer off and leaving a bar of some kind behind. She passed it back to Senara, who took a cautious bite. Not too bad, especially as hungry as she was.

It was devoured in a few seconds. "Do you have more?"

Meri grinned and walked back to the desk. She tossed another to Senara, who peeled it this time. She was in the middle of her third when Sandra came crashing through the door, sending Senara's hand to the dagger hidden in her clothing.

"She's up!" Sandra said, stating the obvious. Were all Swarians this chatty?

"Yep, and eating," Meri answered.

"Great. Is there somewhere we can take you now?" Sandra asked expectantly. "Having you here overnight was bad enough, we don't want to prolong this, whatever it is. We'll help you get wherever you want to go."

"Sandra!" Meri sounded offended. "We can't just kick her out. She said she doesn't have anywhere to go."

"But she can't stay here, not without us informing the hall monitor or we'll all be in trouble. We could be in trouble just for letting her stay here last night." She walked over and collapsed on her bed. "I'm not getting kicked out of school for flouting the rules. I worked too hard to get in here."

"It's fine, we aren't going to get in trouble. Lots of people have friends spend the night." Meri turned to Senara. "We'll need you to register if you're staying any longer though. We can tell them you're from back home or something."

Registering meant being on record. Even under an assumed name that could turn out badly. But this friend of Meri's might not keep quiet if she didn't cooperate. She would have to run the risk of using an alias. "As you wish. What do I need to do?"

"It's really easy," Meri said. "You just need your license."

License? License for what?

Meri must have seen her blank expression. "Your driver's license?"

Senara just shook her head, forcing her face to remain motionless as the bracelet went crazy against her arm. Meri heaved a big sigh. "We can't do it without a license, Sandra. It's just for a couple days until she figures out what she's doing." Meri turned toward her. "You'll have to hide all the time. We aren't really supposed to have guests stay here without permission." She wrinkled her nose. "And you may want to take a shower."

That was typical of any school. At hers no one was allowed to visit, even family. But that seemed to be an extreme. "I could leave today if I could find someone to help me with this accursed bracelet," she muttered under her breath.

Meri cocked her head. "What bracelet? Why do you need it off so bad? Is that why you wanted to see a blacksmith?"

So far Meri had seemed nothing but kind and helpful. So of course, she could not be trusted. No one was truly like that. She had an ulterior motive or she was observing. But she would have to take yet another chance with the girl. She had to get rid of the bracelet. A wave of dizziness hit her. That had only started happening since she'd been cut off from magic, when her handler was killed. The bracelet was trying to make her return to Uthoria so a new handler could be chosen. She would die before doing that.

"I'll only show her," Senara said, nodding toward Meri. She trusted her only slightly more than Sandra, but there was no need for both of them to be here.

Sandra stared at Meri for a second, who shrugged. Then Sandra shot daggers out of her eyes at Senara. "I'll be right outside the door if you need me." She walked out slowly, shutting the door behind her.

"She's just being dramatic. She's an English major," Meri said, like that explained everything. "She can't be that worried, she left us alone up here while you slept."

"If I show you, you swear to never speak of it with anyone?" Senara said, ignoring the girl's rambling. "Swear."

Meri let out a nervous giggle, causing Senara to roll her eyes.

"Fine, fine, I swear!" she said, holding up three fingers like that meant something.

The girl would know. As soon as Senara showed her the bracelet, she would put it all together. Then the truth would come out. If Meri truly wished to help her, or if she would have to kill her and Sandra, right here in the room they shared.

———

Senara reached to her left sleeve and shoved the odd material up to her shoulder, twisting it a little so it would stay there. Meri moved forward and grabbed her hand so she could turn her arm toward the light. Senara squirmed a little at her touch, but tolerated it.

The bracelet was the strangest thing she'd ever seen. It obviously wasn't modern, but neither did it resemble anything she'd covered in class. Even the metal was weird, nothing she recognized right off. Not that she knew much about metal. It was thick and twisted, almost braided. She poked it. It was warm from the other girl's body heat. Meri pulled the older girl's hand to her to get a closer look. Senara made a move as if to pull away, but Meri just pulled back. When the girl finally relaxed, Meri bent over her arm. She tried to twist the bracelet on her arm, but was met with resistance.

"It can't do that," Senara said. Her accent still sounded strange. But Meri was getting used to it.

Meri bent back down and used the light on her phone to brighten the area of Senara's bicep beneath the bracelet. Her stomach flipped, nausea flooding her throat. The bracelet had several small spikes that were embedded into the girl's flesh, like she'd grown around them since she was small. "Who did this to you?" Meri demanded.

Senara raised an eyebrow but didn't answer.

"We're going to the cops." And she wasn't taking a no for an answer. And back to thinking Senara had been held in a basement or something for years and was slightly crazy.

"What will we find at the cops?" Senara asked.

Meri blinked a few times, trying to figure out what she meant. "Oh! The cops. You know, police?" Senara didn't look like she knew. "The ones who put bad guys in cells and help people who can't help themselves?"

She crossed her arms in front of her chest. "I am to believe that your guard can be trusted?"

As in the cops wouldn't hurt her? "Well there are some dirty cops, but it's really rare no matter what the movies say."

She tilted her head, reminding Meri of a puppy trying to figure something out.

"What's a movie?"

"Wow, you must have been in something deeper than a basement."

"I just want it off."

The only thing that betrayed how Senara felt about this was a slight twitch of her eye. How long had she had this thing on? Long enough to not be freaking out about it anymore.

"I totally get you wanting it off. Of course you do. I just don't know how to go about doing that without some outside help."

Sen reached under her and pulled something out in one fluid motion. Meri dropped her hand and stepped back, out of range of the brightly winking dagger.

"Use this. Pry the barbs out and try to break them off."

Meri hesitantly took the dagger from her hand. Did she have any idea how bad this was going to hurt? She had to, but she didn't seem to care. She was obviously desperate. Who wouldn't be? Senara extended her arm and Meri took a deep breath, trying to steady her hand.

"You've never tried this before?" she asked.

"No. I was always being watched."

She would get this bracelet off and then they were going to the police. They were going to find whatever sicko had done this. There might be other people there. "You sure?" she asked. "We could have this done at a hospital. It won't hurt nearly as bad."

Senara grunted but didn't answer.

Meri sighed and slid the tip of the blade between the bracelet and Senara's skin, wiggling it gently to try to loosen its hold. No luck. She dug around for a moment, pushing and prodding. Blood seeped from the area where the barbs connected before she'd nearly had enough.

"This isn't helping," Meri grunted as she pried at the bracelet. Tears welled up in her eyes at the pain she must be causing Senara. The only sign of how much it was hurting her was the sheen of sweat on her forehead and the ashen look of her skin. The bracelet was terrible. They had to find some kind of professional to take it off.

"Then give it to me." Senara grabbed her intricate knife away from Meri. She took a deep breath and before Meri could decide what she was about to do, hacked at her arm.

"No!" Meri shouted. A blast of light fizzled around the knife, growing in intensity. Meri barely got a glance of the knife flying end over end before she had to close her eyes or be blinded. She forced her eyes open after a second and grabbed Senara's hand, hardly able to see past the spots blinking across her vision. "What's wrong with you?" she yelled.

Sandra burst into the room. "What's going on?"

"It has to come off," Senara said, voice dazed.

"Not like that!" Meri jerked Senara's hand over and studied her arm. Nothing. Not even a mark. "What just happened?"

"That's what I want to know!" Sandra yelled.

"I thought that perhaps the spell would not work here. I was wrong." Senara wouldn't look at her. Just stared at the wall. What had driven her to such lengths that she would be willing to cut off her own arm? And what had stopped her? Maybe there was something to this whole magic and spell thing. She checked Senara's arm again. Nothing at all. No injury. Magic? Like, for real? Because it had totally looked like the knife had touched her arm. Maybe there was just some type of electrical mechanism in the bracelet, like a Taser. Yeah, right. But still a better explanation than magic.

"What did you do?" Sandra asked.

"Nothing," Senara muttered.

"I told you, we have to take you in to get it off. A doctor will be able to help."

Sandra started to move forward, but Meri waved her off. It wouldn't be good to make Senara feel crowded right now. While Senara had her head down, Meri gestured toward the knife, stuck deep in the wall. Sandra's eyes went wide and she took a step back.

"I was a fool to think it could be removed, even here, without the

Crafter." Sen continued staring off into space, speaking in a monotone. "I have to go back."

"Go back? Are you crazy? Whoever did this to you obviously is. You can't go back."

Senara looked at her then, and it was the most intimidating look Meri had ever been on the receiving end of. "I will go back. And they will remove the bracelet. I'll make them."

She obviously wasn't thinking straight. Who would be, after everything she'd been through. "Well I'm going with you." She'd go, get the coordinates, take pictures, then call 911. There was no way she'd be able to stop Senara if she tried to go back, and no way she was going to break her trust by calling the cops on her.

"Going with her?" Sandra squeaked.

"Ha," Senara said, looking away again. "Why would you come with me? You wouldn't last a day."

She wouldn't need to. It wouldn't be a day and she wasn't going to get caught. If whoever did this was hiding out in the swamp where she'd found Senara, she'd be perfectly fine. She knew all about surviving out there. And if it was something magical... nope. Not going there.

"I'm in, Sen. If you want to leave without me you'll have to tie me up." The look that flashed through her eyes was, admittedly, somewhat freaky, like tying her up would be too much work. But she seriously needed help. Sen pushed up off the bed and moved stiffly toward her knife, wiggling it until it slid out of the wall. What was wrong with her? She moved all weird. If she had an injury and ended up dying alone in the swamp, Meri would never forgive herself. "Plus, you'll never find your way back to where I found you without me."

Sen paused. Apparently that had caught her attention. "My name is Senara."

Meri glanced down at her watch. "It's 7 o'clock. Early on a Saturday. No one will be around. Give me a minute to throw some stuff together. Sen."

Senara looked like she wanted to say something, but didn't.

"What is it?" Sandra asked.

"Got any more of those granola bars?"

It took about fifteen minutes to pack her stuff. What did one take on a crazy person stakeout? And was the crazy person Sen, or whoever had done this stuff to her? Or both? Both, probably. Even in a deep sleep during the night, the girl was slightly scary. But she needed help and didn't trust anyone. The least Meri could do would be to go and get some evidence before going to the cops. They probably wouldn't believe her right now anyway because they wouldn't be able to just take Sen's word that something weird was going on, and Sen probably wouldn't even speak to them if given the chance.

She double and triple checked her bag. Camera, check. Four batteries, just in case, check. Phone fully charged, extra charger packed, check. Venom kit, flashlight, always packed.

The door behind her creaked open, making her jump a little. She laughed quietly. So nervous in her own room. Sandra shoved the door open a little more and maneuvered through with a tray of food. Meri gestured toward the tiny counter opposite the beds.

"Score, Sandra brought breakfast. Real food, instead of just granola bars."

Sen sat up on the bed, moving stiffly. Okay, the bed admittedly wasn't the most comfortable thing ever, but that seemed extreme.

Sandra took one of the plates off the tray and held it out to her. She nodded her thanks and started eating without comment.

"So, you still planning on just going back without calling the cops? Because I still think calling the cops is the best plan. By a lot, like, seriously the best plan," Sandra said.

No comment from the weird girl sitting on the bed. Okay, no, apparently still no cops. Without warning, Sen started to gag.

"Oh no, no, no, not in our room!" Sandra yelled. She grabbed a plastic bag and dumped the contents, shoving it toward Sen.

Sen grabbed it just in time, vomiting in the bag. She laid her head down on her knees, silent. Okay, so weird seeing someone be this quiet about being sick.

"Are you okay?" Meri moved forward and hesitated, exchanging looks with Sandra and then putting a hand out to rub her back. Sen gave her a slight scowl, but it was nothing compared to some of the other looks she'd gotten from the girl. "What's wrong? Don't like to food?"

She dropped her head back down. "It isn't the food. The food was good."

Meri and Sandra exchanged a glance, waiting for her to continue. She didn't.

"So, it's because..." Meri said.

"Because my essence is no longer connected. I have to go back."

Another look passed between Sandra and Meri. "What does that mean, Sen? Your essence?"

"It means that the longer I stay here, disconnected, the sicker I will become." She stood, only wobbling a little, and straightened. "Thank you for your hospitality. It will be remembered." And then she started for the door.

"Just like that? I said I was going with you!"

"I'm going too," Sandra said.

Sen's face tightened, but she gestured toward the door as if to say lead the way.

Right now she was really wishing she had a gun or something. Even Sen's ornate knife. Going out into the swamp to try to get evidence on a crazy person was in and of itself, crazy. But she had to. She couldn't leave Sen to face this on her own.

———

"Here. This is where we met." Thankfully, Senara had thought to have her mark it, or Meri would never had been able to tell this section of the swamp apart from any other, even with all the exploring she did almost daily.

Senara glanced around and started into the trees without a word.

Meri sighed and followed. "I'm not sure what we're after back here." Senara didn't answer. "Did you live back here?"

"No. I have to find someone to take the bracelet off."

"You said that, but I don't think this is the place to find your black-smith or whatever," Sandra called from way behind. She'd stopped to try to get mud off her fancy boots and Sen hadn't waited. Meri was kind of tired of hearing Sandra freak out about seeing a gator every five minutes anyway. Northerners.

Senara ignored her and kept going. Meri followed after her and Sandra jogged to catch up.

After walking a short distance, Sen stopped. "Here. The portal is waiting. Farewell."

"Wait!" Meri grabbed her arm. She dropped it when the girl glared. "You never said anything about a portal. Portal to where? I don't see anything that looks like a portal."

Sen gestured at a denser clump of brush.

Sandra sighed and rolled her eyes, marching over to where Sen had pointed and walking through. Nothing happened. Should she be relieved or disappointed? Relieved, obviously. But disappointed seemed appropriate too.

"It won't work for you," Senara said. "Not from this side anyway. I assume it would allow you to return."

"Of course it won't, because it isn't real," Sandra answered. She jumped back and forth through the admittedly strange looking knot of trees and moss. "See?"

Meri could feel the disdain drifting off Senara, but the girl didn't even roll her eyes. What kind of teen was this? Or early twenties, or whatever.

"Do we really have to watch this?" Senara asked her.

Another world? Almost impossible to believe. But it was the most logical answer now that she was getting to know Senara a little bit. As much as Senara was allowing her to anyway. There was no other way to explain what had happened when she had tried to cut her own arm off. She was insane, she was playing them for some reason, or she was right. She didn't seem insane, or like the type to run a joke like this.

"Don't follow me. You won't like where I am from. You won't survive." With that grim announcement, Sen took a step and disappeared.

No way. Absolutely no way. Maybe they were on some Punked show or something. Her gaze swung to Sandra. Her wild expression no doubt mirrored her own. No way.

"Now what?" Sandra squeaked out.

Seriously, now what? If this place was as bad as Sen seemed to think, it didn't really sound like somewhere she wanted to go. But she didn't really want Sen going there alone either. And there would probably never be as big a discovery as this, like, ever. Even aliens. People were looking for aliens. They weren't looking for portals. Even if she just stepped through, grabbed something that wasn't from here and went back, something that could prove she'd left Earth, she could be a millionaire, have school paid for, whatever she wanted. Book deals, maybe a movie. All the funding she could ever dream of for the Everglades projects she wanted to start. Hey, she might even be able to do something for the ocean.

Decision made. "I'm going through."

"What?" Sandra squawked.

"You tried it and it didn't work for you. We don't have to time to weigh the pros and cons."

"But-" Sandra started to say, but Meri ignored her and ran at the portal. What if it closed since she'd waited to decide what to do? She hit it at a full out run. Instantly her forward momentum slowed, the air grabbing her and trying to drag her back. She swam forward, movements sluggish, time slow. Then she broke free, slamming into a stone wall of some kind in the pitch black of night or cave.

The dark was deep enough to make her shiver all the way down to her bones. She blinked several times, trying to help her eyes adjust from the bright Florida sunshine and climbed to her feet, wincing. Was she underground, or was it a different time of day here? She grabbed her upper arms and slid her hands up and down, trying not to hyperventilate. Maybe this hadn't been a great idea.

Something flashed and she was hit from behind, nearly knocked over again.

"Oomph!" someone yelled.

"Sandra?"

"Yes, where are we?"

"Uh, I guess I don't really know. Sen?" No answer. Where was she? After that flash her eyes were trying to adjust again, nearly back to where they had been when she'd first come through. "Sen, where are we?" Shoot. Where was she?

"Senara?" Sandra yelled.

"Shhh!" Sen hissed from somewhere above them. "We don't know who, or what is here. You want to get us all killed? I told you not to come."

Meri clamped a hand over her own mouth. What had she gotten herself into? It was okay, she didn't have to stay long. Help Sen, grab something, go back. But seriously, did she really want to go back? What chance did she have of the portal opening for her if she went home and then changed her mind? Probably none. Speaking of, the portal went both ways, right? It had to; somehow Sen had gotten to Florida.

Oh crap, what if it didn't?

Keep it together, Meri. Keep it together.

The deep dark finally began to have different shades of greys and blacks. Her eyes were adjusting. There, on the other side of the tiny room. A set of stairs. That explained why Senara's voice had sounded like it was coming from above them.

"Should we follow her?" Sandra asked.

Meri shrugged and then realized Sandra probably couldn't see her. "We don't really have much of an option, do we?"

She pulled her backpack around where she could get inside and pulled her camera out.

"Shhh!" Sen growled from above, much louder than the last time. She must be getting mad. At least she was still there and hadn't left them.

Meri patted the wall, moving along until her hand hit air. The stairway, hopefully. She started up. A squeak escaped when a hand grabbed onto her shirt from behind. Sandra, trying not to get separated. At least she hoped so. There weren't any zombies here, right? She hadn't thought to ask.

"I can't believe this is happening," Sandra muttered behind her. She couldn't agree more. A slight, nearly non-existent possibility still hovered in the back of her mind that this was all a prank of some kind. But that would be pretty hard to pull off. She'd know in a minute, as soon as she made it up these stupid stairs.

The stairs were uneven, crumbling slightly underfoot. Light filtered down from a doorway at the top. She slipped for the fourth time and Sandra grunted behind her as she kicked her in the shin. "Sorry," she whispered.

Finally, almost there. She braced herself on the wall and climbed the final three steps, pushing through into a chamber of some kind. Okay, way too extreme for a prank, even from the guys in the art department at school. She shivered. And no amount of A/C could make it this cold.

This had to be the real thing. The room around her was old, super old. Carvings covered the walls. Debris littered the floor. Part of the ceiling was gone, which was where the light was coming from. It had to be at least a century old. She moved forward to one of the carvings, chipped into the rock over a beautiful mural, defiling it. A man with a strange light around him stood over a mound of corpses. She snapped a picture.

"Sick," Sandra said, leaning in beside her.

"Yeah," she agreed. She stepped back and something cracked underfoot. She froze, looking down. A skeleton.

She clamped a hand over her mouth again and jumped back, stumbling into the mural.

"Why are you afraid?" Sen half whispered from behind a column, nearly sending Meri jumping even higher. "He's long dead."

"Yes, I can see that," she whispered back. "But how?" She took a quick picture.

Sen watched her take the picture curiously, then shrugged. Meri got the feeling she wasn't being completely honest.

"I can't stay here. It's a dangerous place. You two can do as you wish." And just like that Senara was gone.

"C'mon, Sandra!" Meri called as quietly as she could and took off after her. They moved quickly through another room, this one even bigger than the last.

"What's the plan, Sen?" Meri asked. Sen had paused at a doorway and was just standing there. Probably trying to get a feel for what was outside. She held in a little shiver. It probably wasn't good, whatever it was. "How do we get the bracelet off?"

Meri took a step back as Sen leveled her with a glare unmatched by any she'd ever seen before, from anyone. And that was saying a lot. Her mom was really good at them.

"The plan is for you all to go right back through the anteroom, down the stairs and into the portal, back home. This is no place for you." She gestured toward Sandra. "She is afraid of the small dragons in your land. Those are nothing compared to what awaits you here."

"That doesn't sound good, Meri," Sandra said. "Maybe we should head back."

That would be the logical thing to do. Absolutely the logical thing to do. But when would she ever have this chance again? To discover something no one else had even an inkling about? Stuff like that was running out on Earth, if not completely gone. She might not be Lara Croft, but that didn't mean she couldn't find something that could shake the entire world to its core. Even with the couple pictures of she'd taken she would never be able to convince anyone where she had taken them. She needed concrete proof. Then came the free ride at school, the book deals, the movies. But first the proof.

And even if she did convince someone, would the portal let them come back? Would the United States government let her come back? Nah, probably not. This was her one and only chance. Plus, could she really leave Sen here alone? Sure, she was from here and obviously knew what she was doing, but still. The older girl always seemed so sad, so on edge. It was obvious she'd been through a lot.

If she could find something to take back as absolute proof, maybe she could convince Sen to go back with her. And then when they showed everyone whatever it was she was going to find, all the great minds around could help Sen get the bracelet off. It was totally disgusting that someone would put that thing on her like that, for no reason.

"Waiting for an answer here, Meri," Sandra said, interrupting her thoughts.

Sen snorted and walked off. Apparently Meri was going to have to get used to that.

"You go if you want. I'm staying."

A good fifteen seconds of silence. "Seriously? You're going to risk your life, for what?" Sandra said, her voice quivering a little. "Fine then.

Your choice. But how do I even know that portal will take me home? There have to be other worlds out there if there is this one, right?"

She did have a point. Was this the only other world out there? Maybe they should focus on getting around this one before they thought about that. Being logical didn't stop the tingle of excitement from zapping through her. Endless worlds to explore. This was going to be so amazing.

"Sen said it would take you home. I don't see why she'd be dishonest. If you take the portal, you'll end up back in Florida."

"Sen's gone again," Sandra said.

Shoot. They moved together, in the direction that they had last seen her going. They stumbled through another room, this one full of bodies. At least they had been dead for a while. Not that it was any less creepy. Pieces of a shattered door hung in the way, blocking part of the view of a snow covered the landscape. Snow? She'd never seen snow for real. Her mom always wanted to go to South America on vacation to get a tan.

The temperature changed as soon as they stepped through the open doorway, sending a shiver clear from her toes to her shoulders. And she'd thought the temperature too low before. That didn't make sense. There was no way a broken door could hold in heat, was there?

Fresh footprints in the snow gave away the direction Sen had headed.

They followed.

The air here felt strange. Fresh. And those trees. What kind were they? A deciduous of some kind, but nothing she recognized. Which really wasn't significant since that wasn't included in her major and she was a city girl from the south. Maybe that kind of tree was common in Canada. Who knew.

They found Sen not far away, kneeling over a corpse. A fresh corpse. She was digging in the guy's pockets.

"Ah, Sen? This guy is dead."

"Yes?"

"As in dead, dead. As in no longer alive." Sandra's tone was rising in pitch.

"Yes?" Senara was staying so calm. Calm was good, right?

"Well how do you think he died? Natural causes, right?"

Meri actually looked at the corpse on the ground. A large hole gaped open in his chest. Sen just gave Sandra a look and moved on.

"At least tell us what killed the guy!" Sandra yelled after her.

"I don't know. Probably the temple defenses. You're fine if you're with me."

Temple defenses? Like turrets, or like magic? What left that kind of hole right through a man? After traveling through that portal, she'd probably believe anything. She jogged over to Sen, trying not to stare at the morbid sight. Sandra stuck to her like glue.

And now that she thought about it, why were they fine if they were with Sen? The defenses didn't work against her, or wouldn't try to attack her?

After the freak-out moment ended, the fact that they had just jumped into another world where it was snowing while wearing Florida clothes slowly set in. They were totally going to freeze to death if they didn't figure something out. At least she had boots and jeans, protection against all the swamp critters at home.

"Ah, Sen?" Meri asked. She didn't really want to keep bothering her, but the alternative was frostbite, so... "We really are going to need warmer clothes," she continued when Sen didn't answer.

"My name is Senara." Sen moved over to one of the corpses. A fresh one, not one that had been dead for decades. Surely she wasn't going to... Op. She did. She rolled the body over and took the guy's cloak, holding it out for Meri.

She took it, but held it out in front of her. It wasn't that cold, was it? They'd be fine without the cloak until they found something else, right?

Just the thought made her shiver.

Fine. It was freezing. But this was *so* disgusting. She pulled it over her shoulders. Instant relief. Impressive. The people here sure knew how to stay warm. They'd have to, living on the North Pole like this.

Sen moved over to another body, this one a woman, and did the same thing, holding the cloak out to Sandra.

"There ain't no way I'm wearing that thing," Sandra said, her voice rising in pitch. "It's from a dead person. A dead person. We shouldn't be here. Why are we here?"

"Suit yourself," Sen said, and dropped it on the ground before taking off again.

"Just take it. You'll want it later," Meri told her quietly. Probably sooner rather than later, actually, but Sandra could get stubborn and might not take it.

"I can't do this, Meri. I don't know why you want to, but I can't. I'm going back. I'm not going to die here in some horrible way, with my parents never finding out what happened to me." Her voice continued to rise until she was nearly impossible to understand.

"Shh, calm down." Meri said. "I'm not staying long." She patted her camera. "Just long enough to get some undeniable proof."

"Good luck with that. It isn't worth someone's life." She brushed at the snow on her shorts, glared after Sen for a second, and then took off back toward the portal.

"Sandra!" Meri called after her.

She just lifted a hand without turning around.

Was she right? Was this crazy? Yeah, probably. But everything good came with a risk. There had to be something around here that could prove she'd been to another world. Something portable, or photogenic.

"Sen!" Meri called, scrambling to catch up. The other girl didn't even slow. "Why are you in such a hurry?" Meri panted out when she caught up.

"Because those men," Sen said, pointing a thumb over her shoulder at the bodies littering the ground. "Were looking for me. And those weren't all of them."

Meri's gut clenched and she stopped. Those soldiers had been hunting Senara? Why? And there were more? She looked around at the trees, at the darkening gloom. Anything could be hiding in there. She eyed Sen from the side. And why were they after her, anyway? What had she gotten herself into now?

A glance over her shoulder showed Sandra had just made it back to the temple. Maybe she was the smart one. But that didn't change anything for Meri. This place was going to change her life. Forever.

CHAPTER FIVE

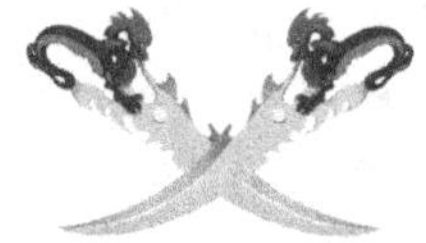

"So, ah, where we going?" Meri asked after slipping on a patch of ice for the seventeenth time. Why had she ever wanted to see snow?

"To find shelter for the night." Sen looked up at the sky. Meri looked too, but she had no idea what she was looking for. "It's going to be cold. We'll have to keep moving until we find somewhere we can stay warm."

"Stay warm? How about get warm?" The giant cloak she'd thought was so warm before wasn't helping much now. And she'd almost lost her fingers to the cold taking pictures. She should have grabbed a pair of gloves. Yuck. For some reason dead person gloves felt so much more wrong than a dead person cloak.

Sen didn't comment, just kept forging onward. Did anything rile that girl up? Actually, she hoped she never saw that. She was scary enough when she was calm. Now that Meri knew Sen's whole world thing was true, what did that mean about the bracelet? It had to be something significant, or whoever had forced her to wear it wouldn't have pierced it into her flesh.

"What kind of shelter are we looking for? Got something in mind?" Meri asked.

"I'll know it when I see it," Sen answered.

"Wonderful," Meri muttered, kicking at a snow drift. This was possibly the dumbest thing she'd ever done, and that was saying a lot.

Would Sen take her back to the portal now, if she asked? She studied Sen's back as the girl marched on, no sign of being tired at all, even with all the stiffness she'd noticed before.

Probably not. Whatever mission she seemed to be on, it was important to her. Meri, not so important. She didn't seem to care about people much. Which just made this even more stupid. If she died here, her mom would never find out what had happened to her.

"Selfish, selfish, Meri," she muttered to herself under her breath.

"What?" Sen asked.

"Nothing," Meri said.

Trudging through the snow was getting old fast. No wonder everyone complained about it, except at Christmas. She thought about kicking another pile, but just couldn't get up enough energy.

It seemed like forever, but finally Sen paused. "Wait here." She took off.

Meri squinted after her, but didn't really see anything. If Sen left her here, she'd die, no doubt. Hopefully Sen wasn't just getting tired of her and decided she wasn't keeping up well enough. Meri moved up to where Sen had been standing when she said it and squinted through the trees. There, barely visible, a small shack of some kind.

Yes! Maybe they could spend the night there.

Unless Sen had already used this chance to abandon her. Sen didn't really seem like the loyal type. Why was she letting her tag along when it was obviously not great for her? It wasn't like she was going to be any help or anything.

She shifted her backpack to a different position and shoved down the urge to pull out her camera. She already had plenty of pictures of the trees. She didn't need one of some random shack that could have been anywhere on Earth. The bag weighed her down, the exhaustion of the day deep in her bones. Maybe her emergency gear wasn't worth it. But it was getting dark.

Dropping the bag on the ground for a moment, she felt around until she found her flashlight. How long was she going to be here? How much battery should she be saving? Was millions of dollars and fame enough to risk her life like this?

Oh yeah. The things she could do for her mom...

"It's empty."

Meri let out a little shriek and tumbled over backward into a snow bank. She just caught Sen rolling her eyes before reaching down and dragging her to her feet. She didn't say a thing about Meri's clumsiness, just turned and headed back for the shack, keeping an eye out the whole time. She shoved open the door and motioned for Meri to go ahead of her.

Meri checked out the tiny hut as she stepped through the door. Tiny was an understatement. But it was already significantly warmer in here without the wind. Body heat and hopefully a fire in the tiny firepit would help, a lot.

Sen dropped a little bag at her feet. She nodded toward a stack of wood along the far wall. "See what you can do about a fire. I'm going to find us something to eat."

And , just like that, she was gone. Meri shoved past a small table to rush after her and yell out into the dark, "I brought granola!" but there wasn't an answer.

At least this would give her a chance to make a quick entry with her camera. Everything that happened over the next couple days was going in a log. She wouldn't forget a thing.

———

Looking for food was a good excuse, and necessary, really, but Sen mostly just wanted to get away from that girl for a while. This was not what she had expected from a Swarian. So far no one she'd seen from that world had shown any magical ability at all. She probably should have just left her at the portal, but she was a Swarian. They were supposed to be the foundation of magic. She should have been able to help her. Maybe not all Swarians had the ability to use magic? If she didn't have any magic, she was useless. Unless she found someone who would want her...

She followed their path back toward the temple. That girl left more of a trail than an entire squad of soldiers. She'd have to cover it up. There needed to be no trail at all. If the Trulathians didn't find any evidence otherwise, they would assume she was still in the temple. She hadn't found him among the dead, but hopefully Titus was still there, his body waiting until spring to rot, or food for scavengers.

Her side ached a little, but it was improving. Just stopping back at the temple had seemed to help. If she'd had time and hadn't had a reason to worry, she would have waited there until the healing completed.

But, back to the girl. With all of the texts and old spells in Swarian, of course it had been assumed that all of them had access to magic. But maybe it wasn't true. Maybe the girl was just useless. Better to give it another day and find out before just leaving her.

A pang hit her. She'd helped Sen when she was in their land, for no reason, without compensation. As much as Sen wanted to believe that she had an ulterior motive, there wasn't one that she could see. Meri had risked getting in trouble to help her, and she couldn't figure out why.

Maybe having someone who would watch her back wouldn't be such a bad thing. Orcus watched out for each other on the battlefield, but only out of necessity. The system pitted them against each other more often than not, to keep them from banding together and fighting back against their masters. Fall too low in the pecking order and bad things started to happen to you.

She needed to stop thinking about that. It was over. The Orcus had been wiped out. Her only concern now had to be getting this infernal bracelet removed. She tightened her bicep, feeling the spikes dig in a little.

The man who had put this on her arm would be able to remove it. She just needed to find a way to get into Ortansa undetected and force him to cut it out of her flesh. Then she would kill him, so he couldn't do it to another ever again. Burn down his shop, destroy all his notes, so no one could replicate it. She would make it her life's work to find anyone that knew the craft and send them into fire and brimstone after the Crafter.

The snow-fall was getting stronger. Wonderful for tonight, to help hide the girl's blunders. Not great for travel tomorrow. But it would make hunting easier, and after the food she'd had in that other world, she was ready for something with a little more substance.

———

Starting the fire had not gone well, to put it mildly. The little bag Sen had tossed at Meri had flint and a striker in it, or this world's equivalent of flint anyway. But even though it had taken forever, it didn't matter. Cheery flames danced in the little fire pit now, and that's what counted. It had gotten warm enough in the shack to even loosen up the dead man's throw she was wearing. She grimaced at the thought. A new cloak would be awesome, so she didn't have to keep thinking of it as the dead man's. It was a good thing that she'd worn boots and jeans. Snakes were the worry in the swamp, but here she probably would have lost her toes to frostbite.

The wind picked up outside, starting to howl. Sen had been gone forever.

"She better not have left me." Her voice got lost in the sounds coming from outside. Sen was just slow because of her injuries. Whatever they were. Or she was having trouble finding something to eat. That seemed pretty plausible in this winter wasteland.

Maybe they could have stayed at that destroyed place where the portal was. It was warm there. But it didn't seem safe, or at all comfortable, with dead bodies everywhere.

Meri shoved another small bite of a granola bar into her mouth. Saving this would have been ideal, but after all that walking and the cold, now that she was warming up she was starving.

The door creaked open and Meri jumped back automatically. She started breathing again when Sen stepped through the door, holding two skinned animals on a long stick.

"Know how to cook these?" she asked, shutting the door.

She didn't even tell her good job for getting the fire going. But then, it was probably something a ten year old could do here.

"Ah, no," Meri answered about the meat.

Sen gave a longsuffering sigh and moved forward, propping the stick up to hang the small creatures over the fire. She took her top layer of clothes off and shook the snow out, pulling a wooden rack close to the fire and slinging the cloak over it. Snow dribbled in the fire, making it sizzle.

This whole thing was surreal. She'd never even been camping on Earth, let alone... wherever this was. Her mom tried to compensate for being a single parent, but camping was something she'd never accomplished.

Not that Meri had been super interested in camping anyway.

It didn't take long for the meat to start to smell really, really good. Apparently Sen was a decent hunter, or she wouldn't have been able to catch two rabbits that quickly. Well, at least it seemed quick, who knew? Being that small, they were probably rabbits. Did they have rabbits here? She leaned over the fire to study the rabbits more closely, just to see if there were any differences to the ones at home. None that she noticed, but it was hard to tell with the fur missing. Not that she'd spent a lot of time around rabbits at home, either.

"Is the snow getting worse?" Meri finally asked. This silence was weird. Being at school the last couple years, without a moment of silence ever, made this uncomfortable.

"Yes," Sen said, but didn't elaborate.

If it wouldn't let all kinds of cold in, she'd go and look outside. Now that things were nice and cozy, the snow didn't seem so bad again.

The rabbit took forever to cook. It started to look done, but Sen just left it on there, rotating it occasionally and flipping the stick over so the one on the bottom didn't cook too much and the one on the top not enough. Meri's stomach protested the wait, rather vigorously. It got to the point where she was about ready to announce that they were done enough for her when Sen took out her giant knife and sliced a piece off. She took a bite and grunted, which must have been acceptance because she then cut off a piece and stabbed it, holding it out to Meri at knife point.

She tapped it, checking the temperature. Hot, but not unbearable. She grabbed it and passed it hand to hand for a second, trying not to burn her fingers before taking a quick bite.

Instantly hot juices flooded her mouth and her stomach protested even louder, waiting for the food to make it all the way down her throat to her belly. It was so good! Unbelievably good. She destroyed her piece within a few moments, and waited to see if she got any more.

Sen almost smiled at her. It was the closest thing to amused that Meri had seen coming from her. She cut off another piece and held it out.

"So much for leftovers," Meri said, reaching out for her next piece too.

Was it the hunger talking, or was rabbit really this good? It didn't matter at the moment. She was going to stuff herself.

"Thanks, Sen," Meri said around a mouthful of rabbit. "This is really good."

Sen shrugged. "Better finish up and get some rest. I don't want to be here much after first light tomorrow. The soldiers will be checking anything that looks like shelter, looking for me."

Meri wiped at her mouth, trying to get some of the juice off. What she wouldn't do for a hot shower right now. "You never really said. Why are these guys after you?"

Instantly the slight humor she'd seen on Sen's face was gone. She almost wished she hadn't asked.

"It's better if you don't know," Sen said, then moved over to the corner and started making herself a bed.

Better if she didn't know sounded kind of ominous. What did she really know about Sen? Not much. What if she was a criminal? That would kind of explain the bracelet, like maybe it was some kind of warning for people, a marker that the one wearing it had done something bad. Maybe really bad. And the way Sen acted, like Meri should know what the bracelet meant...

Suddenly the rabbit didn't seem to want to stay down. Sen could be a murderer for all she knew. Maybe that's why the soldiers were looking for her so hard.

She inched over to the far wall and slowly threw her cloak down. At least the cloak could cover both the ground, and her. It was definitely big enough, made for large men in war gear. And it almost seemed to give off heat itself, which of course couldn't be accurate. No way. A portal could be explained by science, but cloaks that generated their own heat? Nah.

Sleeping would be difficult, after the thoughts that had just occurred to her. Why had she gotten herself into this again? She sighed. Too late now. She'd never find her way back alone, and then would end up starving to death. And she still hadn't found anything that definitively said 'other world.' Sen was her only help right now, and she'd shown no signs whatsoever of meaning her harm.

All that about her being a murderer was probably just crazy. She obviously used the knife for stuff like cooking rabbits, and maybe for killing them or something. No, Sen wouldn't hurt anyone. She had to believe that or this was most definitely going to be the death of her.

———

Sen woke, most definitely not well rested. Aches and pains still coursed through her body, making it difficult to sleep even though she needed the rest. The girl had thought she wouldn't notice that she was trying not to sleep, trying to stand guard. It almost impressed her. That thought was waylaid when she opened her eyes and saw Meri in a dead sleep.

So much for watching her. She was slightly surprised by the way the side of her mouth tipped up in almost a smile. Being fed, warm, and free of Melin, her handler, felt pretty good. If she could get this bracelet off, maybe she could find out what a good life felt like. Away from everything that had plagued her since the first time she'd worked magic. And no one was going to stop her from getting this stupid thing removed. No one.

Wiping every trace of the smile off her face to not give herself away, Sen stood and stretched before going over and kicking Meri lightly in the leg.

"What? Huh?" The girl didn't wake easily, it seemed. Yesterday had been a long day, but nothing out of the ordinary for Sen. What was a normal day to this girl?

"Time to get up." Sen bumped her harder this time. "We need to leave soon."

Meri whined for a second, incoherently, then opened her eyes a crack and noticed where they were. She bolted up, nearly slamming her head into the wall. "I thought this was just a dream."

Sen couldn't stop the snort that escaped. "You mean nightmare? Nope, it's all happening. Now get up and get that cloak situated, it's time to go."

Quite the frown covered Meri's face. Oh well. It was kind of funny, actually.

Sen stamped out the remains of the fire, being careful to separate any embers. They really didn't need the shack catching on fire and the smoke drawing attention. The smoke was invisible at night after dark, but now that the sun was on its way back up there was nothing to hide it.

Meri was horribly slow. If Sen had been that slow getting ready for a morning, she'd have gotten a kick in the face. While effective, she didn't have the time to deal with the whining if she tried that.

"What are we doing about breakfast?" Meri asked blurrily.

Sen shrugged. "If you have something, eat it on the way. You finished the rabbits off last night."

Meri grimaced, then dug around in her backpack. Out popped a couple granola bars. She opened one, then held another out for Sen.

What was this? People didn't share food. You provided for yourself, or you died, simple. She'd shared her rabbit the night before because she'd had extra. But Meri had no way of getting more food after she ran out. Foolish girl.

"Keep it," Sen said roughly, then flung the shack door open and stalked outside. What would it be like to be from a place where people were like that? Were all people there like Meri and Sandra, or were there others, like Titus? Their land didn't seem to be as harsh. Maybe that was why they were able to be a different people. She couldn't begin to imagine Wanha sharing food, or any of the other Orcus for that matter. They earned their rank and the privileges that went with it, such as having the best to eat.

She had to wade through the snow the first few steps. Keeping tabs on Meri while pretending she didn't know she existed was easy. Too easy. She didn't even have to turn and look to know she followed her. So loud, even with the snow muffling everything.

Once they reached the trees, the snow wasn't quite as deep, as she knew it would be. They traveled slowly, Sen forcing Meri to stop and wait while she scouted quite often.

"What's this, Sen?" Meri asked, leaning over a farig plant. The berries were most abundant in winter, but very toxic, their brilliant purple enticing but deadly.

Sen didn't answer, just kept walking, ignoring the girl who ripped a sprig of berries off and stuffed them in her bag.

They made it just a short distance before Meri saw something else that made her squeal and stop, popping out that thing she carried everywhere, then tearing off leaves and twigs to put beside the berries in her bag.

The journey took far too long with Meri stopping every time she saw something she thought was different, going into a tizzy, talking about it how she didn't have anything like it in her homeworld and doing something she called taking pictures.

Sen was not amused.

It may have been almost funny in the morning, but now it just reminded her how the girl would be a liability, not an asset. How had Swarians become so useless? But, unless she truly got in the way, she would keep Meri with her. There was always the chance that she would need to go back to their homeland, and letting one of their people get slaughtered by hers or killed by nature didn't seem like a good way to start. And if she did need to go back, it would be much easier to have an in.

Or so she told herself.

They marched most of the day, Sen occasionally letting Meri take breaks while she went back and covered up their trail. Eventually they hit a road, which made the whole making it hard to follow them thing easier, but it made it much more likely they'd be seen.

The cloak the girl wore was far too big for her, a good thing as it hid her strange clothes underneath. If travelers just passed them, they wouldn't give them a second glance. If they tried to speak to them, however...

Sen paused at the roadway, looking in both directions. Without the feel of the earth to aid her, finding Arnath had gotten much more difficult. Again, the bracelet. She squinted at the sky for a second, the sun just peering out from behind bluish clouds that nearly screamed more snow to come. They would have to find somewhere warm again tonight.

Her stomach clenched. Somewhere warm meant people. Somewhere warm meant possibly Titus. Until the bracelet was off, she had to avoid him at all costs. After that, she'd have a decision to make.

Using the sun to best judge direction, Sen took to the road, going left. "A few things we need to speak about before meeting others," Sen said. She waited to continue speaking until Meri sped up her shuffle enough to catch her. "Rule number one, no speaking when others are around." That was going to be a tough one. She really wasn't very good at being silent.

Meri tipped her head, covered in the cloak. "We're going to meet other people?"

How did she sound so excited? Had she not listened to a word Sen had just said? "I'm sure we'll run into other people along the road. Hopefully eventually we'll reach a town where we can resupply."

Meri nearly bounced in excitement, though it was much more subdued than usual. The poor girl was probably exhausted.

"What was rule number one?" Sen asked.

"No talking to other people," Meri said.

Sen whirled back toward her, eyes going into slits. "No. The rule was no talking, at all, even to each other, when people are around. Is that clear?"

Meri shrugged, making her cloak flop off her shoulder. She shivered and pulled it back tight.

"This is important!" Sen glared at her, driving the point home. "Do you understand?"

The girl nodded, but didn't seem too keen on the idea of being quiet. Oh well. It'd be nice for Sen, if it actually happened.

"Rule two, no looking anyone in the eyes. Don't call undue attention to yourself." Sen started walking again. Number two was pretty self-explanatory. The girl didn't need her to spell that one out. "And number three, if a patrol comes down the road, we are in the trees instantly. Got it?" she looked over her shoulder.

Meri nodded.

Hopefully she actually did, or this was going to be a very short trip.

———

How was everything here so gorgeous? Was all of nature this gorgeous and she just hadn't noticed until now because she lived in the city, or was this place special? It was special to her, no matter what. If she hadn't turned her phone off to conserve the battery, she probably would have the entire memory card full of pictures right now. The camera thankfully had an amazing battery, but she was going to have to be more careful with it too.

Not that the woods like this could really prove anything when they got home, but it was just so beautiful.

A pang hit her. She probably should have texted her mom before jumping through that portal after Sen. But she hadn't really had time to think, which should have made her feel better but didn't. Not that she could just say 'hey Mom, jumping through a portal after a weird girl in strange clothes, don't worry, I'll be back when I get back.' She snorted. That would have gone over well. But maybe she would have been able to come up with something so her mom didn't worry.

Did time work the same here as it did at home? In movies it almost always didn't. But, movies weren't real and this so totally was. She might have to pinch herself again just to prove it one more time, but this was totally real.

They'd been following this road forever. At least most of the day. The chill factor was starting to rise as darkness slowly descended. They needed to find somewhere to spend the night soon. But that wasn't her problem. Somehow Sen always just seemed to know what to do, to know where to go. This was her land, sure, but did that mean she knew every inch of it? Meri knew how to get to Wal-Mart, the local coffee shop all the students loved, and the mall, but that was it. And there were even signs at home!

Sen's brutal pace was slowly settling into a nicer walk. She was clutching at her ribs a bit again, whenever she didn't think Meri was looking. If she even so much as saw Meri's head start to turn that way, she dropped her arm and straightened her spine and continued on. As much as Meri would have liked to believe the slowed pace was for her, she knew it was actually because of whatever was going on with Sen.

A couple of times Sen had seemed to get dizzy. Meri had pretended not to notice, because that just seemed like the right thing to do, but it was worrisome. Even if she didn't care about Sen at all as a person, which she did, she had to worry about something happening to her.

If something was wrong with Sen, Meri would be in big trouble.

A thundering sound, low on the breeze, caught her attention. But it continued too long to be thunder, and it was getting louder.

"Horses!" Sen hissed, then took off for the trees. Meri ran after her, jumping behind a towering giant just before the first of the group barreled around a curve in the road.

Silver flashed in the growing dark. Men yelled to each other, but Meri couldn't make out what they were saying. A team thundered by, pulling a huge wagon. It slid around in the mud. The horses grunted in exertion, heat steaming from their bodies. Where were these guys going in such a hurry? At least they were headed in the direction their little band had come from.

It took a minute for them to pass by. Meri lost count at fifty-seven men, but it was difficult to tell in the growing dark.

Sen kept them there in silence for several minutes after the group had passed. Then she motioned for Meri to stay put and moved out onto the road, carefully checking both directions before waving her out to join her.

"What are those guys after in such a hurry?" Meri asked.

Sen's face went even more closed off than ever, but she didn't answer. The twitch near her right eye gave her away though. They were after her, just like the men at the temple. Which brought back the very interesting question, why? Why were all of these guys hunting one girl?

It was kind of freaky. Okay, seriously freaky. One, because what happened if she was caught with her, and two, what had she done in the first place? Maybe it was time she found someone else, someone that could help her back to the portal. Why had Sen warned her against talking with anyone? Surely she had something to hide if she wouldn't even let her strike up a basic conversation.

Something to hide other than the fact that she was from a different world, of course. Maybe it was a common thing here, but back at home if anyone knew they'd had a visitor from another world, Sen wouldn't be able to move an inch without everyone on the entire planet knowing about it.

Sen started back down the road. Meri followed. Until something better came along, Sen was the only thing keeping her warm and fed. And therefore, alive. She'd have to keep trusting her for now, though maybe a little more cautiously than before.

It didn't take long from when the sun started to set for it to disappear. The temperature plummeted as soon as the sun was gone. Funny how it was impossible to notice the warmth of the sun when it was this cold out, until the sun was gone. Meri huddled into her heated cloak, trying to keep her face somewhat covered. This thing was totally going home with her.

The mud along the road started to freeze, becoming even harder to walk in now than it was before. It squelched at her boots, doing its best to rip them off her feet. "Not today you won't," she muttered. "At least I thought ahead far enough to wear boots."

Not that she'd known when she put them on that she'd be wading around in snow that same day, but she'd been prepared for the swamp.

Another group of soldiers went by. Sen heard the riders far in advance and had Meri hidden.

So many soldiers, and Sen hadn't said a thing about why she didn't want to be seen by them. Back to the whole bracelet thing. What did it do? Or what was it for? Asking why she wanted it off so bad would just be stupid, the thing had to hurt, digging into her flesh like that.

Meri adjusted her cloak, pulling it in as tightly as possible. They had better find shelter soon, or she was going fall over dead. So much walking. She puffed out some air, still fascinated that she could see her breath in the cold.

What would she even ask someone from this world anyway? Why her friend had a scary bracelet on? Nah. But it might look weird if everyone else was talking and she just sat there, silent.

Meri looked up, dragging herself from her thoughts. Light! A few small lights, like maybe houses. She jogged to catch up with Sen, rubbing her hands together. "Is that a town?" she asked when she was close enough she didn't have to raise her voice.

"Hopefully," was all Sen said back. Surprising though, with as much as Sen was trying to fly under the radar that she would want to find a town.

Sen seemed to feel the surprise coming off Meri. "You wouldn't last the night out here without shelter and a place to build a fire. Dry wood is hard to find after a snow like the one last night, and I don't think we're going to be lucky enough to come across another hunter's shack like yesterday. If you can follow the rules, we'll be fine here. Just keep quiet and let me handle everything."

Meri nodded that she understood.

"Wait, so we'll be going to like a tavern or something?" Meri asked.

Sen sighed. She was doing that a lot lately. "Hopefully. We need food. Otherwise we'll find someone's barn to sleep in. The animals let off a lot of heat and we may be able to find a hen still laying."

"Eww, gross, raw eggs?" Meri said.

Sen didn't even dignify that with a response. She just marched forward, slightly faster.

"Let's hope for an inn, then!" Meri said cheerfully. Warmth and food, amazing things that she would never take for granted again. And the chance to actually meet other people from here, to see if they were like Sen or not, to watch the culture. Amazing. If only there was a way to film the entire interaction without anyone noticing.

Record! On her phone. She slipped her hand into her pocket and found the power button, but paused before pressing it. Battery. Had to save that battery. Waiting until something interesting actually happened would be a better plan.

As they got closer it became obvious that the town was larger than she had guessed. Surely there would be an inn here. As much as she enjoyed animals, she didn't fancy sleeping in a barn with them. They passed several ramshackle huts without seeing anyone. It made sense. Anyone with any brains wouldn't be outside tonight in this miserable cold.

She eyed Sen. How was she so unaffected? Did the cold actually bother her but she was too stubborn to admit it?

They were a good chunk of the way into town before the sound of laughter came spilling out of one of the buildings. It was much larger than those around it, and far more brightly lit. A sign hung outside, with no words, only the picture of a pig of some kind.

Sen paused beneath the sign. "Remember the rules?" she asked, almost too quietly for Meri to hear.

"No talking, mostly," she answered.

Sen nodded, and then slipped the door partially open and slid inside. Meri followed and was instantly hit by a blast of hot air. She teared up as her face started to warm. Not tears, for real, she was just actually that cold.

The next thing that hit her was the smell of something roasting. She nearly gagged. It smelled wonderful, but it was making her stomach attempt to eat itself. She'd thought she could never be hungrier than she had been the night before. Today proved her completely wrong.

Sticking to the shadows around the edge of the room, Sen led her around to the counter, keeping a low profile. She was really good at this.

The barkeep glanced up when she got closer. He looked her over for a second, then said something in some weird language. Wait, what language was that? She'd never heard it before.

Of course! No wonder Sen was so adamant about her not saying a word. They didn't speak English here! But... how did Sen speak it so perfectly then? She did have that weird little accent that Meri had noticed when they'd met, but it wasn't enough to scream she was from a whole different world, where Latin hadn't influenced half the languages around.

Okay, this was so weird. She listened intently to the short conversation, doing her best to understand something, anything. Nope, not a word. So much for asking for people's thoughts on Sen, even if she'd wanted to. She looked around the small room. Did anyone here speak English?

Sen motioned for her to follow and moved to a small table in the back of the room. Meri listened to every conversation they passed, trying to find something that sounded even remotely familiar. Nothing.

Crap.

Every hour they got farther into this 'adventure' she felt even more stupid. Sure, this would be more than the discovery of a lifetime. It would be the biggest discovery ever. But for anyone to know about it, she had to live.

Sen dropped into a chair at the tiny table and kicked out another for Meri. Her gaze darted around the room, like she was watching for someone. Meri moved over and sat, waiting with her. Hopefully for food, because Sen didn't tell her what it was they waited for, just leaned back farther so her hood hid her eyes. She probably wasn't talking at all because she was afraid Meri would answer out loud. Or because she knew she couldn't understand her and she felt weird talking to her when Meri couldn't understand whatever language she was speaking.

Looking around to make sure nobody was paying attention, Meri reached into her pocket and turned on her phone. Thankfully it was still on silent, and didn't ding as it booted up. The cold had probably done a number on the battery, but she needed to capture this. Airplane mode did wonders for the battery, and it wasn't like she had any service. Hopefully the power pack she always had with her still had juice. Her camera would be way too conspicuous.

She slid the phone up her sleeve and punched the camera button. View wise she wasn't going to get much, but hopefully someone back at school would be able to recognize that this was a language all the drunks were shouting to each other and laughing in, and know that there wasn't any way this could be faked.

The video, along with the pictures she'd taken of any strange looking, at least to her, fauna, would hopefully be enough to convince people she'd been here. She'd been away long enough to appreciate home, and she was ready to get back. Adventure, great. Probably traveling with a criminal, freezing, starving, not so much.

One of the girls that obviously worked at the tavern brought their food over, dropping it in front of each of them. Meri left her camera running and bent over the blackened meat, sniffing it.

"So gross," she said, almost out loud. Sen gave her a warning glare and she crossed her eyes at her.

A knife and fork with two prongs were on the platter next to the meat. Better than using her hands. She stabbed at the food, which was even worse than she'd thought. Burned on the outside, raw on the inside. She grimaced but cut off a slice. Even if she thought there might be other food available, she didn't have any way of asking for it. And she was starving.

The first bite nearly made her gag. What was this stuff? Sen's rabbit from the night before had been soooo much better. How was that possible when all she'd had to work with was a fire and spit? This tavern seriously needed a different cook.

Chewing furiously, she looked around the room, trying to distract herself and not think about what was in her mouth.

Her history professor would kill to be here right now. Sure, this wasn't Earth history, but it seemed to closely resemble it. Except for maybe the meat. Was this some kind of weird animal that wasn't back home?

The girl came back and sloshed two cups down onto the table, spilling quite a bit all over the meat. Hopefully that would help the taste, but doubtful. That girl totally needed fired.

Now that her stomach roiled for a completely different reason, Meri went back to looking around the room. She kept her hand hidden, but followed her gaze with her phone. There were twelve people packed in here, and if there had been a fire marshal in this area, the max allowed would have been, like, seven. Not that these people seemed to care about safety, with the amount of alcohol they were drinking.

That seemed universal.

Speaking, or thinking, of. Meri grabbed her cup and took a swig, expecting water. It wasn't water. It was the grossest stuff that had ever entered her mouth, and that was saying a lot after that meat. She couldn't help it, it spewed out of her mouth and all over a slightly less inebriated patron at the next table.

He stood, knocked his chair over, and turned to her. He started screaming something in that other language, spittle flying out of his mouth.

She looked wildly to Sen. Sen calmly stood and started speaking, no trace of emotion whatsoever.

The giant from the other table continued to yell for a moment. When Sen didn't respond in anger, he slowly calmed down, his shoulders relaxing and the cords in his neck un-bunching. At least a little. He turned around and righted his chair, falling back into it and going back to his conversation.

The rest of the room started to buzz again. She'd been too freaked out to notice that everyone has stopped talking for a moment there, breaths held in anticipation.

A guy at the table next to them almost looked disappointed as he went back to his meat.

Sen let loose a breath and sat back down. Was she... relieved? Of course she was, but this was the first time she'd shown anything close to that emotion at all.

She took a sip of the gross stuff this time, instead of a swig. Still nasty, but she could get it down. Ale, maybe? It did kind of taste like beer.

They worked on their meals in silence, Sen keeping a close eye on the room. It was weird sitting here like this, not talking. And the people around them probably thought so too, but there wasn't much they could do about it.

If they were walking long hours tomorrow, Sen was going to start teaching her the basics of the language, whether she wanted to or not. And she needed to know more about their plan than just get someone to take the bracelet off. She'd help Sen, unless she found out she was a criminal, and then head home. She had some pictures and video, but she really wanted something else to take with her, maybe a mug or a coin or something. Hopefully it was made out of something they didn't have on Earth.

The tavern girl came bustling by again, this time with a tray of steaming cups. One of the men said something to her and she giggled. She turned away from him and ran into a table, spilling the contents of her tray all over Meri.

"Oww. That's hot!" She frantically wiped at the singed skin, grabbing a rag from the barmaid. It took a second but Meri noticed something was weird.

The room was silent.

One of the strange men said something in that other language. Sen ignored him and kept eating, so Meri dropped back into her chair, threw the rag on the table, and followed her lead. *Please let it go, please,* she begged internally. It didn't work. The man stomped over and put his hand on Meri's shoulder, spinning her toward him.

"Hey!" Meri said. "Don't grab me like that!"

Anyone who had gone back to eating stopped. Not a sound came from anything in the room, other than the crackle of the fire. She glanced at Sen, who had a terribly sour expression on her face. Oops. So much for rule number one.

Chairs around the room scraped back from tables. The big guy hissed something at Sen. She hissed something right back. His eyes went wide and he let go of Meri like he'd grabbed the wrong end of the poker coming out of the fire. He put both hands in the air, like he was saying he didn't want a fight, and backed off.

Sen just eyed him and went back to eating her meat like they hadn't just about gotten murdered, just because Meri had said something completely fine out loud.

The room stayed pretty quiet, compared to the level the noise had been at before.

"We can no longer spend the night here," Sen said, so quietly. "Finish your food, but don't appear like you are in a hurry."

Meri's stomach roiled. She wasn't particularly fond of the food anyway, but after what had just happened she was nauseous. Really nauseous. But she didn't know when the next time they would get to eat might be, so she picked at the food.

After a couple of minutes, Sen dropped a cloth on the table and put what was left of her meal in the middle. She motioned for Meri to do the same.

No one in the room looked directly at them, but she could practically feel fear and disgust seeping from their bodies. What had Sen said that made them back off so quickly? That had made them leave their little duo alone? She desperately wanted to ask, but rule number one was never going to be broken again.

Sen stopped at the counter and spoke to the barkeep. He snapped something back, not nearly as accommodating as he'd been earlier. She argued for a second, but the room was going quiet again. Not that people had really gone back to normal after the last little spat, but the sound level was still definitely dying down.

Sen practically shoved Meri out the door. Instant freezing air slammed Meri, making her gasp. Now that they'd warmed up, it felt even worse out here.

"Let's go." Sen sounded angry. She started off down the road, her pace brisk.

"I'm sorry, Sen, it just popped out," Meri said, stumbling along behind Sen. She adjusted her cloak to cover every inch of skin, and buried her hands in it.

"Two rules, and one important," Sen muttered, "you couldn't even follow that."

"I said I'm sorry. What more do you want me to do? It just popped out. I didn't even have time to think."

"There's nothing you can do. Let's just hope this is behind us and try to find somewhere else to spend the night."

"Can we offer to pay one of the townspeople?" Meri asked.

"Even if one of them would have us, the innkeep kept the last of my coin," Sen answered.

Great. Meri shivered under her cloak. It was still fairly early. How were they going to make it all night? "What did you tell them?" she asked. "That made them leave us alone after they heard me speak?"

Sen looked over her shoulder at Meri, then looked past her back to the tavern. "I told them you are an initiate. That's how you know Swarian."

"Wait, what? What's Swarian?"

"Swarian. The language you speak. You made me lose ten coppers on a room. I wanted to take the food up there, but it was in use for another hour."

"Swarian is your word for English?"

Sen shrugged. "Is that what you call it?"

Meri nodded.

Sen shrugged again.

"Why is that significant?" Meri asked. "You speak English."

Sen stared at her for a second, still marching forward at a brisk pace. "Exactly."

"Exactly? What does that mean?" Meri muttered.

They'd made it to the tree line, leaving the edge of town behind.

"Where did you learn English?" Meri asked. "And why did those people react so badly to it? Surely there's more than one language in your world, how's come this one seemed to bother them so much?"

Sen didn't answer, just looked behind them again.

Meri stopped, throwing her hands on her hips. "Would you stop being so vague? I really need to understand what just happened, so it doesn't happen again!"

"I'm not being intentionally vague, I'm just trying to listen," Sen answered.

"Listen for what?"

She cocked her head. "Nothing, nevermind." And there she went again, practically jogging. Meri groaned. At least it would help keep their body temperatures up.

"We should probably get off the road," Sen said, still scanning their surroundings. What was bothering her so much?

"It's going to be really hard to walk out in the trees in the dark," Meri said tentatively. "We'd make much better time on the road." Obviously Sen knew her world much better than Meri did, but sometimes the other girl seemed a little paranoid. Maybe if she'd grown up in a world where people hated you just because of the language you spoke, she'd be a little more paranoid too.

With a non-committal grunt, Sen kept to the road, but didn't slow.

They didn't make it far before she was stopping them.

"What's going on?" Meri whispered. Her voice held the same fear that trickled down her back, nervous sweat chilling her under her cloak. Sneaking around in the dark like this might seem cool in movies, but it was so not cool in real life.

"I thought I heard..." Sen paused. "Get down!" She slammed into Meri, knocking her into the brush alongside the road.

A whine went by. It took a second, but the sound registered. She'd seen the Hunger Games like fifteen times. An arrow.

"Stay here," Sen hissed. She stayed crouched, but took off.

Meri froze in place, not even twitching. Fear rose, sour in her mouth.

A deep male voice yelled something from the direction of the town. He kept talking as men fanned out around him, all holding weapons. A flint struck, and one of the men lit a torch, passing it around to the rest to light their own. They'd probably not lit the torches until now so they could just shoot Sen in the back. Oafs.

There was a brief pause.

A cold laugh came from the trees. Sen's tone as she answered was nothing Meri had ever heard from her before. Even knowing they were on the same side, she couldn't hardly stop her knees from giving out.

Fifteen. Fifteen men out there, to one. No way this could go well for Sen. And if it didn't go well for Sen...

The men kept yelling, some type of insults no doubt. But then one of them asked a question. A confused murmur went through the crowd, the men looking around.

"Inan?" the big one said.

"Optar?"

At that point the men seemed to do a roll call, getting more and more agitated.

Sen said something snarky from the trees.

Sen! Hush up! Don't get yourself killed.

An arrow shot from a bow and twanged into the forest in the direction the voice had come from, followed by two more in quick succession. Meri's stomach dropped. She strained to hear a whimper, a cry of pain, but there was nothing. Really, this being Sen, that didn't necessarily mean she hadn't been hit.

The giant guy from the tavern bellowed something, and the men rushed forward. One yelled a word that Meri had heard back at the inn, followed by some more she didn't know.

He barely got the words out of his mouth before he was slammed in the face by a rock, thrown from the darkness. His body chased the rock to the ground, the air in his lungs releasing in a huff. The guy groaned, but didn't get up.

The giant yelled, running toward the tree line, a staff raised in his hands.

The archer hung back, arrow nocked in his bow, no doubt waiting for Sen to pop out and give him a chance to take a shot.

She didn't give it to him.

A shadow darted across the road. Was that her? Apparently Sen really was dangerous. Which was both terrifying and reassuring at the same time.

As the men searched through the trees where Sen had just been, the shadow flitted by again. There was a thud and the men stopped moving.

One man started to say something, but was cut off, his sentence ending in a gurgle.

Meri's stomach dropped. Four dead for sure, and one unconscious on the ground. She'd never seen someone die before. Dead people, sure, at funerals, but she'd never watched the life leave a person. She found herself grateful for the dark.

Sen whispered something in the darkness, her voice terrifying. Okay, that one was totally creepy, even if she was on her side.

One of the men shrieked something, waving his axe in the air.

Sen laughed. Ouch. Seeing her laugh like that was even worse than just hearing it from the trees.

The man growled and flailed around at the darkness with the torch. Meri would have felt bad for him, if he wasn't trying to kill her and her... traveling companion? Friend?

Strong arms grabbed her from behind, jerking her out onto the road. The man ripping her shoulder out of socket yelled to the others.

She shrieked and struggled, punching at him, but his many layers of clothes kept her from getting a good blow in.

He dragged Meri down the road to where the archer still stood.

He tightened his grip on Meri's wrists hard enough to bruise. She dropped all her weight backward, making him grunt at the sudden movement. He jerked her against him and grabbed her under her arms. She wiggled, fighting the fear down as much as fighting him.

He smacked her in the head, then tightened his grip, nearly crushing her. He grunted out something at her.

"I can't understand you! Just let me go!"

A stream of men with torches came out of the woods, jogging toward them.

"Run, Sen!" Meri shrieked. "Run!" She couldn't see her anymore in the dark. Tears spilled over. The men had better not have hurt her.

The thought hadn't even finished when Sen popped out of the brush beside them, a huge branch in her hand. She bashed the guy holding Meri over the head without a word, then disappeared in the dark again.

He crumpled to the ground, falling halfway on top of Meri. She tried to shove him off, but he was hugely heavy.

The men down the road shouted and started to run faster.

She frantically shoved at the guy, and finally he budged.

The hiss of an arrow caught her attention and she dropped back to the ground. But the arrow didn't come for her. One of the men with a torch stumbled and fell, an arrow planted firmly in his back. The whole group stopped and looked behind them.

Somehow, while Meri had been distracted, Sen had taken the archer out. Now she had his bow. She didn't even pause before another arrow knocked another man from his feet, and then a third. The group of fifteen was down to six.

Sen grabbed at another arrow stuck in the ground and the men scattered to the trees, leaving Meri in the middle of the road.

"Over here. Now," Sen yelled.

Scrambling to her feet, Meri stumbled toward Sen, ignoring the pain in her shoulders from being dragged. She slid to a stop beside Sen and bent over, panting. Relief washed through her, warming her whole body. Sen would keep her safe.

A head looked out from behind a tree and the last arrow instantly flew in that direction. The man was too fast though, and the arrow embedded itself harmlessly in a tree behind him.

"Hold this," Sen said, shoving the now useless bow into Meri's hands.

Sen's daggers slid simultaneously from their sheaths, silent. *So that scraping noise in the movies is totally fake.* The thought was near hysterical. She took a deep breath trying her best to calm herself. Look at Sen. She didn't seem like this was bothering her a bit. Which was yet again, scary.

The man's head looked out from the trees again. He said something.

"What was that?" Meri asked.

"He noticed we're out of arrows."

They filtered out of the trees, anger and fear twisting their expressions. Who were the men that had fallen to them? Sons? Brothers? But this was their fault. They should have just let them go.

One of the men rasped something after they were close enough to speak without yelling. He held an old rusted sword, probably not used in generations, the tip resting in the frozen soil. These men weren't soldiers. Why were they being so stupid?

Sen didn't answer. She just ran at them in a twirl of steel. The first man went down with hardly a whimper. Meri covered her mouth to keep from crying out.

The last five men broke away, trying to surround her. She would have none of that, darting away every time one of them moved to block her off.

The giant swung at her with a two-handed scythe. Not made to be a weapon, but an effective one none the less. Sen easily dodged out of the way and ignored the huge man, slamming her shoulder into one of the others that was off balance from a bad swing. As he fell her dagger flashed out and he hit the ground as a corpse.

The urge to close her eyes fought with the need to make sure Sen was okay. Nothing she'd ever seen at home was anywhere close to as horrifying as this was turning out to be. No movie, no game could compare to seeing this in real life.

It didn't take long before two more men were on the ground. Sen didn't truly engage any of them, just dancing back and waiting for a second to pop in and end a life.

Finally the giant made a mistake. He swung at Sen, roaring in anger when she dropped another of his friends. He missed, of course, and the blade of the scythe buried itself in the ground. Sen instantly jumped forward, landing on the haft and splintering it from the blade before jumping back out of range of the giant's long arms.

He fell back, arms raised. The other man left followed his example.

Sen paused, then lifted her blade and put the flat on her shoulder. She spoke, turning and walking past them, then back, pacing in front of them like an enraged cat. She swung her dagger and pointed the tip at Meri, yelling at the remaining men.

The man's gaze flicked over to her and then right back to Sen, who was practically vibrating with rage.

The giant's face screwed up in confusion and he spoke.

Sen glared at him and snapped something back. She spit at the man's feet and lifted her blade.

"Sen! Stop! These men have families!"

Sen looked at her, more through her, and put her knife straight through the man's gut. The giant nearly fell over himself trying to get away, but Sen was on him like a flash and soon his lifeless eyes were gazing at the stars along with the others.

"How can you just do that?" Meri asked, tears in her voice. She moved over and retched into the bushes.

"Because it's necessary," Sen answered. She sounded almost apologetic, which really clashed with the blood dripping down her blade, splashing on the face of the man she'd just gutted. "They would have turned me over."

Tears froze to Meri's face. "Would getting turned over be so bad? You could stop running, stop hiding."

Sen just looked at her incredulously.

Well they were practically in the dark ages, like medieval times. Justice was brutal, without mercy. Whatever Sen had done was bad enough that she would kill to not be captured.

Sen pointed her dagger at Meri. "This isn't my fault. It's yours. You should have listened to me. If you had, these men would still be alive."

Meri stood there with her mouth hanging open for a second, then blinked back tears. She was an idiot for coming here, where she didn't belong. Her stomach roiled.

"If I was my master, I would go back into the town and finish this," Sen said, her voice really weird as she stared back down the road toward town. "I would find every person that had been at the tavern and erase the fact that I was here from the town's memory."

"Ahh no, we aren't doing that." Meri walked over and grabbed Sen's arm, giving her a tug. "Right? We totally aren't doing that, right?"

Sen looked over at her and her eyebrows raised at the hand on her arm.

Meri dropped it.

"Correct. Let's just get out of here before a patrol comes along." She took the bow from Meri and slung it over her shoulder. "Even if a patrol doesn't come, it won't be long before the villagers start to wonder where these men are."

With one last glance down the path, Sen moved forward, stopping for a second to grab the archer's empty quiver.

There was no choice but to follow Sen. If there was any chance before of finding someone else in this world to trust, it was probably gone now. The inn keeper thought she was an initiate, whatever that meant. She was on the wanted list right there with Sen now.

Two more quick stops to wrench spent arrows out of bodies, and they were on their way again. Meri avoided watching, bile rising in her throat.

"Prepare for a long night. We are going to have to get far from here before we stop."

Prepare for a long night? Hadn't it already been long enough? It had been the longest night of her life, and that was saying a lot.

Sen never spoke without there being a need. And there was no one else to help pass the time, pass the journey. It would be a long night indeed.

CHAPTER SIX

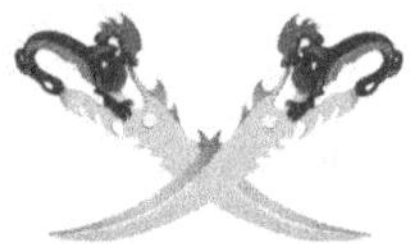

A long night had translated to several hours of the bitter cold before Sen had deemed it safe to find an old barn to collapse in for the night. Sleep had come instantly. Meri groaned and rolled onto her side. Why was she waking up when she just wanted to sleep?

Ouch. A boot in the ribs, that was why.

"It's still dark out," she muttered. "Go away."

"The farmer will be out soon to care for the animals. We need to be gone before he gets here."

She got the feeling that she was going to hate Sen before this was all over. Okay, not hate, because Sen could have easily left her to die the night before. Meri would have been a great distraction while she took off if she'd wanted to. Why was Sen still letting her tag along everywhere? Honestly, if she could have found her way back on her own, she would be long gone by now. Other than the fact that she'd starve to death before she got there, even if she had known how to find the portal.

And asking Sen to take her back seemed pointless. No way that would happen.

Meri finally opened her eyes, jumped back and slammed into a wall with a yelp.

A giant ox thing looked down at her, its expression slightly surprised, hay hanging out of its mouth. After staring for a second, it went back to chewing, eyes half closed.

"What. Is. That," Meri asked Sen, leaning into the wall as far from the creature as she could get.

"You've never seen a cow before?" Sen asked. "I told you when we were looking for a barn to sleep in that they work well because the animals give off so much heat."

"That," Meri raised a trembling finger, "is not a cow. I don't know what it is, but it surely isn't some ordinary cow. Not that I've seen many at home since I live in the city, but yeah, not a cow." She was rambling now, but she hardly noticed.

Wait, she totally needed a picture of this thing. She took her phone out of her pocket. It had three bars of battery when it turned on. Why, oh why, did they not have solar powered phone chargers yet? She snapped a couple of pictures from different angles.

"Any other weird things in here I should look at?"

"No?" Sen answered, but it sounded like a question. "Is my Swarian incorrect? This is not what you call a cow in your world?"

"Swarian is your word for English, right?"

Sen looked confused. "Yes?"

"Then no, absolutely not a cow. But we don't have a word for this thing, so you can call it that if you want."

"You don't have cows in your world?" Now Sen looked really confused.

Meri put a hand to her forehead. "Yes, we have cows, but they don't look like... that. Is it... dangerous?"

Sen looked at her and blinked, still confused. "Are your cows dangerous?"

"Well, in a stampede or something."

Sen looked at the cow thing. It was calmly chewing whatever was in its mouth. "I don't think that's a problem."

Meri snorted and stood. "No, probably not." She stretched, her muscles protesting every move. And here she'd thought she was in good shape back at school. So much for that. She'd have to try out for the track team when she got home. If she got home. "What's the plan for today?"

"Find someone to ask for directions," Sen said. "I didn't get a chance yesterday."

"Why don't we just wait for the farmer to come out?" Meri asked. "Maybe he can help us."

Sen hoisted her pack of stuff up on her back and slid the bow and nearly empty quiver to hang where they were easily accessible. Meri cringed. Hopefully she would never have to see them be used again.

"I know the general direction," Sen said. "But if we find someone that can tell us the easiest route, it would be helpful. Waystations along the path as well."

"What's the plan, anyway?" Meri asked. "You just keep talking about getting this bracelet off, but no whys or hows. And what's the plan once we get that thing off?"

Sen squinted at her and Meri could practically hear her talking with herself about how much of the plan to reveal to her. Apparently she reached a consensus, because she opened the door, motioned for her to follow and started talking.

"The how is to find the Crafter who placed the bracelet on my arm in the first place. He is the only one that can remove it." She glanced over her shoulder as she walked back toward the road they'd left behind the night before.

"And the why?" Meri asked, shutting the barn door behind them.

"This accursed thing tells everyone who sees it what I am." Her voice went dark, tight. "And it reminds me of the masters I've had over the years."

"Masters?" Oh crap. That probably wasn't good. Was slavery a thing here? Duh, it was like the Middle Ages. Of course there was slavery here.

Sen didn't answer, just kept walking. They reached the road and turned.

"How far away is this Crafter? And what's the plan once he gets the bracelet off?"

Sen's face went blank. That was weird. Sure, that was her normal face before, but that had been slowly changing.

"Two more days journey. Once the bracelet is off, I will be free to start a new life. I'll take you back to the portal, then strike off and find somewhere to leave all of this far behind."

A pang hit Meri. Until this moment she would have been ecstatic at the thought of going home. But right now, she wasn't feeling it. If everything went like Sen said, she might only have three more days here. That didn't seem like enough. If she didn't find something groundbreaking, no one would ever believe that she'd been here.

———

Would she really take her back to the portal? Sen pushed on, ignoring the sting of the winter wind, and the angry gurgle her stomach kept throwing out. It seemed foolish to just let her go back. What some of the people here wouldn't give to have a Swarian in their grasp...

But, she knew what it was to be a slave. Knew the horrors that were done to a person when they weren't considered human. She wouldn't do that to another unless it was absolutely necessary. She glanced back at the girl following her. How naïve she was to just believe Sen had her best interests at heart. But part of the reason she was so loathe to turn her over in exchange for whatever she wanted was that misplaced trust.

Had anyone ever truly trusted her before? No, and rightfully so. There was the trust of being on the same side in a battle, the give and take of defending each other. But not this full trust, for absolutely no reason other than she was the first Uthorian she had met.

Harington had been the closest thing to a trusted companion she'd ever had. Mostly since he'd been in her care since the day he was brought to be trained. Young, far younger than most, he'd accidentally shown his power as an infant. His parents had turned him in that hour.

Stop. Stop thinking of him. An Orcus did not cry.

She trudged on, tired of all this walking. Tired of waiting to be attacked. Once she got this bracelet off, she would be the one on the offensive.

If she got the bracelet off without needing to trade the girl, she would return her as she'd promised. Meri wouldn't approve of her plans once she had access to magic again, if the night before was any indication.

Find the Crafter, get the bracelet removed, find out if any Orcus were still alive at the palace training grounds. Find out if one specific Orcus was alive. Then back to the portal. Or find someone who feared her enough for her to trust to take Meri back without her.

Or, maybe she would try going back with her. Maybe, with the bracelet removed, she could stay there safely and not get sick. She was beginning to think that their world didn't hold any magic. How was it that all of the old spellbooks were written in Swarian, but the people she met there had no idea it even existed? Maybe in their world she could live without everything from this world hanging over her head. All of the things that she'd been forced to do. All of the things that had been done to her. And worst, all of the things that she had done willingly.

They'd found a peddler several hours back, and when she asked for directions she'd asked for another town, close enough to the capitol that she could adjust to where they really wanted to go, but far enough that the peddler wouldn't straight out guess where that was.

Her stomach growled in protest again. The girl had groaned when she pulled out the leftovers from the tavern for breakfast, but she'd eaten a healthy portion. Sen had to admit she didn't find it very appetizing either and would have preferred Meri's granola, but they needed the meat to keep going on a day like today.

The wind howled through the trees at them, the weather angry. She shifted her cloak up to cover more of her neck. It was going to be a cold night. Even worse than the one before.

Meri was being quiet enough to nearly make her worry. She glanced over her shoulder at her. Still there, stumbling along behind her, eyes half closed either against the cold or because of the exhaustion.

For as soft as she was, she complained far less than Senara would have expected. Even some of the soldiers complained more. But what else did soldiers have to do while tromping the miles between camps.

"Hungry?" Sen asked, raising her voice to make it reach Meri over the wind.

Meri shook her head. Sen frowned. She should be ravenous. But sometimes exhaustion masked hunger.

"I'm going to hunt anyway," she said. She moved off the road into the trees and found a large fir. She hacked off branches with her dagger. Not something she liked to use the edge on, but it seemed to stay sharp. Maybe there was a spell of some type on the ancient weapons.

"Here, weave these together." She showed Meri how to make a shelter.

Meri sluggishly tried to copy her movements, but didn't get far. Senara sighed. Was the land she was from always as warm as it was when she visited? No wonder she had no idea how to keep herself from freezing to death. Hunting would have to wait.

Weaving branches she had cut with branches still on the massive tree, she slowly built a wall to shield them from the wind. It wasn't large, but it would do. The dried needles would make excellent kindling.

"We will stay here tonight," she announced. It was still early, but the girl looked like she could drop dead at any moment. She'd had many cruel officers lead her band of Orcus, and she never wanted to be anything like them.

She scraped the loose needles into two piles once she had finished making them a roof and three more walls. Not airtight by any means, but it would help.

"You find wood while I hunt. It needs to have been down for awhile, old and dry. Do you understand?"

Meri nodded but didn't speak. She'd never thought there would be a day when she was worried that there weren't words spilling constantly from the girl's mouth. She handed her the flint and steel.

"If you can't get it started, I will when I get back."

Meri nodded, but she still looked half asleep, hiding her chapped lips and skin behind the ruff of the cloak she wore.

"Don't go to sleep. If you don't get the fire going, move around in the shelter until I return. If you stop shivering, that's a bad thing. Jump around, get your blood flowing."

"Got it," Meri said. She looked a little more with it, like she had figured out that they were in danger if they allowed themselves to be.

"Good," Sen nodded. "You'll be fine in here if you can get the fire started. You'll be surprised how much heat this will hold in. Especially if it snows."

She walked out of the shelter and waited a second for the girl to follow. "Don't get out of sight of this place. I don't want to have to come and find you. If you don't find wood right here, make sure you leave yourself a path to follow back, but don't stray far."

"Got it," Meri said again.

Sen sighed. She hoped she did, otherwise somehow she knew she'd be out looking for her.

It was surprisingly hard to leave her, standing there in the snow. Somehow she seemed so much younger than her, though they were probably about the same age. Age was relative.

The snow was at least good for hunting. She didn't have to go far before she came up on deer tracks. A deer would do, but it seemed like a waste when they wouldn't be able to carry much and she didn't want to stay long enough to dry or smoke the leftover meat.

Ah, there, rabbit again. The girl had eaten the last two well. Hopefully she liked it and wasn't just hungry. Not that it mattered to her. Of course it didn't matter to her if she liked it or not.

Hunting was so much easier today. For one, though the snow was coming down and it was windy, there was so much more light. And two, the bow. It didn't take her long to find two rabbits. And then she happened across a third on the way back, and brought it along for good measure. She gutted them a ways before she got back, not wanting to attract animal predators with the leftover guts. They had enough human predators, they didn't need to add nature to the list.

The first thing she noticed when she got back was that snow had gathered over their little shelter. Good. Other than a hole they would need for a chimney to roast the meat, snow would block all the gaps wind could work its way through. And once it melted some and then refroze, they would have a mini version of the homes the people in the north lived in all year, where the snow never melted and wood was hard to come by.

The second thing she noticed was that the girl had thought to make herself a hole for the smoke to go through, and that there was indeed smoke. She almost smiled. For not knowing anything, she was catching on fast.

Sen shook the loose snow off her cloak before opening the side of the shelter and moving in. Meri had done her bed thing again, and was half asleep.

"Rabbit!" Meri said as soon as Sen got in.

"Sure, sure, yell about the rabbit, not that I'm back," Sen said.

Meri blinked at her for a second. "Were you just teasing me?" She blinked several more times before saying out loud to herself, "I think she was teasing me."

Sen rolled her eyes and bent even further to hang the rabbits out over the fire.

"I didn't know you could do that," Meri added.

"Cook rabbit?" Maybe the cold had been harder on Meri than she'd thought. "I just did it the night before last."

"No. Tease, be happy, have fun," Meri explained.

Sen just rolled her eyes again, not sure how to respond.

The fire was actually well made. The girl must have been paying attention when she'd fixed the one the other day, because the wood was neatly tented, the kindling mostly gone but the flames working on the medium sized sticks and starting to eat into the logs. Wood was stacked along the east wall, providing more fuel and a better windbreak.

"Nice work with the fire," Sen said, hanging the last rabbit.

The shelter went quiet.

Sen looked over at Meri. "What?" she asked. The girl baffled her.

"I didn't know you could do that either," Meri said.

Sen sighed. "Do I want to ask?"

"Be encouraging like that."

Sen straightened as much as she could under the low ceiling. "You thought I couldn't be encouraging? Why?" This was almost insulting. She didn't even know her. But she had come to know her at one of the worst moments of her life.

Meri shrugged. "You just don't seem like the encouraging type."

"I'll have you know that I was one of the best trainers at the palace grounds. Every kid that came in wished they could train under me."

Meri just lifted an eyebrow. "Just because you're the best doesn't mean you know how to be encouraging. How did they feel when they actually became your pupil? And what did you teach, anyway?"

Well there was something she'd never really thought about. She'd had many seconds over the years, but only two she'd really cared about. Michl, long gone, and Harington. Her heart clenched. Harington, who'd almost become a son, with his sweet smile and always happy mood, even with all of the things the officers put the Orcus through. He was alive still, back at the palace. She was going to believe that until proven otherwise.

That part of the plan she'd never mentioned to the girl. Get the bracelet off and make a quick detour to the palace training grounds, to see if any Orcus were left.

The shelter was silent. She looked up. Meri stared at her expectantly. Ah, she'd asked her something.

"What did you teach?" Meri asked again.

"Firsts teach their seconds everything here. How to survive in the wild, in battle. How to fight in close combat or ranged. How to identify poisons and how to counteract them. What do your firsts teach you?"

"This is really exciting though! You already know how to be a teacher, a mentor!" Meri bounced a little and clapped her hands. Oh no. She shouldn't have left her alone to think. "I was thinking, maybe you can start teaching me the language you were speaking to those men? You know, in case I need it?"

Surprisingly, not a really bad idea. She shouldn't be around long enough to learn much, but teaching her a few phrases would pass the time, without Meri constantly asking her questions about herself that she didn't want to answer.

"Fine. We can start with something easy."

Meri's mouth dropped open. "Just like that? You just said yes? I'm understanding you correctly, right?"

Sen bristled a little. "All I've been doing since you got here was helping you."

"That's true, I guess," Meri said. "Thanks."

Slightly mollified, Sen shrugged. Sure, she didn't know that Sen had her own reasons for wanting to keep her alive, at least in the beginning, but that meant even more that she should be thankful she'd put up with her this long. "Besides. You should wait out here tomorrow. I'll only be a few hours, and then we can head back to the portal. It would be good for you to know some basics while you're alone."

"Alone? What if something happens to you?" Meri asked. "I can't even talk to anyone here!"

"True, but if something happens to me in there, it'd probably happen to you too. You still stand a better chance staying out here."

"Ah, no. Follow you inside a city to talk to someone, or stay out here in the ice and snow and shiver, waiting to see if you come back? I'm going with you."

Sen sighed.

Meri crossed her arms in front of her chest. "You can give me that longsuffering sigh, but it doesn't change anything. I might be annoying, but going with you could save my life."

A wave of dizziness hit Sen, and her stomach rolled. What was this? It hadn't happened since she'd come back through the portal. She curled up, clenching her eyes shut.

"Sen?" Meri's voice barely came through. "Sen, are you okay?"

"Hmm?" People. Or person. She couldn't let her see a weakness. "I'm fine. Just thinking about where to start."

The bracelet prickled, almost sending her to the ground. It was calling her. Calling her to a master.

"Are you sure?" Meri asked.

Sen nodded, but didn't risk speaking.

"Okayyy," Meri said. She didn't sound like she believed Sen's statement, but that was the best Sen could do at the moment.

She closed her eyes, a different kind of pain going through her. Tomorrow, she would find the Crafter, get the cursed thing off and go on with her life. After dropping this one at the portal.

"Let's get started then. How about Hello? That's what we did in Spanish class," Meri suggested.

What was Spanish? Probably another language that she didn't know the name of. "Fine then. Let's get started."

CHAPTER SEVEN

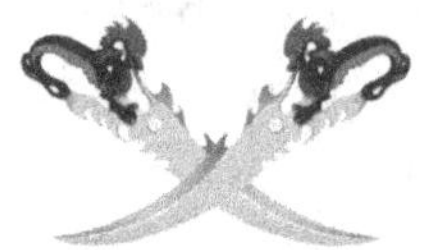

The rabbit they'd had for breakfast was trying to hop its way back out. It had gone down without a fight, which made Meri think that the whole nausea thing was caused by nerves. Which was really not cool. Surely she should be getting used to being in death defying situations by now, and have nerves of steel. Maybe it didn't work like that.

Staring up at the imposing rock wall in front of her was making her think it definitely didn't work like that. They'd tunneled out of their shelter this morning after breakfast and walked, again forever, with Sen helping her work on her Uthorian. It was confusing, but still easier than the Russian she'd tried to take in high school.

They'd stopped outside the city by late afternoon, just behind a hill. Waiting to see what an actual city here looked like had been almost torture. Now she pretty much wished she could go back to the waiting part.

If the bodies hanging over the sides of the walls were any indication, this place wasn't very friendly. No wonder Sen didn't blink an eye at killing people.

She gulped in a breath and adjusted her hood to make sure it covered as much of her face as possible. Not that anyone here would recognize her, but Sen had said not to take any chances. Good thing it was cold enough that everyone else was covered up as well.

They shuffled along in line with farmers and loggers, miners and peddlers, all coming in for the night. Sen had told her that many of the people normally lived outside the walls, but with the war going on everyone felt safer inside.

Of course she had to go and find another world that was in the middle of a war, not one where everyone got along. Were there any of those?

She had been able to snap a couple of pictures before Sen had noticed her phone out and frowned at her until she put it away. It was a good thing she'd thrown in a couple of those extra battery packs, or she'd be crying right now. She still had a full one for her camera, too.

Everything that she'd snapped a picture of so far could have been made up, fixed with Photoshop, and therefore, not proof of another world at all.

It was going to be really hard for someone to explain away an entire city and castle like this.

Carts in front of her pulled by massive horses looked like toys next to the wall. Horses were all she could come up with to call them, even though their legs had claws on the bottom, and the hide looked more like scales. Barbed metal spikes ran in patterns up the side of the wall, pointed down to stop any invading force. The road that they'd come in on seemed large compared to anything they'd traveled on so far. Until they got close to the gates.

They had to be at least thirty feet high. And that was just a conservative guess. Meri paused to look at the chain system that must be used to open and close them, but didn't take long. Getting separated from Sen would be a disaster. She couldn't even ask for help, and if she tried in the wrong language she'd probably end up hanging off the wall next to the other bodies.

The pace seemed to slow even more once they made it through the gates. Soldiers guarded the entranceway, but they didn't spare her a second glance.

Sen had told her not to get too close. To make it seem like they were both traveling alone. She wanted to believe it was just so that they were less noticeable, but had the bad feeling it was also in case one of them was stopped for questioning, the other wouldn't be caught as well. Sen wouldn't be able to save her here.

Sen finally ducked into an alley. Meri waited, checking for anyone tailing her before sliding in behind her. She caught up quickly, trying not to let her breathing give away the fact that she was about to freak out. She crowded in close to Sen, so her English wouldn't have to be spoken very loudly. "Whew, okay, we got this far. Now what? Any chance of someone on the inside who can get us in closer without being seen?"

Sen stiffened. "No. No one."

"Didn't you say you grew up here?" Meri asked. "Don't you have friends we can ask for help? Maybe they can find the guy and bring him to you so you don't have to take the chance of being spotted."

Sen's face blanched for less than a second before her mask slipped into place. "Orcus don't have friends."

"What's an Orcus? That doesn't translate." The implications of what she'd said were a little scary. The reason behind the fact that Orcus didn't have friends couldn't be a good one. At least not one that she could come up with. Besides, what did that make her to Sen? Hopefully not expendable.

What about family? Sen had never mentioned her family. Neither had Meri, so that was okay, but her family would help her for sure, right?

With practiced ease, Sen ignored her question about what an Orcus was and ducked and dodged through the city, sticking to dark dirty alleys with people Meri would be seriously freaked out to walk by if Sen hadn't been there. As it was, she was only slightly freaked out, which was a step up, in her opinion.

Sen had said this was her city, but when she said that Meri had just thought it was the city she most associated herself with, like Meri and Jacksonville, Florida. If a person were to ask her where the closest drugstore was, or how to find fast food, she'd be able to help. But to cut around the city like this, obviously knowing exactly where she was going? No way. She'd be so lost.

At least it was warmer here, with no wind. Not warm by any means, but warmer.

The alleys they moved through slowly became cleaner. The buildings they passed by, nicer. Soon they were at another wall. This one not nearly as large, but just as imposing.

"We won't be able to go through this gate," Sen whispered after Meri moved in to huddle. "The guards watch it too closely. I know a place we can go over the wall." And just like that, she was gone, like that was enough of an explanation. Meri sighed. Well. It was more than she'd gotten in the whole first day she'd been here, so she'd take it.

Going over the wall didn't seem great though.

Sen led them along the wall for a couple of minutes and then stopped and pointed at a tree. A tree that would be no help at all, because it was on the other side of the wall. What was she thinking?

Hold that thought. Hopefully she wasn't thinking what Meri was thinking she was thinking, because this was just plain stupid. Ah. Yep. She totally was.

Sen scaled the building closest to the wall with ease, pulled herself up onto a small balcony and paused, then launched herself over the wall and caught the tree. She stopped up there and waited. When Meri didn't immediately follow, she waved her arm, urging her to hurry.

Well, this was not ideal. She looked in both directions up and down the street. It was getting darker and she seriously didn't want to stay out here alone.

"Wonderful," she muttered, squinting up at the building. The bricks were slightly uneven, leaving nice handholds. Better than some of the trees she'd climbed, looking for panther signs. Well. Here went nothing. She scrambled up the side of the building, with so much less grace than Sen had just shown. Less speed too. She could practically see the aura of impatience radiating around Sen's stiff body.

"Hold your horses, I'm doing the best I can." That was a long jump. Really long. She peeked over the balcony rail. And that was a long way down.

Okay, now she was just stalling. She ran through all the different possibilities of what could happen with this jump. Most not good, and it wasn't like there was a hospital nearby. Oh well, such was life. Without letting herself think about it any further, she launched herself in the air.

It was forever, but also an instant before she hit the tree, scrambling to find something to grab onto. She slipped and would have fallen, but Sen grabbed her by the back of her cloak and hauled her closer to the trunk.

She made it to the ground and dusted the bark off her clothes, trying not to pant. Sen dropped down beside her. "We better have a different way of getting out of here."

Sen smiled, looking like she wanted to laugh. Since when did that happen?

"We will. Once I get this bracelet off, we'll be able to just walk through the gates if we want." She paused. "Not that we will, since I still don't want anyone to know how to find me, but we'll have plenty of options."

How did taking a slave bracelet off make so many options open up? Now was not the time to ask, but she was curious. She'd find out shortly.

Taking off with determination in her stride, Sen led the way around the wall, still sticking to the shadows. Several times she'd stop, waiting for a couple of guards to pass.

Finally they reached a small building. So unassuming compared to the others surrounding it. But from the way Sen stopped and took a second, then set her shoulders and marched in, the place was significant.

It was warm inside, much more comfortable without the bite in the air outdoors.

They moved down a short hallway, turning left into a little room without pause. Sen knew this pathway well, apparently. She stopped to draw her daggers before pushing the door open and slipping inside.

There was a stooped older man leaning over a worktable when they pushed their way into the room. Without giving him a chance to notice them first, Sen jumped forward and knocked him to the ground, kicking whatever he was working on out of reach.

"Sen!" Meri yelled. "He's old!"

"And dangerous," Sen growled, all hints of the smile and laughter from a few minutes ago completely gone. She was back to being the girl that had slaughtered the men the night before. Cold and unfeeling.

"How is an old man like this dangerous?"

The man on the ground started speaking in Uthorian, babbling on in fear. Sen's eyes just hardened and she shoved him into the ground harder. "Stay out of this. I'll explain when we're done, but know he deserves anything I could do to him, and more."

The look on the man's face nearly made her sick. The fear, defensive anger. But she was beginning to trust Sen, and if she said she had a reason, then she did. But there was no way Meri was letting this get out of hand. She never wanted to see anything like back at that road the night before again.

———

She would have to hurry. In this city, her city, she couldn't be seen. Any moment in the open was a risk. Everyone in this city knew her face. Before and after every battle the king paraded his Orcus in front of the entire city, doling out medals like that made the blood on her hands worthwhile.

Soon enough the king would get what was coming to him. If not from her, then from the Trulathians. Without the Orcus the war could not be won. The city had been somber, already feeling defeated. Somehow she couldn't bring herself to care. Here was not home. Trulathia was Uthoria's enemy, but did that really make it hers?

Not anymore.

She held her arm out to the man, pushing her sleeve up. "Take this off." Speaking in Uthorian almost seemed strange after talking with the girl in Swarian over the last few days.

The Crafter's eyes widened, the blood draining from his face. "It can't be. You all died."

"None live at the palace?" she asked, afraid of the answer.

"No, every Orcus was killed in an attack at the pass near Tarsh Vannen. The young ones had even been sent along to observe."

She closed her eyes for a second, the last little hope she had that

Harington might be whole and well, still bull-headed and untrained but alive, was gone.

"They were all killed but me. Now take it off."

He scooted back from her a little, his hands going up in the air. "I would help you if I could, truly, but there's nothing I can do. There's no way for me to remove the bracelet."

Her vision swirled, the daggers dropping to hang in her hand, the familiar weight of the blades suddenly more than she could hold. He couldn't remove it? Could anyone? Would she just waste away until she died from not having access to magic?

"You have to. I need it off, now."

"Are you starting to fall ill?" the old man asked. He almost sounded gleeful. "Orcus don't do well when they don't have a master."

There were questions she wanted to ask, things she needed to know, but she wouldn't give him the pleasure.

She bent over him, sliding the blade close to this throat. "Take it off," she whispered.

"I cannot help you remove the bracelet. Even if I wanted to, it would be impossible. I only make them, I cannot remove them."

"Then of what use are you?" Sen slid her blade farther forward.

"Wait, wait!" The man's hands twitched in the air. "I have no knowledge of how to remove the bracelet. But I have something else that may help. The binding words, so you can pledge yourself to another."

Sen grimaced. "I will never again be a slave. Die."

"Sen?" Meri's voice, calm, yet timid. "Are you really going to kill him?"

The girl couldn't understand Sen's words. But her body language shouted her intentions. She stared down at the Crafter, anger boiling under the surface of her skin. "You have no idea the things he has done. What he's done to me, to others like me. He deserves to die."

"Probably. But what about the things you've done to other people? Like the men back at that village? Surely they weren't all evil. They had probably been told all kinds of things about you that weren't true, things that made them scared enough to want to turn you over."

Things that weren't true? Maybe. But probably more things that were true. Innocent people she'd cut down, wars she'd started, all because of the whisper of her master.

"He can't be allowed to do this anymore," she ground out from behind gritted teeth. Even if it wasn't for revenge, wasn't because of the hand he had in forcing her to do all kinds of horrifying things, that was reason enough.

"Isn't there another way?"

Sen tore her eyes off the Crafter for a moment, looking over at the girl. She was teary eyed, almost looked sick. Was death so rare where she was from that she couldn't stand it? Sen looked back at the Crafter, considering. Was there another way?

"What would one of your bracelets do to a normal person?" she asked.

He blanched. "The effect would be the same as if it was placed on an Orcus, without the blocking of course. That's why the king ordered me to continue crafting them, even after the Orcus were slaughtered."

She allowed one side of her mouth to tip up in a smile. The girl was going to have to live with this. It was poetic justice, after all. Though she was glad that she only spoke Swarian and had missed the last part of what the man had said. No reason for her to know about the magic. No reason for her to go back to her world and tell everyone about it.

"Good." She nodded toward the basket of completed bracelets sitting near the work bench. "Put one on. Pledge yourself to me."

The Crafter shuffled to his knees, tears filling his eyes. "No, please. I have children, a wife. Don't do this to me, please."

She bent over and grabbed him by the hair, tipping his head back. "You think the people you do this to don't have families? That they want to be enslaved?"

"I'm sure they don't want to be, but they're dangerous!" His voice lowered to a whisper. "You're dangerous. Orcus need to be controlled, so another doesn't become a Garanath, ready to destroy the world if that's what it takes to bend it to their will."

"As if we are all just a moment away from snapping and killing hundreds of thousands," Sen bit out. "The bracelet. Now."

When he didn't move, she grabbed his jacket and dragged him over to the basket. "Take your pick."

He reached out a trembling hand and picked one up, clumsy fingers dropping it right away.

She pushed him closer with her boot. "Take. Your. Pick."

The one he chose looked too big. She knocked it out of his hand and grabbed another, more suited to the size of his bicep.

"Please, the spikes, it's going to-"

"Hurt enough you want to die?" Sen ground out. "I know. Now are you doing this, or am I?"

He leaned up and looked at her face, apparently deciding there was no going back from this, and rolled up his sleeve.

Bitter anger crawled up her throat as she stepped forward and loosely fitted the bracelet to his arm. She wanted so badly to feel good about this, to feel like she was avenging the pain that this man had put so many through.

But she didn't. She just felt weary, all the way down to her bones.

"Take a deep breath," she ordered. It was exactly what she had been told. It probably didn't help, but it was something.

The Crafter obeyed, and she snapped the bracelet closed on his arm, blood spilling down his wrist and over his hand.

He fell to the floor, writhing in pain. It wasn't just the pain of the metal, but the sheer agony of the magic of the bracelet taking control of the body, forming ties, waiting to be knotted to a master.

Meri stared at Sen accusingly.

"You wanted me to leave him alive," she said. Meri just crossed her arms. "What? He's done this to my people for generations!"

Meri didn't say anything, but her silence shouted enough. Sen was beginning to think she was even younger than she'd originally assumed. She had no idea how the world worked.

It took a moment, but the movement on the floor ended. She reached down and hauled the Crafter onto his knees. "Now give me the binding words."

Hate flashed in his eyes, but it didn't affect her in the slightest. She'd been on the receiving end of that look since the day she was born. Born to be a weapon to protect the people of Uthoria, but they didn't see it like that. All they could see was what they didn't understand.

The only person who had never looked at her like that stood behind her. The outsider, who didn't know better than to be her friend.

When the Crafter didn't give her the words, she shook him.

He glared, but told her, the words foreign to her even with all her training.

She ran them through her mind, committing them to memory, then said them out loud with all the authority she could muster.

The bracelet sizzled and cauterized the wounds it had caused, the stench of burnt flesh filling the room. "Who is your master?" she asked.

"You are," he glowered.

She motioned toward the basket of bracelets, the form of her nightmares. "Destroy them. All of them. Right away. And never create another, understood?"

"Understood," the Crafter ground out.

"Now. Ideas. How can I get this thing off?"

"Like there is only one Crafter, there is only one who can remove the bracelets as well. Her name is Adeen, and she lives in Trulathia."

Her stomach dropped to the floor, eyes slamming closed. Of course. Nothing could ever go right for her. Of course the one person that could help her would be in enemy territory. "Where in Trulathia?"

"At the palace, in Treyor. She is descended from a strong, devout Uthorian family, but the royals here decided that it was too dangerous for someone who could remove the bracelets to live in proximity to the Orcus, so they relocated the family generations ago. Even now, when we are at war with Trulathia, the family is left in peace because the Trulathians rightfully fear they may need her services one day."

It was what it was. Either stay, and die a slow painful death, cut off from the very essence of her being, or go and take the chance of being enslaved again. She would never be a slave again. Binding herself to another would never happen. She straightened. This weasely old man would not see her weakness.

"Destroy the bracelets right away, then go back to your family. Find another job, a decent one, that helps and doesn't harm others. And tell no one that we were here."

Surprise colored his face. "You will let me live?"

Sen shrugged toward the girl, who was still silent. "Thank her. It's better than you deserve." She moved for the door, leaving him lying on the floor of his shop. "Again. Tell no one about us."

"Wait. It's affecting you, isn't it?" The Crafter pushed himself up, leaning heavily on his workbench. "Not having a master. Being cut off from magic."

She paused but didn't turn around.

"I always assumed that would happen, but I've never truly seen it. I've been around enough Orcus in my day to see when something isn't quite right. You hide it well."

"How long until it truly affects me?" she asked quietly.

"Without any history of this, I can't say with any accuracy. It could be months. It could be days. But it will kill you."

She looked at him over her shoulder. "Why are you telling me this?" Without her specifically asking, the bracelet wouldn't have forced him to speak.

He shrugged, but was forced to answer. "Penance, maybe."

There was no answer for that. She moved down the hall and out the door into the waning light of dusk. Happiness that they had survived this far warred with what had to come next.

"How do you know he'll do what you told him after we leave?" Meri asked, breaking her out of her thoughts.

"How do you know I told him to do anything?" Sen asked.

Meri rolled her eyes. "You were ordering him to do stuff right and left. That comes through, even when I only understand one word in a hundred."

"The bracelet will force him to do as I've instructed." She didn't feel like talking, but the girl would just badger her until she answered. "He's now my slave."

Meri's eyes widened. "Your slave? So it's magic? Like real magic?"

So much for her not finding out about magic. But at least she didn't know Sen could control it. When she got this bracelet off. If. The chances of that were beginning to look slim. And now she needed to decide what to do about Meri. Hauling the girl around Uthoria was one thing. Taking her to Trulathia? Something entirely different.

"What did you guys talk about for so long?" Meri asked. "Why didn't he take your bracelet off?"

"He couldn't," she answered, short without meaning to be. "He told me of someone else that may be able to help." She slid down a dark alley, avoiding the main street. All of her plans on how to get out of here were in ruin. Magic had been her go to, because the bracelet was supposed to be gone.

Now what would she do? Risk her life going to Trulathia? Risk slavery? Or slowly die, a painful death. She could feel it, deep inside. Magic sustained an Orcus, and without it...

The girl followed behind her, uncharacteristically quiet, like she could feel the emotions burning their way out from under Sen's skin. Why could things never go the way they should? She'd been cursed from birth with being different, and she couldn't change that.

If she did decide to try Trulathia, what would she do with the girl? Leave her alone to die, because she would, or waste two days taking them back to the portal? Two days could make a huge difference, if the tremor in her hand meant anything.

Time enough for that once they were outside the walls. For now she needed to focus on getting them out of the city. She ran her hand along the wall as they walked. It almost quivered, like the earth inside it knew she wanted through, but the bracelet kept it from leaping to obey.

It would be a long drop, but the tree they had used to come in was the only way out now. The only reason she even knew of the tree in the first place was that she'd had her master tell her she couldn't use magic for a month while she was in training, so she focused on swordsmanship instead of the elements. She hadn't let that stop her from sneaking out into the city to explore.

The girl groaned quietly when they got to the tree, but climbed it just fine. Sen dropped on the other side first, the cobblestones making the landing hard.

Meri jumped after her without pause. She was getting better at this life. Sen wasn't sure if that was a good thing or not.

The city was quiet. Much quieter than she would have expected with all of the extra people staying in the city limits at night, terrified the Trulathians would attack in the dark. People lined the alleys, small families huddled together for warmth. She passed by them without looking, but she could practically feel Meri's dismay.

When they reached the main gate, it was closed. She nearly cursed under her breath. Of course it was closed. They were waiting for an attack. In times of peace the main gates stayed open all night. Only the gates to the upper city were closed.

But this was definitely not a time of peace.

Staying overnight in the city couldn't end well. Someone would recognize her at some point.

She walked past the gate like that had been her intention the entire time. They wouldn't be able to find an inn. She had no coin left after the fiasco at the last one. They were about to become those people Meri was pitying a few minutes ago.

Unless... Yes. That would work.

She picked up her pace now that she had a destination in mind. The city had its own water supply, underground in case of attack. It would be much warmer down there. She walked by the first two entrances because there were people nearby. The third, they were in luck. The alley was empty.

She jammed her knife into the hinge holding the small trapdoor in place. The lock was fairly new looking, but the mortar the hinge hooked into was crumbling. It only took a second of wiggling before the hinge popped free. She moved to the next one, and it succumbed even more quickly.

After throwing the door open, she motioned the girl to jump down. Again, she did without pausing. If she'd let herself, her heart would warm at that. Meri was truly starting to trust her.

One last glance around. No one. She jumped down the hole, pulling what was left of the door over it as she went. It was only a short drop down, and it was instantly warmer. The dampness would have made building a fire difficult, but they didn't have the supplies anyway.

Meri shifted to the side and let her go ahead.

"Where are we?" Meri broke the silence.

Ah well, it had to happen eventually.

"The aqueduct system that runs under the city. It stays much warmer down here. And there may be a way out at the other end. This time of year the water is low." There would be a scout watching, but that was easily taken care of. Unless they had replaced the old grating that had rusted and broken in spots, they would have no problems sneaking by.

"Watch for movement. There are many things down here we'd prefer not to meet."

———

Many things they'd prefer not to meet? Well that was just great. Not a thing, or even some things, but many things. So far she'd been doing really well tonight, keeping it all under control, not talking in case someone would overhear them speaking in English, just doing what Sen asked without questioning. The not talking part had been particularly difficult, considering whenever she got nervous she spouted nonsense.

They moved along slowly in the dark, carefully. Wait a second, why were they in the dark when she had a flashlight? "Wait a second," she said, and dropped down to rifle through her bag. "Ah, here it is." She flicked the light on and shone it toward Sen. Her face would be comical in a different situation. Okay, it was kind of comical even now.

"Is that a miniature of the light in your home in your world?" Sen asked, moving closer.

"Kind of?" Sure, she'd been to a bunch of science classes, but still. She didn't super understand how it worked, she had no idea how to explain it to Sen.

"Is it magic?" Sen asked, tapping the glass.

"No, just science." She fought the urge to smile, knowing she'd make Sen mad. Too bad magic wasn't actually a thing. Other than the portal. But that might be science too, just not that she understood. Sen obviously believed in magic, for some reason she thought the bracelet was a magical item. But most people from the Middle Ages would believe in magic too, what they didn't attribute to God. The bracelet she didn't have an explanation for, but if she could get one of those to take home with her...

She'd doubted for a moment, up at the Crafter's home. But that was just because she was tired. Nothing magical had happened, other than some colorful sparks.

"Can you make it not so bright? There are things down here we don't want to attract."

Oh shoot, she hadn't thought of that. She quickly covered the front with part of her cloak, muting the light. "Is that enough?"

"Adequate."

They moved along the tunnel more quickly now, but still cautiously. The left was rock, curving at shoulder height to arch over to the other side. On her right water flowed, but in the dark it was impossible to tell how deep it was.

The little walkway they were on was stone, slick from the dampness surrounding them. She turned the flashlight for a second to get a look at the far side of the tunnel. The same rock as on this side. It was probably six feet across to the other side, with no walkway over there.

"What do they use this for?" Meri asked, pulling out her camera and starting it rolling.

"It's only used in emergency, during a siege. There are rooms down here for civilians, and the water is fine to drink even if it tastes somewhat foul."

"Is it a stream?"

"No, it's all rainwater. That makes it more difficult for the enemy to pollute or poison. The gate we are heading for is only for overflow, and to get people out if the city falls. Mostly the royal family, but once they are out anyone could use it."

It was strange that Sen knew so much about the city, so much about the royal family. Really, she didn't know much about Sen at all. Had she grown up here? She'd called it her city. Did she have family here? Now wasn't the time to ask, but she would. Eventually.

She panned in on how the rock looked odd, then shut down her camera. She only had one battery left for it, and one charged up power bank for her phone. She needed to conserve.

"What's the plan now? Since that guy couldn't help you with the bracelet?"

"He pointed me to someone else."

"Far away?"

"Far enough."

Meri groaned. "More traveling. How I miss cars right now."

Sen paused and looked over her shoulder. "You don't want to go back?"

That was a good question. Did she? If she was smart she would. Why would anyone want to stay in a place like this when there was a place like home to go to. But really, what did she have there, other than her mom? School? Somehow, after seeing things here, school didn't seem nearly as important.

"Nah, not yet."

Sen still hadn't moved forward. "Things are only going to get worse. The country I need to go to... it isn't safe."

Meri couldn't stop the snort. "And this one is?"

"Compared to Trulathia? Yes."

Well that wasn't intimidating at all. Crap. But Sen didn't have anyone. She'd been through so much. What it was, Meri had no idea because the frustrating woman didn't talk, but it was obvious. She was past the point of doing this for the fame and fortune. Sen was her friend now, and her friend needed help. Not that she could do much more than support her, but still.

"I'm going with you."

Sen shrugged. "Suit yourself." And started back down the tunnel.

Well a thank you or something would have been nice. Not that she'd been expecting one.

Did she know what she was getting herself into? Probably not. But it had worked out so far. Not that that meant it would continue to work out, but she'd never do anything like this again. And something was starting to seem off with Sen. The blank looks, the suddenly acting like she was dizzy. It was happening more often. Something wasn't right.

Not that Sen would ever admit it. A shiver went through her. What if something was seriously wrong with her and something happened? She'd be stuck here, unable to find her way back to the portal, not able to even talk with anyone. Maybe she should be trying to convince Sen to go back with her instead of just tagging along all over this world.

Surely with everything doctors could do now, they could help with whatever was wrong.

"Have you thought of, you know, just a possibility, I mean, it might work…"

Sen looked over her shoulder with a raised eyebrow.

"How about instead we just go back to where I'm from? Someone there has to be able to help you."

Sen's attention snapped back forward. "No."

"No?" Just like that? Without even thinking about it?

"Your world makes me sick. I need to be here. I need to get this bracelet off."

Well that explained some stuff, actually. It must have been why she'd wanted to leave Florida so suddenly. Had she picked up a virus of some kind? Wow, even a cold could be dangerous if her body didn't know how to fight it. Which meant that Meri was probably susceptible to stuff here, too.

"The doctors at home can help you with anything you caught there, I'm sure of it. They'd be much more likely to be able to help you than anyone you're going to find here."

"It isn't like that." Her voice was sad, resigned almost. "The bracelet cuts a person off from accessing magic. I need magic to live."

Okay, what was she supposed to say to that? Obviously she couldn't say anything about magic not being real without offending Sen, and she seriously didn't want to do that. This was the most open she'd seen her so far and she didn't want to ruin it.

"So if getting the bracelet off doesn't heal you, you'll come back with me and try it my way?"

Sen snorted. "Sure. If my way doesn't work, we'll try it your way." She was quiet for a few steps. "Why are you helping me?"

Apparently walking in the dark was really conducive to tough talks. Why was she helping her? She had to put it into words that didn't make Sen think she pitied her, or that would be the end.

"I think you're great, and I don't see anyone else trying to help. Do unto others, right?"

"Do unto others what?"

"Do unto others as you would have them do unto you. It's a passage from one of the holy books on earth."

The look Sen threw over her shoulder was totally disbelieving. "Who would do that?"

"A guy thousands of years ago. It's just a saying now, to most people, but my grandma had it drilled it into me, taking me to church. I think it would change the world, if people listened to it."

"Seems impossible to me."

"It is tough. But if it's important to you, you do it."

They shuffled along in the dark in quiet for a moment. "That still doesn't explain why you came with me in the first place."

Ah, why could she not just let it go? "To be honest it started out because I thought I could tell everyone at home about here and make a bunch of money. But I think we've become friends and I don't want to see you try to do this by yourself."

Sen looked at her, right down to her bones, like she could totally tell if she was lying or not. She must have decided not. "The first part makes sense, but I don't understand the second."

"What, that we're friends? People do that."

If it had been anyone else, they would totally be getting a hug right now. But a hug wouldn't go over well, and would probably make Sen huff and stop talking.

No answer. Did she seriously not know how friends worked? Maybe not. This whole world didn't seem conducive to friendship. Allies, yes. Friends who you cared about, not so much. She'd seen more death in three days here than she could even imagine at home.

They came to a branch in the tunnel, a small bridge going over the water and another pathway going to the right. Sen paused. This was the first time Meri hadn't seen her completely sure of what to do.

"Haven't been down here in a while?" Meri asked.

"Not since I was a child."

"Oh." That wasn't super encouraging. But it was interesting. Sen as a kid was a funny thought. She'd never really seen her be anything but serious. Had she been a serious kid? Marching around giving orders and just expecting people to obey? She could absolutely see it.

Somehow coming to a decision, Sen took off down the left branch.

"I'd prefer to sleep here tonight and leave the tunnels before sunrise since the temperature is better down here than above. But we need to find the exit before we rest so we're ready to go in the morning."

The moment the word rest left Sen's lips, Meri's muscles changed to water. Well and truly exhausted, and not in the nice right-after-a workout kind of way. Like giving voice to the word made it all set in.

These tunnels had better not go on forever.

They moved along in the dark, on and on. At this rate they wouldn't even get a chance to sleep before the sun came up. She had to force every step, her muscles not wanting to cooperate.

Then something splashed in the water, and suddenly she wasn't nearly as tired. "Sen? Did you hear that?" she whispered.

"Yes. Saw it too. Just a snake."

"Ew!" Meri let out, involuntarily moving so Sen was between her and the water. "I hate snakes."

Sen let out a noise that Meri had to process for a second. Was that... a laugh?

"What? They bite! And they're just gross."

"These don't bite. You're perfectly safe from them, I promise. They just like the mice."

"I'll still stay over here, thank you very much."

She could barely make out Sen rolling her eyes in the dark, but at least this time it seemed like it was in an amused way and not a frustrated one.

Time was impossible to tell down here. They traveled and traveled, Sen occasionally pausing for a few seconds to think at forks, but somehow always seeming to know where to go. Or at least she put off enough confidence to play it like she did.

Though how in the world she knew where she was going down here was a complete mystery.

Apparently she did, because eventually they found their way to a room with a huge pool. Meri uncovered her flashlight for a second to try to see to the other side, but it was useless. The cavern stretched on farther than the light could reach.

Down below the pool stayed completely still, about a fourth of the way up the wall. Different levels went down the side, like long shallow stairs.

"There's still a lot of room down there for water," Meri whispered. Whispering just felt safer in this vast of a space. "It's huge. That's enough water to take a jet-ski in. And no gators."

"The gate is only to allow overflow," Sen answered. "Supposedly it has only been filled to the brink once since it was built."

"How does a space like this get built anyway?" Mind boggling, really, that this could be built without all the power equipment at home. But so had the pyramids. The walls were really strange. The exact same color, the same exact unnatural smoothness the whole length.

Sen didn't acknowledge her question. Did she not know the answer or did she not want to say? Weird. She motioned below and Meri slid down the first part of the wall to reach the first level. They went down two more before light showed through a section of the wall.

Meri moved to the gate and looked up into the moonlight.

"Don't let anyone see you," Sen said from behind.

She stepped back. Sen dropped her pack and started getting ready for the night. Meri walked over and dropped hers close by. There was a slight draft from the open gate, but the bowl shape of the pool helped keep it off them.

Sen curled up in her cloak. Just like that she was ready to sleep.

It would be super nice to just wind down like that. Her body still buzzed from sneaking through the city and climbing around in the dark. It would probably be a little while before she could sleep. "Night."

"We should keep watches," Sen said. "Do you want to sleep first?"

"No, go ahead. I'm not going to be able to sleep." Exhaustion set into her body, but her mind was a different story. "Night. Sleep well."

Sen grunted in acknowledgement and settled in deeper. "Night."

———

She really had no idea what time it was. She'd traded off watch with Sen, got some sleep and then Sen woke her when she needed to rest. That had to have been at least an hour ago.

What had caught her attention? Something rustled. Probably just her imagination. Sitting here in the dark really wasn't good for her, especially when she had no idea what kinds of things there were in this world and her mind was filling in blanks in scary ways. She'd almost woken Sen up about five times in the first hour, but had managed to stop herself.

Nope, the sound gently echoed around again. So not her imagination. Snakes didn't make sounds like that, did they? Oh crap. She flicked her flashlight on. It hadn't left her hand since Sen had woken her.

A quick sweep didn't reveal anything. But there, the sound again. She scrambled up into a sitting position. The light quivered as her hand holding the flashlight trembled. Something scraped on the stone to her right and she snapped the light in that direction.

Beady eyes looked back at her. She blew out a breath. At least it wasn't a snake. Maybe a rat. The thing stood up on its back legs, glaring at her. A mink, or something similar. Definitely not a rat.

"Aww, aren't you adorable."

It looked at her and cocked his head.

"Aww," Meri practically squeaked. "Are you used to people? You seem pretty friendly." She dug around and found a little scrap of left-over meat, tossing it over.

The thing gave it a little sniff and snatched it up in a tiny paw, glaring at her again and then taking off back into the tunnel.

"Hey! Come back! That's rude." It ignored her, scampering away. "See if you get any more when you're done with that!"

All the excitement over, Meri settled back down into her cloak and shivered a little, flicking off the flashlight. Underground was much warmer than up above, but still not Florida weather.

Her muscles were just starting to relax, her mind wandering when the scraping started up again. "Back for more?" she asked.

She got the flashlight back on and shone it over in that direction. Five sets of eyes this time. "Brought friends? Well I'm not sure we can waste that much food. Sen would kill me when she woke up." She glanced over at the sleeping girl. She was really out, sleeping more deeply than Meri had ever seen her sleep so far. Hopefully that meant she was starting to trust her.

She dug around for more scraps, but there wasn't much left. "Sorry guys, I need what's left for breakfast. I'm already kind of hungry."

They all cocked their heads at her, looking decidedly grumpy. One of them got brave and moved closer, chittering at her. It sat back on its back legs and stared expectantly.

"You're the first little guy, aren't you? You shouldn't have told all your friends. I might have had more for you."

The look he gave her back was rather insulted. It looked back and chittered its cute little noise at them. They answered. He turned back to her and showed his teeth, giving her a little snarl.

"Hey now! I gave you all the extra I had. I probably shouldn't have given you that much. Just be happy."

It did not look impressed. It dropped back on all fours and stalked forward, legs rigid and angry. The ones following started hissing, advancing behind the first. Five rodents. She could totally handle this. No reason to wake Sen. She needed sleep, and would be so impressed that Meri had handled this herself.

Scrambling started behind the mink things. She flashed her light. Oh crap. There were a lot more than five. A lot.

She barely heard a sound behind her before something hit her in the back. She yelled and jerked around, trying to knock it off, but the thing had a hold of her cloak with its teeth.

"Sen!" she yelped.

Sen jumped up before the echo of her name even started, knife in each hand. It took her less than a second to evaluate the situation. In that second three mink flew at her out of the shadows. One slice with her blade and all three hit the rock in pieces.

"Don't let them bite you!" Sen snapped, ripping one trying to get to Meri through her clothes off her cloak and slamming it into the wall behind her.

"Like I'm just going to let them bite me," Meri snapped back.

Sen's blades flashed in the dark and more tiny bodies littered their camping spot. "They're venomous," Sen got out before a chittering war cry started up all around them. "Pack up our stuff." Sen eyes scanned around them.

Meri scrambled to obey, fingers clumsy as she tried to stuff all of their things into bags.

"Get to the gate," Sen panted out, wildly swinging, catching one of those things in mid-air as it leapt for Meri. Meri jumped backward and sucked in a breath. So much for handling it on her own.

Meri ran for the gate as fast as she could, nearly bouncing off it when she hit.

"It's locked, Sen! What do we do?" she yelled. She turned in time to see one of the things coming at her fast and punted the furry little beast away. Its body splashed into the water behind Sen.

"Senara!"

Sen was a little busy. Thankfully some of the creatures were stopping to chew on their fallen comrades. They hissed and spat at each other, fighting over the bodies. Some gave up and took off after Sen again.

"Aleos acanos!" Sen yelled, not stopping her swinging. They were close enough now that Meri could hear the hiss of the venom dripping from the things teeth.

"Crap, crap!" she flung her bag up between herself and the raging horde of miniature horrors.

Something started to grind and the gate slowly dropped into the ground, inch by exhausting inch. "Seriously?" Meri yelled, kicking the stupid thing. She didn't even have the brain power at the moment to wonder how the gate had started to open at Sen's command.

Ripping her cloak off, she beat at a couple of the things trying to get in close to her.

A squeak caught her attention and she jerked back just in time for a creature to go flying in front of her face. Her gaze snapped to where it had come from. Surely those things couldn't jump that high. Nope. They were climbing the walls, as agile as the rats she had originally thought they were. That she wished so badly at the moment that they were.

She turned her back to the gate. Open enough.

Sucking everything in and making herself as small a target as she could, Meri leaned into the gate as it slowly slid down. A foot of open space at the top would have made her relieved, except it had a good seven feet to go before it reached the ground.

A splatter made her let out a yelp and jump sideways as body parts thudded against the wall to her right, squelching as they slowly slid to the ground.

"That is so gross," Meri moaned.

The little beast that had attacked her a moment ago ran past, stopping to stand at the bottom of the wall with its mouth open. How terrible that they ate their own kind. Terrible, but fortunate, otherwise Sen would be dealing with a lot worse than she was right now. Sen!

The warrior grunted as she dove forward, taking out a swath of five in one blow. Thankfully they were small creatures, or this battle would have been over with already.

All that seemed to be left were the desperate ones, the ones not strong enough to fight with their comrades over the bodies of the fallen. They were much more cautious now though, starting to think ahead.

Feeling useless, Meri groped behind her, trying to feel how far the gate had come down. About halfway. Maybe four feet up, four feet down.

"Climb over," Sen grunted, getting her long knife up just in time for a creature to impale itself on her blade. She flung it off to the side, close enough to attract some of the others.

Meri turned to obey, jumping up as far as she could, and then climbing the last little bit. She flung her bag over the top and waited before jumping down, straddling the gate.

Sen tried to follow, but wave after wave came at her, not giving her a chance to get over the gate. The gate was opening too slowly, she was going to be overrun before she could back through. She was going to watch her friend die, right here.

No.

She jumped down and frantically dug around in her bag.

"Meri, run," Sen panted, sounding exhausted.

Meri ignored her and fumbled around for another second before her hand closed over the end of her flashlight. She whipped it out and clicked it on full force, shining it into all those beady little eyes.

The front row froze, chittering to each other and blinking, turning their heads to try to shield their eyes from the bright light. That quick second of a distraction gave Sen enough time to jump up and pull herself over the gate, crashing ungracefully to the ground beside Meri.

Meri bent down and put her arm under her, letting Sen brace herself against her.

On the other side of the gate the monsters started to climb.

"We need to get out of here. Like, now." Meri dragged Sen to her feet, vaguely surprised that such a small woman could weigh so much. Probably all the weapons. "Come on, Sen, we have to get out of here. They'll be coming through soon."

"Aconsi, Aparte," Sen whispered. The gate ground to a stop for just a second, then started back up.

One of the little beasts fell over the top, dropping to the ground at their feet. Meri grabbed Sen's knife out of her limp hand and skewered it to the ground. It convulsed for a moment, angrily spitting at them, then finally stopped.

The gate went up much more quickly than it went down, probably because if there was an invasion up was pretty important. The doorway was soon sealed, covered by little bodies, paws sticking through the gaps in the gate. What would individually be little screeches made a din with all the tiny voices put together.

"We need to get out of here," Sen said. "This ruckus will bring the royal guard down."

"Don't need to tell me twice," Meri muttered. For some reason Sen still allowed her to help. Fighting off those things must have worn her down. She hadn't been like this even after fighting off those men back at the village. If it had been anyone else Meri would have been worried, but worrying about Sen seemed to be a waste of energy. Somehow no matter what, she was always fine. Meri grabbed the knife sticking out of the small creature and handed it to Sen.

"We need to keep moving. To the trees." And Sen took off, leaving Meri to follow.

Which she did, quickly. They weren't even to the tree-line before torches appeared on the wall above the gate. Two men, armor clanking, rushed down the stairway.

Sen grabbed Meri and dropped near some bushes, putting her finger to her lips. Like she didn't know this wasn't a time to talk. But then, she'd known at the inn too.

"They'll think haryrets caused all the noise. They go on a rampage like that occasionally," Sen said. Her voice sounded funny.

"Are you okay?" Meri asked. Something definitely wasn't right.

"Fine," Sen answered, but it sounded like she was gritting her teeth. She stood and started for the trees, but stumbled. Meri jumped forward and caught her part way down.

"What's going on?" Meri hissed.

Sen just swatted her away and stood again, moving slowly but at least moving.

"If you don't tell me what's wrong I'm going to turn my flashlight on and find out."

"Don't. The guard will see it."

They reached the trees and as soon as they were in cover, Meri pulled Sen to a stop. "I don't care if the guard will see it or not. If you won't tell me what's up I'm just going to have to figure it out for myself. Are you hurt?"

"One of them nipped me. My cloak took the brunt of it."

Oh crap, like seriously oh crap. "How venomous are those things?" She wrapped her arm around Sen again, and wasn't shoved away. Oh crap, this really was bad.

"Pretty venomous," Sen answered. "We have to get away from here though. Patrols will be out once the sun rises, and if they find me it will be worse than dying from a haryret bite."

Seriously? Them finding her would be worse than her dying in agony from a venomous bite? She'd seen plenty of movies and documentaries to know it wasn't pleasant.

"Which direction?" she managed to pant out as she half dragged Sen deeper into the trees.

"Follow the sun." Sen had no trouble with one leg, but the other didn't seem to be supporting any weight. The bite must have been on that side.

They plowed through small drifts, stumbling along far slower than was ideal.

"When do we eat granola?" Sen asked, her words slightly slurred.

"What?" So random.

"Are we going to eat it at your place?" Then she went off in Uthorian.

A tear froze to Meri's cheek. She draped Sen over her, pulled off one of her own gloves and felt her face. Enough heat to warm her hand radiated off the warrior's forehead.

She flopped Sen around. "Don't you die on me." Meri slid her glove back on, adjusted Sen's weight and then pushed on, doing most of the work at this point. "You hear me, Sen? I'm serious. Don't even think about it."

Sen went quiet and limp. She must have been carrying more of her own weight than Meri had thought, because she pulled them both to the ground.

"Shoot, shoot, shoot, what do I do?"

Meri rolled Sen over to feel for a pulse. When she'd taken CPR classes a year ago she'd never thought she'd be using that knowledge in a different world on someone bitten by a creature she'd never heard of.

There. A pulse. Erratic, but still strong. Did people from here have the same pulse rate? She pushed up to her feet. Obviously they couldn't deal with this by themselves. But she didn't even speak the language, let alone know where to go to find help. If she left Sen here, there was always the chance she wouldn't be able to find her again. But she couldn't possibly pull her along, even with the snow to help.

Sobs shook her body. This was it. Sen would die, and then she would. Her mom would never know what had happened to her, what she'd discovered. She rolled Sen onto her back and propped her head in her lap, letting the gently falling snow cover them both.

No. This wouldn't be how it ended, for either of them. She pulled Sen's cloak up a bit so her head wasn't lying in the snow and gently sat her head down. Taking one of Sen's daggers out of its sheath, she avoided as much of the blood as she could, and whacked at branches, cutting enough down to make a small one person shelter.

She wove the branches around Sen. She took her own cloak off, instantly shivering, but tucked it around Sen.

"We need help." Meri squeezed Sen's hand. "This close to a city, there has to be a farm or something around here somewhere. I'll be right back, I promise." She tucked Sen's cold hand into the warmth. She slid Sen's sheathed knife under the cloak, practically in her hand, but took the second one.

Every few feet as she stumbled through the trees, she chopped off a branch or cut a chunk of bark out of a tree. Somehow the dagger slipped through anything she swung it at, which had to defy some law of physics or something. But at least she'd be able to find her way back to Sen once she got some help.

Stumbling around in the snow took a toll on her already exhausted body. She rushed as much as she could, her legs trembling, her lungs feeling like they were about to burst. But finally she fell into a small clearing.

A nice sized cabin stood in the middle, smoke puffing out of the chimney. She whacked a chunk out of a nearby tree, wincing as the dagger chafed across blisters forming on her hand.

What had looked like a small clearing seemed much larger as she waded through the snow drifts to reach the door. She sucked in a deep breath, then lifted a fist and pounded, keeping the blade pointed at the ground.

Voices sounded inside. She pounded again, just for good measure.

A moment later the door flung open, revealing a giant of a man on the other side. She looked up at him and felt her head swim. Hopefully he was friendly. Even with a dagger she wasn't going to be able to do a thing against a guy that size, not after the night she'd had.

He looked down at her, and said something, but of course she had no idea what.

If she shook her head, that would seem like she was saying no. What if he was asking if she needed help? Hot tears splashed down her frozen face. To make it this far, and then not be able to actually ask for help...

A woman's voice came from behind the man, and he stepped out of the way. A small lady bustled past him. As soon as she saw Meri she exclaimed something loudly and grabbed her hands, trying to pull her inside.

Meri started crying harder. She was such a wimp, but this day was just so horrible. She tried tugging the lady out the door, but the man stepped in, glowering at her. She grabbed his massive hand instead, pulling him toward the door.

His wife said something to him and he heaved a huge sigh, grabbing a cloak and some gloves off a peg by the door. A smile nearly burst Meri's face, her frozen cheeks screaming in protest.

She rushed out the door, pausing to see if the big guy followed. He did, though far slower than she would have liked. He paused to pull an axe out of a stump and hefted it up onto his shoulder. Intimidating, but fair, considering she was asking him to follow her into the woods with no explanation.

The trip back seemed to go much more quickly. Now that she knew where she was going, kind of. They followed her trail of chopped up branches and trees. She tried to tamp down the tide of fear pulsing through her system, but it just kept steadily rising. What if Sen was dead when she got back? What if someone had found her, and she was gone?

By the time they reached Sen, her hands were shaking. Fear, adrenaline, exhaustion. Maybe all three. The makeshift shelter she'd built over Sen was mostly covered in snow.

She rushed forward and shoved the shelter off and tipped the branches over, careful not to speak. What had happened at the tavern wasn't going to be forgotten.

As soon as the man saw what she was trying to do, he shoved the handle of his axe at her and bent over. Meri hovered, unable to force herself to check, to see if Sen was still alive.

The man reached forward and felt for a pulse, then grunted and said something. He lifted her, the sight of her body hanging limply from his arms nearly making Meri puke. She'd never known someone who had died before.

Without stopping to see if she followed, the man trotted off back towards the cabin, following their tracks with ease.

Meri tried to copy his hold with the axe, putting it up over her shoulder, but the thing weighed a ton. She half carried it, half dragged it after him, not willing to let Sen out of her sight again.

———

Heat. So much heat. Wait, did that mean... Surely she would know if she was dead, wouldn't she?

She opened her eyes and blinked, forcing them wider. The crusty stuff that said they'd been closed for a while made it difficult. The need to drink slammed her a second later, the dryness in her mouth almost making her sick.

"Water," she managed to mumble. A face popped into view. Meri. Well that ruled out her being in hell. A girl like that wouldn't be there. "Water," she mumbled again, before remembering she should be speaking in Swarian.

"Now, now, I've got it here for you, but just little sips in the beginning." A woman's voice, one she didn't know. Speaking in Uthorian.

Meri smiled and squeezed her hand, probably trying to convey without words that it was okay. Meri didn't have the best survival instincts, but at this point Sen had to trust her. She was going to die if she didn't get something to drink.

Meri went behind her and propped her up while the woman dribbled a few drops of water from a skin into her mouth. For a second it made things better, but then the raging thirst gripped her mouth again, worse than before.

"More," she whispered.

"Alright, but just a little," the woman said, tipping the skin up again.

When she took it back away, Sen licked the little bit of moisture dribbled onto her lips, the thirst no longer overpowering but still strong.

Meri buried her face in Sen's shoulder, body shaking as she held her up from behind. What was wrong with her? If this woman had done anything... She glared at the lady, who didn't seem to notice.

"I'll just give you two a moment," she said, moving away toward a small kitchen.

"What's wrong?" Sen asked as soon as the lady was out of earshot. "Did someone hurt you?"

Meri smacked her in shoulder, sitting straight back up. "What's wrong?" Her voice rose a little. "What's wrong? You almost died! Why didn't you tell me sooner that you were bitten? When did it happen? Will you be okay now?"

Sen winced at the smack. She'd only been bitten once, but she'd been slammed around a bit, and that fall over the gate had not been one of her best moments. "Where are we?" A cabin of some sort, nice and tidy, well stocked.

Meri leaned back down, glancing over at the woman. "She thinks I can't talk." The words came out funny with Meri trying not to move her lips.

"I doubt she thinks you can't talk anymore," Sen answered, trying feebly to sit up. "You kept your mouth closed? You must have been scared."

Meri smacked her again. "I don't really know where we are, exactly, just that I found this place and they helped us go back and get you and bring you here. That was two days ago."

Sen snorted. "You mean you've had to go without talking for two whole days?"

Meri sat up, an indignant expression on her face. "Hey. I saved your life."

Well, that was true. Not much she could say about that. But it didn't change the fact that thinking about Meri not talking for two days straight was nearly mind-boggling.

"Did they have the antidote or did I just pull through?" It did make a difference, because it told her how long it would be until she got back to feeling normal. A few days, at the very least, just because of the dehydration. Her stomach growled. And lack of nutrition.

"She didn't have any antidote, but she had some herbs. We've been giving you broth," Meri said, nodding toward Sen's rumbling stomach. Wonderful. She'd heard that. "But since you were probably already hungry before, you're going to need a lot of food for a while."

"Yeah," was all she said back. This wasn't the first time she'd been out for a couple days. Probably not the last either, unless she died before it happened again.

The lady came back toward them and Meri shut up right away. Good. She'd hate to have to kill this woman after she'd helped them. She carried a steaming bowl of soup with her, handed it to Meri and went back to the kitchen.

Meri dipped the spoon in the bowl and held it out to Sen. Sen raised an eyebrow and held both hands out for the bowl. The lack of visible trembling almost made her proud.

The first spoonful slid down easily, flavor bursting across her tongue and making her mouth water even as she ate. But she didn't make it far into the bowl before she couldn't take another bite. She handed it back to Meri, trying not to look.

Returning for the bowl, the woman bent down and felt Sen's forehead.

Sen clenched her hands into fists, physically holding herself back from slapping the woman away.

"I'm glad you're feeling better," the lady said, pulling up a chair. She was probably in her early fifties, covered in pelts, long hair braided down her back. "My name is Fanel. What is yours?"

"Tash," Sen said. It wasn't like people named their children after Orcus. Orcus were considered a necessary evil, but despised. This close to the capitol, anyone would without doubt recognize her name instantly and as far as she knew, she was the only Senara.

Meri just looked back and forth between the two of them, but thankfully kept her mouth shut. She was getting better at this.

"Where are you from, Tash? And how'd you come to get a hayret bite? Those buggers are nasty."

"My sister and I were just visiting family in the city. We were up early to start our journey home. Not far into the woods a pack of them came at us."

Fanel cocked her head. "Strange. They don't usually like to leave the aqueducts, if they can help it. It's been a bad winter though. Lots of creatures doing things they wouldn't normally do." She nodded at Meri. "So. You're sisters, huh? She's so quiet."

"A little slow," Sen lied. She glanced at Meri, who cocked her head like she was trying to understand what was going on. Perfect. "Sometimes she catches on, sometimes not." She teetered on the thought of lying and saying she spoke Trulathian, but that was dangerous, or Arcasnian, but there was always the chance this lady spoke that as well as Uthorian. It wasn't terribly uncommon.

"Ah. Makes sense. She pounded on our door all in a tizzy. My husband, Garren, didn't want to follow her out into the forest. Things haven't been good around here as of late, and it's hard to trust even the people you know, harder still the people you don't. But she just looked so sad, so scared, we hadn't a choice but to help her."

With that, Fanel stood. "Speaking of my husband, I'd better let him know supper is ready. He's always hungry, even in the summer, but especially this winter cold makes him want to be eating at every moment." She took Sen's bowl over to a wash bucket and dropped it in, grabbed a cloak hanging by the door and went out, shutting the door tightly behind her.

"Meri, where are my daggers and bow?" Sen asked. Trust may be hard to come by for commoners right now, but it was always in short supply for Orcus. Non-existent now that she was the last. She glanced over at Meri. Maybe next to non-existent. The girl had risked her life for her, after all.

"Over there," Meri nodded toward a small cupboard. "I tried to keep them near you, but the man was insistent. What were you and the lady talking about?"

"They were afraid it was a trap of some kind, when you came stumbling up to the door," Sen answered. "That you had people waiting out in the brush, ready to attack."

"And they still came?"

Sen felt her face settle into a frown. "Yes. They still came." Did that mean there were good people here too, not just in Meri's world? Was it really possible that she had lived here all her life and not met them? One family she'd stayed with as a child had seemed decent, but she'd just always assumed she hadn't seen the signs of who they truly were because of her age.

She felt at her arm for a second. The bracelet still hugged it, as tight as ever.

"I didn't let her remove your shirt, though she wanted to check for other injuries." Meri frowned. "At least, that's what I think she wanted. She tried to show me, but I didn't really understand. You're so careful about that bracelet I was afraid it might mean something to her, so I just pretended to be upset every time she was going to change your clothes or whatever."

A flood of relief went through her. Maybe she didn't need to be as on edge as she'd thought. Maybe the couple really believed they were just some stupid girls who'd gotten into trouble. "Meri, you're a genius. You may have just saved our lives."

The girl's face went beet red, and she couldn't seem to hold back a giant smile.

Boots on the porch outside stopped their conversation instantly.

Sen leaned in close and whispered to Meri. "By the way. I told them you are my sister." She couldn't help the small smirk that worked its way across her face. "And that you can't speak."

Meri sputtered for a second. "You told them what?"

Sen shrugged. "I didn't specify why. I just said you can't speak. They can infer from that whatever they want."

Whatever Meri would have said next died on her lips as the door opened. She glared at Sen, which almost made her laugh. It might have, if she wasn't so terribly tired. Really, this healing without magic was torture. Last time she'd been severely injured she'd only been out for a couple days, and she'd had a skull fracture, several broken ribs and a broken collar bone. Stupid bracelet.

Her good mood at Meri's expense faded. In its place, exhaustion prodded her, poking at all her weak points. Voices of doubt that she had crushed years ago, shoved into tiny compartments wiggled around inside, trying to break free.

Eyelids heavy, she leaned back into her pallet by the fire. Garren and Fanel were talking with each other about the deer he'd managed to find, discussing different ways to dress it. Meri was staring at her, biting her lip like she was worried.

She would have liked to tell her everything was going to be fine, but not with the odd couple in the room. Garren was a giant. She fought off the tendrils of sleepiness as long as she could, studying him as he walked around the cabin, trying to decide if he was a threat or not.

He pretty much ignored the two of them, after a nod of greeting. He treated his wife well, which had to mean something.

It wasn't long before she couldn't hold it off anymore. Belly full, body warm, she drifted off into sleep.

———

That was it. Uthorian lessons six hours a day after this. She was so done with not being able to understand what people were talking about.

Meri strained to understand even a phrase, but it was useless. A word, occasionally, yes. Whole phrases? All guesswork.

Five days after Sen had finally woken up, and she still didn't understand any more than she had when it was just her and the cabin owners. She had figured out their names at least, and knew now that Garren and Fanel weren't just words. They hadn't left her and Sen alone since that first day. Intentionally or not, she didn't know.

Sen was very obviously getting restless. Every time the big guy left the cabin, her nerves practically radiated off of her, making Meri almost as big a nervous wreck as she was.

"Hello!" a voice shouted in Uthorian from outside, followed by a string of words that Meri had no idea what they meant. Oh crap, that couldn't be good. Meri looked to Sen to tell her what to do, but the other girl looked like she was about to fall over dead. Her face had gone deathly pale, even worse than the days she had been unconscious. Her eyes were wide enough they looked like they covered half her face and she was panting, like she was freaked out.

Even when it had seemed like Sen was going to die she hadn't even looked nervous. Did she know this guy? Meri jaw clenched. Was he the one who had put the bracelet on her arm? She'd never talked about it, so Meri wasn't even one hundred percent sure what it was all about. But the guy back in the city hadn't seemed very happy about it, even more than just the obvious pain those spikes going into his skin would cause him.

The man outside yelled again, and Garren and Fanel started talking frantically under their breath to each other.

Garren turned and said something to Sen, who didn't answer, still staring at the door. Meri reached over and shook her arm. Her attention snapped back to Garren, and they had a rapid fire discussion.

Fanel moved over and motioned them towards the back of the house. Sen looked wary, but she complied, so Meri did too. She was just going up a ladder into a small storage space when Garren started toward the door.

Sen took longer on the ladder than she normally would have, Meri catching up with her. She was there to grab Meri's arm though, and pulled her up and over the top. They huddled together as far back as they could go.

As soon as Meri's feet were out of sight of the door, Garren opened it and called something out in a jovial voice.

"They are looking for me," Sen whispered. "How is he so close to Arnath unopposed? If Garren gives us up..."

"He won't," Meri whispered, squeezing her hand. "I'm sure they won't. They're good people."

Sen looked over at her, one eyebrow raised. "How do you know that? You can't even talk with them."

Meri shrugged. "I can just tell. Garren came into the woods to help me, even though he was afraid it was a trap. They're good people. They've taken really good care of us. Feeding us even when I don't think they have much."

Sen rolled her eyes and went quiet, listening to the exchange going on downstairs. The voices rang out loud and clear. Stupid other worlds with different languages. Why couldn't they speak the same thing?

"What's going on?" Meri whispered. Sen waved her off and kept listening.

"Farewell," the voice outside called. One of the few words Meri did know, from her one day of work with Sen. Farewell. There wasn't a better word out there at the moment.

They waited quietly for a sign that it was safe to come down. Meri studied Sen out of the corner of her eye. She still had no idea why these men were chasing her. Did Sen always have these feelings of fear bottled up inside and had just let them out now because of her injury?

After a couple of minutes, Fanel came to the bottom of the ladder and called something up. Sen started down without answering.

The couple waited for them at the bottom of the stairs, eyes cold, arms crossed. She hadn't seen them like this, ever. They'd been so willing to help. What had the guy told them that would make them turn against her and Sen so easily?

Garren moved over to Sen, talking in an angry voice. He grabbed her arm and jerked the sleeve up. She didn't fight back when she could have easily leveled the man, even after being hurt. Sleeve up, Fanel hissed and stepped back after seeing the bracelet, spitting toward Sen.

"He's angry because we could have gotten him and his wife killed," Sen's arm was still up in the air. She didn't fight to take it away. No doubt if she did, there would be a serious confrontation. "If it had been Uthorian soldiers at his door instead of Trulathian, he would have given us up." Hearing Sen speak in front of them was a bit of a shock. But apparently now that they knew about the bracelet, there wasn't any reason to keep them in the dark about the English.

Fanel shivered a little, staring at Sen as she spoke. What was it about the English language that made people hate it so much? And how did they know about it anyway? It wasn't like there were no other languages in this world than Uthorian, so why did they recognize it and hate it, instead of just thinking that it originated somewhere strange and they just had never heard it before?

"Pack up," Sen said after a moment of glaring between her and the two others.

Meri went to obey. She slid sideways to get past Garren, but he let go of Sen and grabbed her.

Instantly Sen was there, punching him in the throat. He dropped to the ground, gasping for air. Fanel shouted something and jumped between them, hands in the air.

Sen glowered for a second, but Meri tugged her back towards their stuff.

From the floor, Garren tried to say something as Sen went for her weapons. Sen grunted but didn't answer.

Meri shoved stuff into their bags, not worried about orderly packing.

Moving slowly, hands still raised, Fanel inched toward Meri. Meri paused and let her, Sen watching closely from where she was strapping on her weapons.

Fanel said something, Meri just shook her head. Hesitantly the woman reached forward, and slipped her sleeve up. She looked about ready to cry in relief when there was no bracelet.

Okay, first thing to happen when they were alone was she needed to know more about these bracelets. Obviously. And second, she looked over to Sen who had that cold mask on from when they'd first met, she needed to find out how Sen was taking all this. Find out why everyone hated her without even knowing her. Garren and Fanel had seemed to like her just fine until they found out about the bracelet.

Garren escorted them to the door, mostly recovered from Sen's blow. She could have easily killed him, hitting him in the throat like that, but Meri had to assume Sen knew that. Knew exactly how hard to hit without being dangerous.

Originally she'd thought everyone from here probably knew how to fight, probably carried weapons like Sen. Now she was starting to think otherwise.

They walked out without a word. Meri adjusted her pack and looked back as Fanel came out the door. Sen didn't look, she just started walking.

"Thank you," Meri said in Uthorian. Hopefully it sounded right enough that Fanel could understand her. Sure, today hadn't gone well, but they had taken them in when Sen needed somewhere so badly. She'd always be grateful for that.

Fanel pulled her into a hug, surprising her and making Sen stiffen, even as she continued to stalk away. That woman was paranoid. Fanel motioned her closer.

"Bad," Fanel said. Wait, was that English, or did the word mean something different here? She nodded toward Sen. "Bad." She reached forward and touched Meri's cheek, then grabbed her hand. "Good." She pointed at Meri, then at the cabin before making swooping motions around her, Meri, and Garren.

Um, okay, did she just ask her to live with them? She glanced at Sen, whose pace had slowed enough to make her think the other girl was keeping them in earshot. Staying here until she learned some Uthorian and it warmed up before heading to the portal probably would be the wisest thing to do. But that left Sen trying to get that bracelet off by herself. Maybe if they found a way to get it off people wouldn't hate her so much. Maybe she could just have a normal life.

Meri eyed Fanel, then looked to Sen, who had kept moving and was now a distance from the house. "I don't think I can just let her go by herself. She's hurt. I know you probably can't understand me, but I have to go. She doesn't have anyone. I can't imagine what it would be like to not have a single person in your corner." She turned back to Fanel and smiled, shaking her head no. "Thank you," she tried in Uthorian again.

The woman patted her face, looking pretty upset. Meri smiled, barely able to force her lips to move. Then Fanel handed her a bag. Meri pulled it open and found it full of food. Dried meats and fruits of some kind that she didn't recognize right off.

"Thank you." She took the bag, gave Fanel a tight hug and waited, just for a second, the decision weighing on her mind.

Then she jogged off after Sen.

"You know you can stay if you want," Sen said. "We don't owe each other anything."

"I know," Meri answered. There wasn't much to say after that.

CHAPTER EIGHT

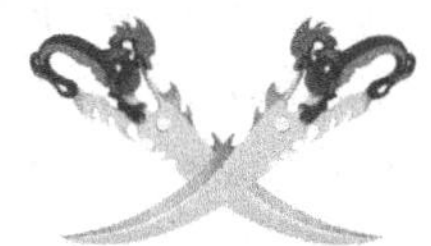

Not only did Meri want Uthorian lessons now, but also instruction in basic combat. It was probably wise, but it made her think of being back in Uthoria, teaching her seconds. She didn't like it.

It was a hard balance. She wanted Meri to be able to take care of herself, but she didn't want her to turn out hard. Bitter. Angry. And that's what this world did to people.

Meri'd been sad ever since they'd left the cabin. She'd seemed to really connect with Fanel, even though they couldn't speak. How must it feel to be able to make choices like this girl could? Come and go. Help or hurt. Everything was on her own terms. Sen had never had a friend, only allies. Somehow, that had changed. Now she had one, and didn't know what to do with her. What fool wouldn't have stayed behind in a warm cabin, fed and safe, instead of traveling who-knew-where with Sen? Only Meri, apparently.

A small sea with a channel that went into a river separated Trulathia from Arnath. If they'd been able to board a ship at Uthoria, the journey would only have taken two days. But with both sides looking for her now, going back to the capitol was out of the question.

Ships weren't going to Trulathian territory anymore anyway, so they would have had to make a detour to Arcasnia, which had remained neutral in the war. Really not a bad plan though, as the Arcasnians had nothing personal against Orcus. At least not in the last one hundred years or so. Garanath's destruction in his time had touched the entire world.

Meri did surprisingly well working on Uthorian. She took to it fairly quickly, forcing Sen to work with her on it for hours at a time as they traveled.

As surprisingly well as she did with the language, that was completely compounded by how badly she did with combat. She was next to hopeless, by far the worst student Sen had ever tried to teach.

The sad thing was, that almost made Sen happy. While it was important that Meri be able to take care of herself in case something happened to Sen, combat changed a person. To willingly hurt another human being twisted something inside. Hopefully it would never come to that with Meri, because Sen wouldn't let it as long as she was alive.

It took them longer than it should have to reach the small fishing village Sen was aiming for. There, hopefully they could find someone to get them over the channel that separated Arcasnia and Arnath. If she figured out some incentive other than money, because that she had none of.

The food that Fanel had sent for Meri lasted them several days. Sen would never admit it out loud, but it may have saved their lives. She would have been hard pressed to find them enough food, the way she was feeling.

The dizzy moments were getting more and more frequent. And no longer was she just dizzy. She could feel it coming, moments before it hit, and usually was able to make up some excuse to leave Meri for a few minutes to suffer through the attack without the other girl seeing what was going on.

Piercing pain through her head, followed by nausea. They couldn't take their time, it was getting worse and she needed this bracelet off. But they couldn't hurry either, because hurrying led to carelessness, which meant they would get caught.

Arcine was completely empty when they arrived, which was to be expected since they got there mid-afternoon on a sunny day. Nearly everyone would be out at sea. Fish was as good as gold in the cold months when things didn't grow.

Winter's grip was loosening, thankfully. Being on the run in the wild went much better in warmer weather. The sun shone brightly today, enough to make her want to take her cloak off. But not enough that she wanted to figure out how to carry it instead of wearing it.

And she may need it to hide her face. Coming back here was a bad idea, but she didn't have the time to come up with a better plan.

They made their way through town, Meri taking everything in. She was doing well enough here now that sometimes Sen forgot she was from another world, that all of this was new to her. Not for long. She'd seen almost all there truly was to see of Uthoria. Wilderness, ruins, small towns, the capitol, and now a tiny fishing village.

Meri stayed silent as they walked, even without people in sight. The girl was getting smart. She learned from her mistakes, something not everyone could claim.

The docks were empty when they arrived, every ship down to the smallest rowboat, gone. Sen sat down on the dock, dangling her feet over the water. Meri followed.

"So that's it, we're just going to sit here and wait?" Meri asked.

Sen nodded.

"Whoa. I kind of forget what that's like. Except for waiting for you to wake up, of course." Meri smirked at her.

It was strange, being teased in a good natured way. It had never happened until Meri, and sometimes she still didn't recognize it right away. "I'd have woken up sooner, but I needed a break from your endless babbling." She kept her face stern for a second, then let the corner of her mouth tip up in a smile.

Meri burst into laughter, the sound floating out across the water.

She could definitely get used to this. Having a friend, someone to watch her back. Someone that cared if she died or not for her, not because of how it would affect them.

Always before friendship had been dangerous. To have someone she cared about was foolish. She'd even done her best to not care for her seconds, though that had been impossible. She frowned. Had they known though? That she cared? Probably not.

Meri put the toe of her boot in the freezing water and flicked a little at Sen. "Where'd your mind just go?"

Sen grunted but didn't answer. Meri didn't push.

With the sunshine so warm on her face, it was beginning to feel like spring instead of winter. Sen closed her eyes and just soaked it in. When was the last time she'd been able to do this? Just have a moment where nothing was expected of her, where she had nothing pressing.

She couldn't remember.

Meri shivered beside her. "Hey, I know you're used to this kind of weather, but my Florida blood hasn't adjusted yet. Isn't there an inn or something we can find to wait at?"

"This town doesn't have an inn. One of the fishers has an extra room in her house she rents out on the rare occasion the town has visitors that don't stay with family. She's probably out there with the rest."

"Fine," Meri muttered, pulling her legs up from the side of the dock and tucking them under her cloak.

Sen dropped her face into her own cloak, not for the warmth but to hide the grin. Who'd have thought someone who had originally been so annoying could make her laugh now.

It was still winter enough that the sun hurried towards the horizon early. The light above the sea like that made the ships all coming in from different directions stand out, their multi-colored sails full of the winter wind.

"They go out together in the winter, and come in together, so they can make sure every ship makes it back to port," Sen told Meri.

Meri cocked her head, looking over at her. "How do you know so much about this place?"

"I spent some time here, once. As a kid. I'd been injured and my first left me here to heal so he could return to the army."

"Return to the army?" Meri frowned. "Are you some kind of soldier? And how did you get injured if you were only a kid? Aren't you afraid someone will recognize you?"

"No, it was long ago. Don't your firsts take your seconds into battle?" Meri's face twisted in confusion at Sen's question. "If a second isn't taken into battle, how do they learn?"

"Well I guess that's an answer to my question about you being a soldier, right? Where I'm from no one is allowed to even make the choice to be a soldier until they're eighteen. How young are we talking here?"

Make a choice? This was getting confusing. "Your soldiers aren't conscripted?"

"No. All volunteers. You still didn't answer my question."

All volunteers? That was just crazy. "Why would anyone choose to be a soldier and follow the whims of whoever is in charge? To give up your life in service to someone who may have bad intentions?"

"It's not really like that at home. Sure, the president," she must have seen the confusion on Sen's face, "The guy in charge, kind of like a king but not really, has to share power. We don't just have one man telling everyone what to do. We have a bunch of people, and those people are only supposed to do what the normal people in the country want. Not that it always goes like that, but still."

How was that possible?

Meri popped out that strange thing she was always 'taking pictures' with, and held it up, the horizon going by on its small 'screen.'

"What does that do?" Sen asked.

"It's called a camera. It records things, so I can see it all again. So I'll always have a memory of what I saw here. But the battery is almost gone. I won't be able to do it much longer." She turned it toward Sen. "Have anything you want to say?"

"You can play it back, whenever you want?"

"Sure." Meri leaned over. "You just push this button," she tapped on something and the screen changed from Meri and some guy to Sen and Meri sitting next to each other on the dock. "And then you push this button to start." She pushed it, and then smiled at the camera. "Just sitting here on the dock of some fishing village, waiting for the ships to come in for the night. This might be my last entry, I'm almost out of battery." She waved it at Sen. "Got anything to say?"

Sen just grunted.

"Yep, that's how I'll always remember you." She laughed and Sen rolled her eyes, then Meri hit the same button again. "And that's how you stop it. If the little red light stops blinking, it isn't filming anymore." She held it out in front of Sen and used her finger to move the screen around until it played back what had just happened. Now this, this was amazing. Even better than her portable light. "And here's where you turn it on and off. I'm gonna turn it off now, to save the battery. That's all there is to it. Easy."

"Sure. Easy. I would like very much to learn about how this works, at a better time when we're alone." She nodded to the closest ship, which wasn't far from the dock.

"You got it. But that doesn't mean you've gotten out of telling me some more stuff about how you guys do things here."

Sen grunted, not committing to anything.

Meri gave her a look that said she was on to her, but she let it go at the moment. The ships were close enough now that soon they would be able to hear them, even over the sounds of the water slapping the boat and the sails snapping in the wind.

Surely no one would recognize her. All of their faces had faded from her memory. So many years had passed, and even more than that, so many things.

Once the ships were close enough, the largest slid up to the dock beside them. One of the men jumped over the rail, landing on the deck with a thud. He lashed a rope to one of the posts rising out of the water, then ran back to the far end of the ship to do the same there.

Men and women practically poured over the side once the ship was secure, making Sen tense up. Crowds were dangerous. If she had her powers, she could take on practically any size of crowd if the attackers were average people, but she didn't and so she had to think about things like exit strategies more than ever now.

People eyed them as they went about their jobs unloading the ship and helping the others that came in, but no one tried to talk to them. That was fine by her. It gave her time to assess, to be the one that did the approaching when she found the person she wanted to speak with.

And there she was. Flame red hair gave her away, even though Sen hadn't seen her since she was a kid. Since they were both kids. It had been her family that her first had left Sen with. Bruna wouldn't recognize her, she was a couple of years younger, but it didn't matter to Sen. The only kindness she'd found in this world had come from the girl's parents. They were paid to keep her, to feed her and look after her wounds, but not to care for her the way they had.

"Hail," Sen said when Bruna was about to walk by.

"Hail," she answered, looking confused as to why Sen was talking to her after ignoring the large number of people who had flowed past already.

"I have a favor to ask of you." She'd decided to just come out and say it. To be completely blunt. She had nothing to offer the girl for passage. Hopefully some of the kindness of her parents flowed through her veins. Were they still alive? Still so happy together, even when they were incredibly poor? She'd find a way to ask, later. Right now it would be too conspicuous.

Bruna squinted at her, assessing. The girl had indeed grown up. She had been absolutely naïve when they were children, believing everyone only had good intentions. The world changed that fast, as it did to everyone.

"And what would this favor be?" Bruna asked. "If you're looking for a room, I'm not the one to ask, but I can point you in the right direction."

Sen shook her head. "We haven't the coin for a room. And it's not a room that we need, badly. It's passage. To Arcasnia."

Bruna cocked her head, looking her over again. "And why would you be wanting to go there? And why should I be wanting to take you?"

It really was too bad Meri didn't speak Uthorian yet. She was so much better at dealing with people. She probably would have had this lady not only talked into giving them passage, but a room for the night as well.

"We'll help you fish all day. You'll be going close anyway, won't you? Once the day of fishing is over, you can drop us off. You'd have free labor for the day, with nothing to lose."

"Other than the fact that you two are obviously ground lovers and would have to be taught something to even be useful."

"How about scaling fish? I'm a quick hand. Then they'd already be gutted when you reach shore, and you'd have extra bait ready."

Bruna considered that for a moment. "Seems like a deal to me."

A man walked up beside her. "Who's this?" he asked Bruna, wrapping an arm around her shoulders.

"Our newest hands, apparently. Though just for a day."

The man studied them quietly for a moment. Who was he to Bruna? He was awful close to her to just be a deck hand, even a first mate. His bracelet matched one on Bruna's wrist. Her husband.

"There were men through here the other day." The man's gaze went to Meri and back to Sen. "Looking for a girl about your age. That one of you two?"

Bruna crossed her arms in front of her chest and lifted an eyebrow.

"What kind of men? And why were they looking for a girl?"

"Soldiers. Trulathian soldiers."

Sen let her face go shocked and confused. "Trulathian soldiers this close to the capitol? Did you report it?"

"What do we care who rules. Trulathia, Uthoria, it's all the same to us."

Okay, that was much different than her parents. Or at least what she remembered of them. They had taken her in for the money of course, but they had seemed loyal. What did they think of their daughter's lack of allegiance?

Not that she truly cared. Both countries wanted to use her, to force her to fight for them. They could both burn for all she cared.

Now that she thought about it, there was nothing here she cared about. Which should make her sad, but didn't. She'd never been out in the world, other than coming from or going to battles. She'd seen a lot of this section of the country, but it was always torn by war, shattered and ugly.

Maybe after this was over, she'd go south. See for herself if the stories about dragons and water sirens were true.

She glanced over at Meri. After she got her back to the portal, of course.

An awkward silence had settled in while everything ran through her mind.

"When do we leave in the morning?"

"At dawn. First light." Bruna nodded toward the ship. "You can sleep on there if you want. Two other of the hands do. Sons of farmers that spend a few days working in exchange for fish to take home to their families."

"Many thanks." They would just have to make do with the food they had left, because they still had no coin.

Bruna nodded. "Why is your friend so quiet?"

"She can't speak. Born that way."

Meri squinted at her, more like a small glare. Ha. The Uthorian lessons were doing some good apparently. She seemed to understand that. Or maybe it was just prior history that gave her an idea what was being said.

"Sleep well," Bruna said, and started up the dock.

Sen went for the gangplank, knowing Meri would follow without prompting. Thankfully the sea was calm tonight, the ship only lightly rolling. The few times she'd been on a ship, she hadn't cared for it much.

They went down the short stairs to the lower deck, having to stay bent over because even though this was the largest of the ships here, it still wasn't big by any means. Sen checked and there was no one here. The two men Bruna had mentioned must have gone to find supper. Not that she could blame them. After spending all day on board, she'd want to get off for a while too. Especially with them having to repeat it on the morrow.

"Hopefully you're okay on boats," Sen said to Meri, moving to the back of the ship and dropping her pack.

Meri smiled. "I grew up in Florida. Of course I'm okay on boats."

Sen shrugged. She didn't really know what that meant, but okay.

They settled in for the night in silence, both tired. The ship blocked the wind well, but it would still be a chilly night without a fire. Better than a shelter in the woods though, and no way of being left behind in the morning if they overslept.

A scuffling above drew her attention. The two men back to settle in for the night? Hopefully they preferred the open sky. But it didn't really sound loud enough to be two men.

A small form started down the stairs. It was dark enough that Sen couldn't make out much about it. She slid her dagger out of its sheath, just in case.

"M'lady?" a boy asked, voice timid.

"Yes?" Sen answered, waving him over into the shadows.

"Bruna sent this for you." He held up a tray with two bowls covering it, a ray of moonlight making it just visible. He slowly sat it on the deck and scurried back up the stairs.

Sen walked over and picked up the tray, sniffing. It was just stew, fish stew no doubt, but it was far more than she would have even hoped for. Maybe Bruna was more like her parents than she'd thought.

She handed a bowl to Meri, who wrinkled her nose. "This smells terrible."

"It tastes worse," she hadn't had it in years, but it was unlikely the recipe had changed. "At least it's warm."

Meri gave it another dubious sniff before dipping in her wooden spoon. She held it up to her lips and blew on it, while Sen watched with amusement. Meri gave her a little half-hearted glare, and then took the first bite.

She gagged, spitting it back into the bowl. "Ew, gross! I like fish, but this is disgusting! Why is it so bad? If they eat this all the time they should know how to make it taste good!"

"It's the amount of salt they use to keep the fish from going bad," Sen said, trying not to laugh. "You get used to it. If you grow up on it, apparently you love it that way."

"So gross." Meri held her spoon up and let some stew drip back into the bowl. "Nasty."

"It's that or the last of the dried meat. If you won't eat it, I'll eat your share too."

Meri looked shocked. "Don't tell me you like this stuff?"

"No, I don't, not at all. But you learn to eat it if you live here very long, and like I said, it's nice and warm."

"Fine, I'll eat enough to warm up my insides, but you can have what's left," Meri muttered.

Sen smiled. "Sounds good to me. I'll sleep well tonight, warm and full." And with a goal in sight, even if the path to get there was grim. Right at this moment, she could let herself feel optimistic, for the first time she could remember.

———

"Sen. Sen, wake up. I think something is going on." Meri poked her again, but Sen was sleeping far harder than she'd ever seen her before. She tried to straighten up more, but the woozy feeling nearly knocked her back fully to the ground.

What was in that fish stew crap?

"Sen?" Meri tipped over and fell on top of Sen, who still didn't move. She had to keep herself from panicking, trying to control her breathing. She wasn't dead, was she? After everything they'd been through, she couldn't be killed by fish stew.

Heavy boots thudded across the deck. They paused at the top of the stairs, and several voices starting talking. Stupid Uthorian. Why hadn't she had Sen start teaching her the moment they had popped out of the portal?

Probably because she hadn't known there was another language here, which she totally should have. Not important at the moment.

"Sen, wake up. You have to wake up, please!" The whispers were getting more frantic. Once again she was leaning over Sen feeling for a pulse. Seriously? Who was supposed to be the awesome warrior here? Why was she knocked out so thoroughly and Meri just loopy?

Because she'd finished the stew. Because the stew was gross and Meri had barely touched her bowl. Sen had gotten a double dose.

The boots made their way down the stairs, lit by a couple of lanterns. She couldn't tell how many men there were, with her vision swimming all over. She closed her eyes.

One of the men came over and bumped her with his boot. She didn't acknowledge it. No reason for him to know she was semi-awake.

Hands grabbed her around the waist and she was tossed over some guy's shoulder. The force knocked the air from her lungs and she had to keep herself from crying out.

As soon as she could breathe again, she looked for Sen.

There, thrown across another guy's shoulder. She flopped as he moved, eyes glossed over and arms dangling. Was she dead? She couldn't be dead. She couldn't.

Meri gagged, tears dripping down her forehead as she hung upside down. If they didn't know she was awake, she would have the advantage. She had to keep it together, had to keep them from noticing she was still awake. Still alive. If the poison had been meant to kill...

Checking on Sen again didn't help. It had only been a few seconds. She shouldn't have expected change, but somehow, she had.

They reached the end of the dock and Bruna was there, waiting for them. She held a torch, and in its light Meri got her first look at the man's face behind her. Bruna's husband.

They spoke as they walked, but she could only make out a few words. Put them. Tomorrow.

This was so not good. She twisted a little, making it look like she was swaying from the movement of the brute who carried her, so she could get yet another look at Sen. No movement whatsoever.

You had better not be dead.

No kidding she had better not be dead. If she was, it was literally a matter of time before Meri followed. She closed her eyes, fighting the vomit that wanted to explode from her body. What had she been thinking? No amount of money was worth this. Her mom... She'd never know where she'd gone, what had happened. She'd be left for the rest of her life, wondering.

It wasn't fair. And it was her fault.

The tears fell silently as she fought hard to not let the sobs wrack her body. This guy couldn't know she was awake, couldn't know she wasn't completely out of it. It was their only chance.

Bruna said a bunch of stuff as they bumped along, stopping after what seemed like forever. The only word she recognized was dead.

The husband said no, so that was good. She cracked an eye, just as Bruna opened a shed door, took Sen's weapons straight off her belt, and her husband tossed Sen inside. Literally threw her.

Biting her lip to keep from crying out, Meri kept it together enough to stop herself from beating on the back of the man carrying her. He followed the husband over and sent Meri sailing.

Her stomach flipped repeatedly and she crushed her eyes closed, terrified to land. But her landing was broken by a body. Sen. Still warm, at least.

The door closed and a lock rasped on the outside, the others still talking. She rolled over and shook Sen.

"Sen? Sen? Are you okay? Are you alive? Come on, anything, please."

No answer.

She felt for a pulse. There it was. Thready, as they said on TV, but there. At least hopefully it was Sen's, and she wasn't doing something wrong and it was hers.

She moved down and cradled Sen's head in her lap, leaning over, letting the tears flow. "Don't die, okay?"

No answer. And that was almost an answer in itself.

CHAPTER NINE

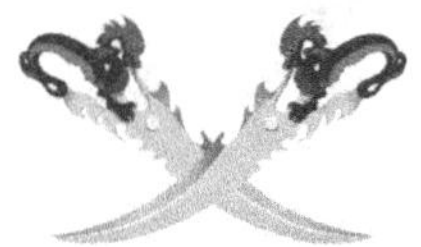

The world spun. She needed to pass out. That would be the only thing that could help her. But passing out could get her killed. Was it the bracelet? No. The bracelet wasn't causing it this time. She'd been on a boat. With Meri. Meri.

"Meri?" That wasn't her voice. Was it?

"Sen? Sen, are you okay?"

Relief made the dizziness bearable. But that was a scary thought. She shouldn't care so much. Friends were a liability. Friends got a person killed.

"Not okay." It was all she could get out. But even that admission of weakness made her stomach turn. "You okay?"

"A little nauseous, but not too bad. I think the soup was poisoned."

Poison. That made sense. But not the kill a person kind, no. Titus wanted her alive.

"And you got a double dose, since you ate mine. I was afraid you were going to die!"

That wasn't off the table yet. She tried opening her eyes, but the dark shifted around her, making the dizziness worse. "Where are we?"

"A shed or something, just off the dock."

Her stomach sank, even farther than the poison had sent it. "Bruna?"

Meri's voice was teary in the darkness. "I'm sorry, Sen. I don't know what she was thinking."

She was thinking she was protecting her village. From the Trulathians. From Sen. She was thinking of the reward money that would pay for years worth of food. They'd played together as children, that was hardly reason to not turn her over. If Bruna even remembered her.

That didn't make it sting any less.

"It's fine. It's what I would have done."

"I don't believe that."

Sen settled back against the wall, her muscles trembling, head spinning. "Then you don't know me."

———

A bit of time passed. How much was hard to say, but the dark still blocked out everything. Sometime after midnight, probably. Sen had gone unconscious again, and no matter what Meri did, she couldn't get her to respond. She'd pounded on the door, screaming for help, but had given up after no one came.

Something scuffled outside.

Meri shrank back to the door, tugging Sen with her. Something was scraping at the sandy earth under the back wall. A small chunk pulled free, grinding enough to make her cringe, and whoever was on the other side to stop.

Propping Sen against the wall, Meri shuffled along the floor of the shack. There had to be something in here she could use as a weapon. Something she could at least bash a person with.

Nothing. Bruna had probably been pretty careful to remove everything, considering who they were throwing in here.

A hand pulled more sand under the wall, dirt stuck in the fingernails. Surely if this person was with the others, they'd come in through the door, right? Meri moved between Sen and the deepening hole.

Not that there was much she could do against an assailant. She was basically hopeless when it came to this stuff. But she couldn't just let them go after an unconscious Sen.

"Hello?" A voice asked. At least hello was one of the words she recognized. The person didn't sound aggressive. "Hello?"

Meri scooted closer, squinting in the dark. A head was through the hole. An old man, but she couldn't make out his features.

He started speaking again, his tones hushed, but she didn't catch much.

"Help?" she asked in Uthorian.

"Help," he agreed. "Senara?"

"She's hurt," Meri said in English, on instinct. She slapped a hand over her mouth. Stupid. Sen had been very clear about never speaking English.

The old man's head disappeared. Oh no. Now he was going to leave them. Because she'd done something stupid again.

But she was wrong. The tip of a shovel came through the hole, dragging dirt out the other direction, the space under the wall getting bigger and bigger. Then the old man's head popped through again, this time facing the ceiling as he pulled himself through the hole on his back. He jumped up unlike any old man she'd seen at home. He caught sight of Sen and his hands flew to his face.

"Senara!" It was odd hearing her name with his accent. But he rushed over to her limp form and gathered her up in his arms, cradling her as he looked down at her face. He spoke to her in their language, but it was far too quick for Meri to even catch a word.

He half lifted Sen, and half dragged her, heading for the hole under the wall, her feet leaving grooves in the sandy flooring. Meri followed behind, kicking the sand back into place. "You better be here to help her," she muttered. The sand thing though, she'd have never thought to do that on her own. More than Sen's language skills seemed to be soaking in.

The old man positioned Sen's shoulders next to the hole and then said something. When Meri shrugged, he picked up Sen's feet and mimicked pushing her through the hole, every movement exaggerated like he was talking to an idiot.

"I'm not stupid, I just don't speak your language," Meri said.

The old man rolled his eyes and dropped onto his stomach, scrambling through the hole like he was ten instead of... however old he was, it was hard to tell. His hands came right back through the gap, patting around until he found Sen, and grabbing her cloak. He wiggled her towards the hole.

Surely the situation they were about to get into couldn't be any worse than the one they were in already, could it? The old man seemed nice, seemed like he was trying to help. But so had Bruna. Now she was starting to understand why Sen was the way she was. These people were supposed to be like family. Kind of.

Meri snapped out of her weary thoughts and jumped forward to help. She pushed on the bottom of Sen's boots, but only managed to make her legs bend at the knee. Wow. This was not the kind of thing college prepared you for.

The old man must have given a giant heave on the other side, and been much stronger than he looked, because suddenly Sen was gone, boots and all.

Oh crap. What if that was a bad thing? What if Bruna had come back, and found the poor old man trying to help Sen? Bruna obviously had no qualms when it came to hurting Senara. Would she if the person she was beating on was old?

Scrambling forward, Meri went to throw her body through the hole head first, but paused. Did she really want her head sticking out there, completely vulnerable? No. Not really. She put both hands on the dirt floor of the hut and shifted so she was about to go out feet first.

Wait. Feet first presented its own set of problems. She shook her head. Now was not the time for this. Sen was on the other side of the wall, and something bad might be happening to her. She turned back over and dove through the hole, army-crawling out the other side.

Somehow the old man was already twenty feet away, dragging Sen with arms hooked under her armpits.

Meri clamped a hand over her mouth before the instinct to yell for him to stop got the better of her.

He paused for a second and waved her after them, leaving Sen listing towards the ground until he readjusted his grip and took off again.

Meri scrambled to her feet and followed.

Who was this guy? And why was he going against the town's wishes to help a stranger? Nope. Not a stranger. He'd known Senara by name.

He reached the water just as Meri caught up. Not that reaching the water meant much, when the water was close to everything here. She nearly stumbled into the man before she saw what they were aiming for. A small boat, barely visible in the dark. He got Sen close enough he was able to prop her shoulder against the side and maneuver himself in, muttering something Meri didn't understand, but took as grab Sen's feet.

Now they were talking. It wasn't her kayak, but she could make do.

She dumped Sen's legs into the boat, panting a bit. All this freaking out was exhausting.

She fell into the boat after Sen, making sure to not let go. She still didn't know this old guy's motives. It wouldn't do to get Sen loaded up for him and have him take off with Sen, and without Meri.

But apparently he was doing the opposite of that. He tenderly set Sen's head on a cushion that must have been there just for that, because no one carried a cushion in a fishing boat like this in the middle of winter, and then jumped out. He said something, then pointed out over the water.

"I can't understand you." The words came out teary, the frustration of not being able to communicate coupled with the fear and exhaustion of the night millimeters away from taking over.

"Senara," he said, and pointed the same way.

"Take Sen that way, huh?" She turned to try and find something to make a map in her mind so that once she was out on the water she'd still be able to find whatever he was pointing at. The stars here were so different, and mostly hidden behind fog. She focused on one in the direction he'd pointed and tried to write all the surrounding stars in her mind. It wouldn't do any good if they were out on the water long enough for the stars to shift, but it would have to do for now.

"Thank you," Meri told the man in Uthorian.

He grinned, missing teeth giving him a gap-toothed smile.

"Thank you," he answered.

Meri moved to the front of the boat, stepping over a bag. She gasped and dropped down to open it. Her camera, still there. And a pile of Sen's weapons. The old man had more than delivered. She jumped forward and set the oars, ignoring the sail. Here was something she understood. Something that couldn't be much different than at home. She eased the tips of the oars into the water, and braced for the lurch as the old man shoved them out into the sea.

———

A groan sounded. A moment went past, and then there was another. Who was that? Whoever it was would pay the price for waking her. She needed rest. She needed... Another groan. This one sounding close, drowning out the sound of wood creaking.

Wait. Was the groaning... her?

Apparently it was.

Muscles trembling, Sen shoved herself up into a sitting position. Bruna. She shoved down the hurt, physically willing herself to move on. She shouldn't have trusted her. She'd known better. Never trust anyone. They had been close as children, but did that really mean anything? No. It seemed not.

The sun peeked over the water to the left. The water. How had she gotten out over the water?

Dizziness almost sent her back to the bottom of the boat when she tried to sit up. There had been plenty of that the night before. Enough to last a lifetime.

She squinted toward the front of the boat. A small lump sprawled between the sets of seats.

Wait. She knew this vessel well. She'd spent hundreds of hours out in it, helping earn her keep. She put a hand out to the side of the boat and ran a finger over a carving in the side.

Though she couldn't see it in the dark, she knew exactly what it looked like. Two stick figures holding hands. Sisters.

Or so it was supposed to be.

But sisters didn't betray sisters.

"Meri?" Sen rasped out. Her throat protested.

A mop of tousled hair jerked up. Meri blinked wildly at her for a second. "Did I fall asleep?" She blinked another couple of times, then continued without waiting for an answer. "Well that was stupid of me."

"Give yourself a break, we've been traveling hard." Sen waited for a second for Meri to stretch and get back up onto the bench. "How'd we get here?"

"You mean who helped us? Because we both know I didn't do this on my own." Meri's smile strained across her face, like the slightest thing would make it slip off. Why was this girl still here? Why was she helping her? Even her own sister had betrayed her today, even if they weren't sisters by blood. "An old man helped me dig under the wall and drag you out to this boat. Then he pointed and I started rowing. I have no idea where we're headed."

"An old man?" Could it be Halivar? Would he go against his real daughter to help his... whatever she was to him. Not likely. But who else could it have been? No one in that village had ever liked her. They feared her, just like everyone else in this world. Everyone but Titus. Just thinking his name made her shiver.

"Yeah, we couldn't talk, obviously, so I have no idea why he was helping us. But I definitely wasn't going to complain. I'm not sure what he saved us from, but I've seen enough medieval movies to know I wouldn't have liked whatever it was. Not at all."

She was too tired to ask for an explanation about what a movie was at the moment.

This girl had helped her. She hadn't had any reason to, but she had. Sen eyed her when Meri went after the oars. Why? There was a reason everyone made the choices that they did. Meri couldn't be any different. What did she expect to get out of this? There was no advantage Sen could figure out.

"What's in all this for you?" Sen asked. There had to be some underlying reason. No one would go through all this without one. And if Meri said there wasn't, that would just make Sen trust her all the less. They'd touched on this back beneath her city, but Sen wasn't satisfied with the answer Meri had given.

Meri shrugged, looking slightly ashamed. "My culture puts big emphasis on other worlds, but no one has ever been able to prove anything. I thought I'd just have a quick trip here, grab something that couldn't be explained at home, and then go back and get showered in riches and glory. But we left the portal so far behind that I'd never find it, so I couldn't get back."

Studying her, Sen settled back against the bench, still in the bottom of the boat. What she said made sense. But she still could have stayed behind with Sandra at the portal. Come into the world, and then leave right away again.

As if reading her mind, Meri smiled at her. "Plus, I'm in it now. No way I'm letting you do this on your own. Getting that bracelet off is going to fix something for you, even if I don't know what."

And now she was suspicious again. Money and power she could understand risking your life for, but not just for another person you hardly knew. Meri's kindness and ignorance had worked its way under her skin, strongly enough that she'd begun to trust her.

No more. If she couldn't trust the closest thing she had to family, she couldn't trust some stranger from another world.

Could she?

She squinted up at the sky, trying to get a reading of time of day. "How long have we been on the water?"

"I don't know. A couple hours? It's not like I have a clock, and I can't tell by the moon here. It doesn't seem to work the same."

"Then we're going the wrong way. We're going long ways instead of straight across. If we were going in a straight line, we should have hit shore by now."

Meri slumped over. "Seriously? I'm so stupid."

"No." A strange stirring of pity went through Sen, seeing Meri so discouraged. "It was the wisest course of action, considering I was unconscious and you wouldn't be able to travel without leaving me if we hit shore. This keeps the others from finding us."

Meri gave her a look that said she was on to Sen trying to make her feel better. It was a strange feeling, actually caring about someone else's feelings.

But she didn't. Not really. She wouldn't. Caring was a choice.

A quick study of the sky, now that she was more awake, revealed their direction quickly enough. "Point that way." Sen nodded toward where the shore should be.

Silently obeying, Meri tipped the oars into the water and pushed. If they'd been traveling as long as Meri had thought, her arms were probably feeling like they were about to fall off at this point. But she kept on anyway.

They moved on, the only sounds breaking the silence were of the boat creaking and the oars dipping into the water.

The quiet should be welcome after the events of the last few days. But it wasn't. Silence left too much for the mind to work with. Sen curled her legs under her and closed her eyes, trying to find a place of peace somewhere inside. Trying, and failing.

They were almost there. Her last chance of getting this bracelet off within reach. She cracked an eye to watch Meri work the oars, her strokes having less and less strength. Well. Nearly last chance.

The boat lurched to a stop, throwing Sen against the wall of the boat. She groaned quietly and grabbed her head. Whatever Bruna had given her had been potent. She should be recovering by now, but sure didn't feel any better yet.

"You okay?" Meri asked from the front. "Sorry, I couldn't see anything in the dark."

"I'm fine," Sen got out between gritted teeth. "We must have made it to shore. The channel isn't that wide here, and there aren't any sand-bars unless they've formed since I used to fish here."

"Well that's good. I usually love boats, but I'm hating all this today."

"You're just tired." Sen moved toward the front of the boat, pausing for a bout of dizziness.

"Yeah well, one of us didn't get a huge long nap."

She sounded cranky. But who could really blame her. Meri splashed down into the water and grabbed the front of the boat, hovering a bit when Sen jumped down. Sen waved her off.

"What now?" Meri asked.

"Now we get far enough away we don't have to worry about Bruna coming after us. None of those people like to leave the water, so we won't have to go far. And after that we find somewhere to hole up and get a bit of rest before we get ourselves into any more trouble." She reached forward and gave the boat as hard a tug as she could, which at the moment wasn't much. Halivar had risked his livelihood letting them take this boat. She wasn't going to spit in his face and let the tide take it out to sea before he could come find it.

Meri sighed and came over to help. "And with you along, that's only a matter of time."

Sen nodded. "You know that's true."

———

Sleep had come far too easily after they'd found a small den made out of the tangled roots of a massive tree. They'd both collapsed into the hole, not even thinking about staying warm. Thankfully the small space seemed to have held their body heat well, and a nice snow had fallen and covered the opening enough to seal it in, making the cave almost toasty.

Almost. But the cold was something she was used to, so it didn't bother her. Meri, on the other hand, still shivered a bit. The climate she lived in had made her soft. Sen grunted to herself. Two weeks ago she would have used the word weak, instead of soft. Maybe she was the one who was actually going soft, not Meri.

The thought almost made her laugh. No one in all of Arnath would think her soft. Most trembled when they heard her name, even though it was on their side she fought.

But even the common people knew her loyalty was forced and not earned. There wasn't any type of true allegiance here, not to anyone now that she was the last Orcus. Turner would have had her loyalty. Him, and any of her other seconds. Harington... more than just loyalty. But when she thought of him, it hurt. So she wouldn't. Wanha she felt something for, to a certain extent. But that was as far as anything even resembling loyalty could be stretched.

Loyalty was earned, not given. And no one left alive had done anything to gain even her respect, let alone her loyalty.

Meri snored and Sen wrinkled her nose at the sound.

Well. Maybe one.

No. That wasn't possible, and was a stupid thought. She'd only know the girl a short time. Definitely not time enough to owe her anything.

She bumped Meri with the toe of her boot. Not out of malice, but there wasn't enough room to turn around in the tight space. "Meri. Time to get up."

"Huh?" Meri didn't even open her eyes.

"Time to go." A wave of dizziness hit her, and she nearly vomited, rolling over to grab onto a stray root and dig her nails in. It went on. And on. These attacks were getting more and more frequent, and stronger and stronger in intensity. If they didn't get to Treyor soon...

Better not to guess. No Orcus had ever made it this long without their magic, as far as she knew. Which meant there was no one to ask about an outcome.

She grabbed some snow from the entranceway and held it to her flushed face. It melted as in came in contact.

Good thing Meri hadn't fully wakened yet. She didn't need to see Sen falling apart. The fact that no Orcus had ever been able to stay away from their handler, to be cut off from magic forever, made more and more sense. If these episodes continued to get worse, it was find a master or face death.

Pushing down the desperation that wanted so badly to be recognized, Sen shoved through the thin snow wall to the outside, and took a deep, full breath of the frost air. Clean. Free. That's what this bite in her lungs felt like. She could almost taste it. She only needed to get to Treyor, find Adeen, and freedom would be hers. What she would do with it, she had no idea. Not with everyone she knew gone.

No one could stand in her way, whatever it was she decided she wanted to do. Not with the bracelet gone. If people had feared Garanath, they would fall to their fear for her even more easily, if she decided to take the throne. The Trulathians had probably destroyed Arnath by now, sweeping through like the plague that they were without the Orcus to defend Uthoria.

If she returned and freed the city, would she be a hero? Or would they try and cut her down, terrified of her power?

There was no one left there who she cared about. No one to save.

Maybe she'd just disappear into nothing, the last Orcus, dying alone in some wilderness, happy and free.

An Orcus, happy? Even less chance of that than of an Orcus being free.

Death was the only freedom many before her had found. And it was beginning to look like that might be her only freedom too. How could she even consider taking Meri into a situation that she wasn't going to be able to control? Take her into a city she didn't know, trying to find someone she didn't know would help her?

She glanced over her shoulder back down into the cave of twisted roots. Meri had rolled over and gone right back to sleep.

If she left without telling her, than Meri would follow, and it would be for nothing. But if she tried to tell her, there was no way Meri would let it happen.

Ah. The phone thing.

Sen reached back into the small cave and tugged Meri's bag free from under her. That she still had it was a testament to the girl's stubbornness. The phone was in the front pocket, right where she'd last seen Meri shove it. She pulled it out, along with the map Meri carried of her homeland, and tossed the bag back into the cave, fumbling with the phone for a moment, trying two buttons before she found the one that started the magic.

Finding the little square that started the thing was a whole other problem. There it was. She hit it and waited for the red light to start blinking. Was it... yes. It was 'filming.'

"Meri. I've decided you won't be of any more help to me for the time being." Better to keep it mean. If she was honest, than Meri would try to follow. And being honest meant being vulnerable, and there was no way that was going to happen. "If you wish to wait here for two days, that should be plenty of time for me to return if I survive. If you do not wish to wait, I will understand. After two days, leave in the morning and follow the sun to the channel. If you can't find a way across, follow it to the left. It will take an extra day of traveling, but there is a crossing."

She paused. Maybe she was taking the mean too far.

"I realize this seems cruel. That's not my intention. My mission doesn't stand much of a chance of succeeding. You attempting to find your way home on your own is far less cruel than the fate that would await you should this journey end in failure. Once you've crossed the channel, you will follow it until you reach the king's road. It will take you back to where the map I will draw you can get you to the temple. Best of luck."

She pushed the button to stop recording. And paused again. She'd gotten too informal. She shouldn't have added that bit in the middle. Fumbling with the phone, she punched a button. Deleted. That's what Meri called it. Another short video, with only instructions would do.

Finished with the new video, Sen carefully turned the phone off. She took a pencil and laboriously drew a map of Arnath with detailed instructions on the back of the map of the swamp Meri still carried, leaned down and slipped them both into Meri's hand. Hopefully she found it. If not, there was nothing more Sen could do.

She moved quietly away, brushing the snow across her footprints as she went. It wouldn't do to lead someone straight to a sleeping Meri. That girl was completely helpless.

Once far enough away to breathe without the chance of waking Meri, Sen stopped for a second, looking ahead. This was it. Success or death. Did she want to go into the home of the man who had killed everyone she knew?

No.

But the bracelet wasn't going to give her an option.

In and out, and hopefully Titus wouldn't even know she'd been there. Get the bracelet off, and get on with her life. A life of her choosing, for the first time since she was born.

CHAPTER TEN

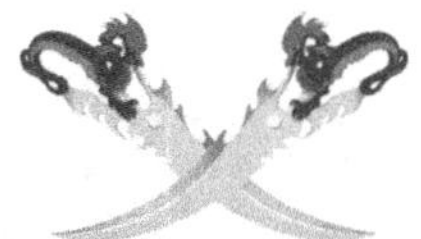

The roads had widened and flattened. Groups of soldiers marched by with more and more frequency, headed no doubt for Uthoria. Unless all of Arnath had fallen without the Orcus, and Titus had turned his conquest in another direction.

Would that make her happy, or sad? Or both? Stupid Meri. Before her, she would never have even stopped to think about it. Life was as it was, it didn't matter how a person felt about it. And yet, somehow, it did.

Both. Happy, and sad. Happy because the Uthorians hadn't treated her well. A slave, forced to fight, forced to kill, for things she didn't believe in, or even care about. Sad, because other than Arcine, it was the only home she truly knew. Whether she liked the place or not, there was comfort in familiarity.

She physically shook the thoughts off. Getting distracted could be a death sentence. Leave it to Meri to be the reason she died, even when the girl was miles away.

That wasn't fair. She had saved her. Probably not her life. Titus wanted her to serve him. No, her life wasn't in danger from Bruna. But there were things far worse than losing a person's life.

Meri had stuck with her, helped her out of a situation that would have been impossible to get herself out of.

She didn't like that.

The thought turned her stomach. She was the one that didn't need help. Other than Wanha, she had been the strongest Orcus. The one to step in when another Orcus was about to go down. But not anymore. Not without a master.

She would die before she had another master.

Her body shivered, nausea blasting her entire being, like the bracelet knew what she was thinking. She braced herself against a tree, closing her eyes. Get it over with out here. Get this episode done, and then get in and get the bracelet off before another hit.

The bracelet didn't like that either. A shockwave went through her, knocking her to the frozen earth. She ground her teeth, still conscious enough to not let out a sound. If a troop of soldiers found her now, it would be the end. Even if she recovered enough to fight back, once they knew she was here, there was no way she could get in and out without being found.

A grim smile quirked up the side of her mouth. In, at least. If she got the bracelet off, getting out wouldn't be a problem.

The pain and nausea disappeared as quickly as they had hit. But the tired didn't go anywhere. Bruna's drugs to knock her out, coupled with the bracelets tantrums were getting harder and harder to ignore.

It didn't matter. Not when her goal was finally within reach.

She shuffled forward, pulling her hood back over her head. It had fallen down sometime during her internal struggle. With how she felt right now, she could probably pass as an old woman and not have to climb the castle wall. Never having been here before was a real disadvantage.

Barreling forward, she made it a good length before almost stumbling out in front of a hunter. He glared, and then slunk off into the trees. She'd scared away game nearby.

Stupid. She paused. Being in a rush at this point was beyond idiocy. It may take a day or two of poking around, but this required a plan. Her hands shook a little, reminding her why she needed to hurry.

In a day or two, would she be functional enough to follow through with whatever plan she came up with? It was almost as if the bracelet felt her intentions and fought against her. If she continued to decline at this rate... She leaned into a tree, pressing her palm into the rough bark until the pain brought her back.

Not the time to devolve into panic. She'd made it this far. She'd never left a mission unfinished before, and wouldn't be starting now. Not when the mission was finally something that benefited her.

Her. That's all she had to think about now. She straightened, the thought giving her strength. No one alive even mattered at this point. Once the bracelet was off, she would have no worries, no one to hold her back.

Freedom.

She stalked forward, ignoring the fact that her hand tingled all the way to the tips of her fingers. Time to finish this.

———

The walls were even grander than she'd anticipated, and that was something with all of the stories she'd heard about this place. Treyor. Here. Right in front of her. The place she would want to avoid the most, unless she was at the head of a conquering army.

That sounded pretty good. Especially after what Titus had done to her. Had done to her people. To the young ones, innocent, in their own home country. Maybe she wouldn't be able to just leave after getting the bracelet off. Maybe there was someone she needed to visit first.

Someone who deserved what was coming to him. She paused. The first person she chose to go after. Did she really want that to be her first act as a free human? Maybe better to see if she made it to that point before spending too much time on this. But on the other hand, having a plan made things go so much more smoothly.

Meri's face popped into her head. With the expression she'd had when she'd seen Sen in her first fight. The disgust. The fear. A pang hit her. She wasn't a monster. Her world was just so different from Meri's. Meri knew that now. She had to. She'd seen what life was like here.

What did she care if Meri knew or what Meri cared about. It didn't matter anymore. She'd never see her again.

That was the plan. Die or be free. Maybe if she did get the bracelet off she'd find Meri and help her get home. But not likely. She'd try to find her. Probably. But they could be even only a few hours apart and never stumble across each other. The girl was on her own now. On her own with a chance at living was better than dead and in the gutter or enslaved, the two options most likely to happen to Sen in the next few hours.

Death didn't even sound that bad anymore. That's where everyone she knew was. She would be in good company.

Death came for everyone. Did it matter when?

No. She wouldn't think like that. The others would wait for her. If there was a place to wait. Maybe it was better if there wasn't. With all of things she'd done, whatever waited for her wouldn't be pleasant.

Turner wouldn't be where she would go. Not if there was any justice at all. He was just a kid, and forced to do the things he'd done. And Harington had far too kind a soul to be placed anywhere near her in the afterlife.

Stop.

She had to stop. Stop thinking, stop feeling.

Now to decide if to wait for dark and try to enter the city in secret, or to stride confidently in with a hood covering her face. Considering the fact that no one really knew her face but Titus, and the other fact that she didn't know the city and didn't have time to explore the edges for a weakness, the former plan didn't make as much sense.

Time to find some cover.

It didn't take long. People flowed by in groups, arms and wagons laden with stuff for market. Until there he was. A man, alone. Her new target.

She moved down to the road, waving at the poor man.

He waved back, and moved her way. The people of Trulathia were so foolish. Easy times had made them weak. No one in Uthoria would behave like this. Not unless they expected something.

If he was expecting anything, he was about to have his expectations destroyed.

"Hello," he called. "Heading for the city? Do you need help? It's just around the bend."

"I don't need help. I just need your goods."

His smile slowly fell. He moved his basket to hold it with one hand, looking around. "I'm willing to sell out here, but I'll still charge market prices. Gotta feed my family, you know."

"I'm not planning on paying. But thank you."

Sen jumped forward. The farmer dropped his basket and took a swing at her, but she easily sidestepped it, then used the butt of her knife to send the man to the ground. He was out cold before he was laid out flat.

"I'm sorry about this." And she actually was. She would have killed him before. Before Meri and all her dumb good-heartedness. But she couldn't now. Now he'd wake up in a few hours confused and with a very bad headache.

She collected the dried fruit that had scattered across the forest floor. A pang hit her. This man had been holding on to this for a while. For it to still be good this late into the year meant he'd put a good deal of effort into drying it correctly, and that it would fetch him a very good price.

"I'll make it up to you, if I can," she told his prone form. The blow she'd dealt him hadn't been too hard. It wouldn't do for him to lie out here until he froze to death after she'd decided to let him live.

But no time to get distracted by that. She had to get this done before she had another episode. An episode inside the castle walls would be a disaster. And she didn't want to wait around until she had another. So fast and hard it was. Time to hit the city.

It didn't take her long to find a weakness. A place this size looked to keep an army out, not one person. The inner walls would be more difficult, but probably not much.

Her bracelet thrummed along with the beat of her heart, like it knew her intentions. It wouldn't be there for long. She'd worn it since she was a small child, the size being updated until she was grown. What would it be like to not have it there?

Like she was missing a limb? Or just a bad memory? It wouldn't be long until she found out.

The people she passed here were happy. So different from Arnath, torn by continual wars. They walked differently. Met each other's eyes. Said hello to strangers.

It was uncomfortable.

And was going to make her stand out if she couldn't figure out how to imitate it. She nodded at a kid walking by with her mother, but the kid just shrank into her mother's skirts, obviously terrified.

Maybe she'd picked someone too young. But no. Another man waved to the child, and she smiled and did a little wave back.

Okay. Apparently she'd done something wrong. This was going to have to be something she worked on.

Or not, depending on how the next few hours went.

A man leaning against a wall caught her eye. He was half drunk, or something was really wrong with him. Either way he wasn't likely to remember any questions she had for him, if he remembered having a conversation at all.

Sidling up to him, she leaned against the wall close enough to smell the alcohol, but not close enough to touch.

"Hey."

Tilting enough he almost fell over, the man looked her over. "Hello." His tone said he'd obviously gotten the wrong impression. She hid her grimace.

"Things are quiet around here without the army, aren't they?"

He grunted and collapsed back into the wall. "Not quiet enough. Wish they'd all leave."

"You and me both." She waited for a moment. Looking too eager would be stupid. "Bet it's left the castle defenses low. So many troops out in the world right now."

"My brother's a royal guard. He can't believe that Titus is fool enough to take so many troops so far from home. And that his father is fool enough to let 'em." He clamped a hand over his mouth and giggled. "Don't tell anyone I said that." His voice came across muffled enough by his fingers that he was hard to understand.

"With the guard count down, they're probably not even getting everything covered, are they. Titus is so arrogant."

"You got that right!" He hiccupped. "Aro... arooo... full of himself. He is. I heard that the garden gate isn't even being guarded most of the time. They just have the gardeners keep an eye on it, and what do they know?"

Sen pushed off the wall and pulled her cloak in tighter. "What do they know, indeed."

"Titus will be back soon. And then the city will be safe. He's the true leader in that family, even if none of them will admit that. And even though he's stupid enough to empty the city. Is what it is, whether we like it or not."

Sauntering off, Sen didn't take a chance by looking over her shoulder. The flow of people would take her in the direction she needed to go. Everything moved toward the inner city.

She hoisted the goods taken from the farmer up on her shoulder. Less guards inside meant that much less of a chance that she would be recognized. And the chances of that were already extremely slim. A few of the soldiers from back at the pass would know her face if she ran into them, but this setting was so different from the one they'd encountered her in before, it was unlikely they'd figure it out in time to catch her.

Titus on the other hand, would be a problem if he made it back before she had the bracelet off. In and out, that was her only option.

And then maybe she'd make it back to Meri before the girl got herself into trouble. One of the few things she was extremely good at doing.

Pulling her hood in closer, she hefted the basket again and started walking with the flow of people. She sidled in closer to a mother tugging a child along, carrying a basket of eggs. They would make the perfect shield.

The next set of walls came up quickly. There were more guards here, keeping a closer eye on everyone as they filed through. But the people didn't seem to fear the guard. A good sign. Not at all what she would have expected.

"Hey, you, stop."

Sen kept shuffling slowly forward. Maybe it wasn't her the guard wanted. Being overly defensive could spell disaster.

"You, with the hood. Stop."

She obeyed, the woman with the child looking her over as she pulled her kid away. The urge to take off surged through her body, but she forced it down. Drawing attention to herself without even knowing why she was being detained would be stupid at this point. "Yes, sir?"

Two guards moved closer, javelins at the ready.

"Hoods aren't allowed. How do you not know this?"

Sen reluctantly flipped the hood back. "I'm sorry, sir. My uncle is ill, and I'm bringing his produce to market for him. This is my first time in the city."

The guard's body language instantly relaxed. "See that it doesn't happen again."

"Yes, sir. Thank you, sir."

Cowering a little to look like what a typical citizen stopped by the guard should look, Sen bustled off after the lady with the eggs.

The next gate loomed up in front of her. Guards kept a watchful eye as people streamed past, but weren't stopping and searching anyone without cause.

This place was definitely different than Arnath.

How was it still so free, even after all of their wars? How did the people seem so normal, after all of the endless aggression?

It didn't matter. She wouldn't be here long. Instead of staying here where people knew who she was by the scar where the bracelet grew into her arm, maybe she'd go with Meri. Her world seemed interesting. Different. Very different. But livable.

Surely they needed mercenaries there. She wasn't good at anything else. A small cottage in the forest far from people was pretty appealing too.

Stupid. Focus. No use dreaming until she knew it would be a possibility. The soul could only take so much crushing before it was ground to powder. No dreams, a much safer way to live until she knew if she would even be alive tomorrow.

Because Titus wasn't taking her alive. The bracelet removed, or death. Meri wouldn't understand, but that was why she'd been left behind.

Another death may be the last one that she could stand. She'd become numb to death, blocking everything down when she lost someone. But it was all on the verge of breaking through. That pain, hurt, loneliness that the deaths of all of her people over the years had brought.

Not friends. She didn't have friends. Not until Meri.

Ugh. She tucked her head down again, avoiding eye contact with anyone, but not pulling up the hood. Meri came up far too often lately. But she'd never had anyone who'd ever chosen to spend time with her in her entire life.

Except maybe Harington. One of her seconds. But knowing his intent was impossible. He might just have been ambitious, and wanted to learn from the best.

One guard eyed her a little extra long. The no eye contact thing. Bad here, instead of normal. She would never get used to that. She lifted her head a bit and smiled at another kid.

This one didn't seem quite as disturbed as the first. Maybe she could get the hang of this. Maybe there wasn't something inherently wrong with her, something people could just sense. Without the bracelet, was she just another person? She knew what she was. But would anyone else? Did she want them to be able to? Did she want to use her powers, to control, or did she want to just blend in?

Blending in didn't sound so bad. Being normal, for the first time in her life.

The clatter of hooves sounded behind her moments before the shouting of the guards to get out of the way. A patrol burst into view, pushing their horses far too fast for this crowded of a street.

The little girl who'd almost smiled at her before didn't seem to notice. Standing in the middle of the street, frozen. Where was her mother?

One less enemy if she died. One less Trulathian to destroy what was left of Arnath.

One less child.

The horses tore forward, and Sen's heart beat faster. Somewhere to the side, the child's mother screamed for her.

It was too late to do anything now. But not too late to try. Sen jumped forward, sick to her stomach. Why had she waited so long? She couldn't reach the girl in time.

A man just a bit older than her snatched the child up on his horse as they ran through, before pulling the whole mass of guard to a stop. "That was pretty brave." His voice carried down the street, the whole crowd as silent as death.

The child stared up into his face.

"Brave could get you killed though, so next time be a bit less brave, eh?" He lifted her to the ground from the saddle as her mother pushed through the crowd to grab her.

"My apologies. Thank you so much for saving her."

The man nodded, but he looked very unhappy. "See that it doesn't happen again. There may not be anyone able to help next time."

"Yes, my lord." Humbled, the mother didn't look up at him, staring at the ground.

Sen melted back out of sight now that the child was safe. What had possessed her to risk everything to help some foolish child she didn't even know?

Whoever this man was, he didn't take the time to say anything else. He clicked his horse into a much more controlled canter, and the rest of the men followed.

News of the war, most likely. The men looked travel-worn.

This could be good. A distraction. If all of the generals and royalty were in the main hall to receive news, that meant that they weren't with Adeen, wherever she was.

Now to just figure that out.

The crowd all burst into life at the same time. She was losing the easy path the riders had cleared for her. Time to up the pace a bit, and take a little risk.

Sen marched forward, passing the small stands that started the edge of the marketplace. Maybe she could pass for a serving girl bringing in supplies for the kitchen.

It wasn't far before the top of a massive wall stretched above the houses ahead. And even less time after that before she reached a ring, at least three of the houses long, where nothing but cobblestone stretched to the wall.

Smart, tactically. Frustrating for her.

The horses had already disappeared, and the portcullis clanged to the ground.

This definitely would be a much more difficult task than getting into the city. Of course. Anything otherwise would be idiotic.

The basket of dried fruit began to weigh her down a bit. It never would have before this cursed bracelet had started her body deteriorating. Slower, weaker, unable to make decisions as quickly. Were these things normal to the average person, or had she sunk even lower than average?

The bracelet lived almost like an organism. It depended on her to keep it alive. Would it kill itself just to kill her? Probably. It obeyed its master, just as she did. And the master who had created it had woven into it what it was supposed to do should a handler get killed. The bracelet itself was a slave.

Pfft. Now look at her, losing her mind. The bracelet wasn't alive. It just felt like it.

Trudging felt odd here. Even in winter, these people seemed happier than the folk during the best of times at home. She eyed them as she moved along the ring of houses, staying out of the line of sight of the top of the wall, though it seemed like there weren't any guards above.

Though some of the people were slightly thin, none of them had the gaunt, starved look that every lower class citizen of Arnath carried with them, the pain of hunger always eating at their faces.

Something differed here from her city, but she hadn't been here long enough to see what that something was.

And wouldn't be. She should be out of the city before nightfall, when the gates closed. At least, they closed in Uthoria. Here she'd begun to doubt anything she thought she knew about city life.

A ruckus behind her made her hunch up and move closer to one of the houses, slowly looking over her shoulder to make out another group of horses moving through the gate and into the keep, even though with the angle she couldn't see the gate itself anymore.

She shuffled forward, ignoring the last of the riders going through the opening and the gate starting its descent again. Unless she could catch a rider unaware and steal his armor and horse, that gate did her no good. And that was far too much of a risk, even if she knew right where one would be for her to stop and lay out flat.

It wasn't far before another gate came into sight. This one considerably smaller. One horse could possibly fit through if forced, but wouldn't be very happy about it.

Unless it served another purpose, this had to be the correct gate. The garden gate. Not the one the servants would regularly bring produce through. That one had to be large enough for a wagon, but one she may be able to trick her way through. The servant's gate came with people, and people who most likely all knew each other.

The lightly guarded gate in the garden would be a better bet.

Closing her eyes for a second and leaning on the wall of the closest house, Sen took a deep breath. This was it. Almost time for her to feel whole again. Well. Like herself. She didn't know who she was without the magic coursing through her body.

Living alone in a cottage somewhere would be wonderful. A cottage it was. No more fighting. No more wars. Just peace, for what remained of her life.

A good thought. But it wouldn't happen. She would never find peace. As long as she was alive, someone would be after her.

But they had better bring a lot of help if she was fighting at her normal level.

A look both ways showed this might be the best time. No one in sight meant no witnesses if she had to get... rough, with the gate guard.

Hopefully it wouldn't come to that. Getting rough meant drawing attention. Drawing attention could very well mean the end of this mission. Not being in her element could get her killed, but she wasn't getting any better without getting the bracelet off. Every minute she waited could cost her. Every minute brought her closer to another attack.

A light knock on the gate didn't bring any results. She shut down all feeling and went into the calm she found before battle. She knocked again, more loudly this time.

"What do you want?" A voice called from on top of the wall. A guard, not just a gardener as she'd hope. But he did look far too old to be a regular guard.

She craned her neck back to look up, letting the guard see her face. He wouldn't know it, and if he only assessed her abilities by her sex and age, she would be at an advantage.

"I have a delivery."

"Then go to the servant's gate, not here at the garden." His head disappeared.

"Sir!" Her mind raced for a moment. "The delivery is for the gardener! The servant's gate sent me here."

The guard looked back down at her. She held up her basket, proof that she carried goods.

He disappeared again.

She waited. Now what? What other options were there for entry? Climbing this wall would be nearly impossible, and almost suicidal with that chance that her body would betray her at any moment.

But there. A grinding on the other side of the gate as someone unlocked it.

"I don't know why no one can warn us when things change." The guard's voice filtered through the door, getting louder as the crack widened. "I realize there aren't a lot of us around at the moment, so it's harder to keep up good communication, but good communication is so important."

The door finally opened enough for Sen to get her first good look at the man. He was much older than she had originally thought, and obviously not happy to be here.

"Now don't tell anyone I let you in here. I know you're just trying to do your job too. In all this ridiculousness we just all do our best, eh?"

"Our best is all we can do." Sen slipped through the slight opening he had left for her.

The door ground closed behind her, but she couldn't make out what the guard said afterward, because she had already moved toward the castle. She held up the basket for the guard to see. "Sorry, in a bit of a rush."

It wouldn't do for the man to memorize her face.

Better for her, but also, better for him.

What was wrong with her, thinking about other people so much. "Meri," she muttered under her breath.

Rough stone walls ahead of her shielded her from view as she made her way across a small courtyard. The stable stood to the left, obvious what it was by the piles of hay just inside the door.

More interconnected buildings ran down both sides of the small alleyway that came up after the courtyard. She slowed, catching her breath, far more tired than she should be. "Cursed bracelet."

As she leaned on the wall for a moment, a door popped open and a woman bustled out with a pot. She dumped it to run down the alleyway and turned to go back inside.

Once she was out of sight, Sen moved forward enough to inspect the slop. Foodstuff, not chamber pot. This was probably the kitchen.

The door felt so far away, the alleyway swimming a bit. No. She wasn't going to get this close and then not make it. Couldn't.

She flung the door open and marched in. A whole room full of cooks, assistants, and scullery girls all suddenly had eyes on her.

"I have an urgent delivery," she told them all. "It needs to go straight up to one of the guests here."

That seemed to placate them.

A short woman with an aura of control waved her over. "Get back to it!" she roared at everyone else.

They jumped to obey.

"I didn't hear of no delivery." The woman wiped her hands on her apron, then put them on her hips. "And I ain't got no one to spare to deliver it upstairs, not with the prince due back and all, gettin' ready for that."

"The prince is due back?"

"Any day now."

There were a lot of princes here. It didn't mean it was Titus. And even if it did, she'd be gone or in power before he arrived. "I can take it up myself, if you just point me in the right direction."

"That'd be appreciated. Things er crazy round here. Who's it for?"

"Adeen? I think that's it."

"Adeen, eh?" The woman looked her over suspiciously for a second. "If you say so. Ain't none of my business, if the guard let you in." She waved her hand towards a door on the far wall. "Take that. Go on straight to the servants stair. Climb up three flights. Turn left, and walk down five er six doors. It's the one with the guard at it."

A guard at the door had not been in her plans. But one guard shouldn't cause too much trouble.

"Thank you." Sen headed for the doorway. "Three flights, turn left, door with guard," she muttered to herself under her breath.

Ridiculous, that she should have to remind herself like this. But exhaustion and pain took their toll, and more and more that meant her mental capacities.

The castle bustled, but no one seemed to notice just another servant girl, making her way to serve some noble. Quietly was not how an Orcus generally did things, but it did prove useful once in a while.

The exertion of the stairs made her suck in breaths, taking a short rest midway up the last flight. The bracelet would kill her if it didn't come off. At this point, she had no doubt.

Death over slavery.

At last at the top, she heaved the basket up with her. It would have been nice to lose its weight, but it did prove a great distraction if she was stopped.

One guard, down the hallway, bored at a door. Perfect. Adeen was in her room.

"Ho there." Sen pasted on a big smile, the muscles in her mouth twitching in exhaustion. "I've a delivery." She held up the basket to prove what she said was true.

The guard didn't look impressed. "I don't recognize you. Just leave the basket and I'll go through it."

"I'm sorry, I can't do that. I've been entrusted with placing this basket straight into the hands of your lady."

His posture slowly starting to stiffen, the guard looked her over. "No."

This was not how this was supposed to go. The guard should be getting blasted away by fire or water after she went into the room and Adeen freed her.

But no. Things could never be that easy.

"As you wish."

Apparently thinking she didn't look like much of a threat, the guard leaned back against the wall as Sen got close enough to sit the basket almost at his feet.

Then, the basket went straight back up, bashing him in the chin.

He went down to his knees, giving her a chance to slam the handle of her dagger against his head. He crumpled to the ground.

"Everyone always chooses the hard way," Sen muttered, dropping what remained of the basket of fruit on his prone body. She opened the door and stepped slowly inside, daggers ready just in case another guard waited there.

No guard. Only a petite woman, sitting by the fire, staring into the flames. Somehow she hadn't heard a thing.

"Adeen?" Sen asked, her heart thundering in her ears. This was it. This was the moment she'd longed for since she was a child, forced to go through drills all day instead of chasing butterflies.

Adeen squeaked and jumped up from her chair, moving to put it between her and Sen. "Who are you? What do you want?"

"I'm not here to hurt you, Adeen. I'm here to help." She held up her arm. "I heard you're the only one capable of taking this off. As soon as you do, I can handle anything they throw at us. They won't even know what hit them. I'll see that you're freed too."

Instead of getting excited and rushing over to remove the bracelet, Adeen went pale and grabbed a pillow, clutching it to her chest, shrinking away from Sen.

"What's wrong?" Sen moved forward, careful to keep her body language soft. "I can get you out of here. Give you freedom. Just get the bracelet off."

"What do you mean, freedom? I'm already free. You're the only one threatening me around here!"

Sen took a step back. "What about the guard?"

"Frendor? What did you do to Frendor?" Adeen's eyes were wide, her breaths coming in pants. "Guards! Guards!"

"Stop!" Sen hissed. "Don't you want out of here? They have a guard on you at all times. How can you call that freedom?"

"They have a guard on me to protect me from people like you," Adeen spat out, then took off for the door.

Stunned, Sen froze. The girl wasn't a captive. She hated Orcus as much as everyone else did. Sen's chances of freedom were slipping away. She nearly smacked herself. Of course they were. They were literally running out the doorway, and with her state of mind the way it was, she was letting them go without a fight.

She never did anything without a fight.

"Stop!" She took off after Adeen. "Help me, and I swear not to hurt you."

But Adeen kept running. She either didn't believe Sen, or had some moral conviction that an Orcus shouldn't be free ground down into her soul.

Shoving the nausea down, Sen tore down the hallway after Adeen. The woman slid around a corner not far ahead of her, and Sen followed without a second thought. Straight into a waiting unit of men.

Full stop, Sen backpedaled, flailing in an attempt to keep her balance. But the dizziness took this chance to hit her full strength, making her go to the floor, unable to see straight.

"Lady Adeen?" One of the guards asked, his voice far off in the distance even though his body stood so close.

Crawling backward, the nausea grew until Sen nearly threw up.

"Grab her! She's an Orcus!"

Even in the state she was in, Sen could feel the tension flooding the hallway.

"She's powerless at the moment," Adeen added.

That seemed to give a couple of the men a bit of a boost in bravery, but none of them seemed to really want to engage. Until the officer shoved one, and then another, in her direction.

"Leave me be," Sen growled, struggling to her feet and pulling her daggers with trembling hands. "Or you'll regret it."

"This is an Orcus?" The guard closest to her asked. "After all of the stories I've heard from soldiers returning from the front lines, this isn't what I was expecting."

Sen sneered at him, showing her teeth. "Get this bracelet off, and then you'll see. I'll even go easy on you. No powers."

The guard looked at her for a moment, then punched her in the face. She fell back against the stone floor, hitting her head hard enough to make the room whirl. He reached down and grabbed her weapons while Adeen screamed and the rest of the guards laughed.

"What's the meaning of this?" a voice she didn't recognize asked, tone harsh.

"She's an Orcus, sir!" the guard captain said, snapping to attention. Sen couldn't see who spoke, couldn't truly see anything. "Probably here to kill the king and queen!"

"Since when do we assume someone's actions based on where they're from or what they are? You're from Heth, Urc. What would most people say about that?"

"Nothing good," one of the other guards said.

But no laughter followed from the rest of the men. They respected whoever it was they were talking with. Sen squinted, trying to make out his face. The voice sounded vaguely familiar, but wasn't one she truly knew.

"Get her up. She doesn't seem dangerous. We'll take her before the king and queen. They can decide what happens to her."

The guards who had come forward earlier pulled her to her feet by her arms, sending her stomach dropping to her toes.

Without malice, but still not very gently, they pulled her along after them, following the man who'd spoken to them all.

This was it. Freedom or death. That's what she'd been saying. Now was the time. With the way her body kept betraying her, freedom would not, could not, happen. Unless Adeen suddenly changed her mind and decided to help. Past unlikely.

Freedom came in more than one form. Freedom in death. Maybe that was where this entire journey had led her. *Turner. Harington. I hope you are there to show me around.* Seeing her seconds wouldn't be so bad. She'd always treated them well. Surely they would be happy to see her. The only regret that would haunt her though... *I'm sorry, Meri. Truly. I hope you've find your way home, and that you find peace.*

———

The throne room wasn't as large as the one in Uthoria, even though the castle was much larger.

Good. Less space to be dragged over.

The men threw her at the bottom of the dais. Sen didn't get up. Pain seared through every part of her body, every cell crying out to be reunited with the magic she could feel, just out of reach.

"Are you okay?" The voice was distant, like it drifted through a canyon or over a lake. Male. The man who'd had her brought in here.

She didn't answer. Couldn't, even if she'd wanted to.

Doors boomed open somewhere, and boots clicked across the store floor, heading in her direction. She didn't waste the energy trying to lift her head.

"Trying to have this meeting without me?"

Now she jerked to attention. That voice. She knew that voice.

"My quarry, and you're here, deciding her fate without me?" Titus. Of course Titus had beaten her back here. He'd had the best means of travel at his disposal, wasn't ill, and didn't have someone from another world slowing him down.

"We haven't started anything," the other voice said. "The king and queen haven't even arrived yet."

Boots made their way into her vision, stopping just in front of her. He reached forward, tipping her face up with a finger to the chin. "You're looking much worse for the wear."

His face swam in her vision.

"That's okay. It just makes things easier for me."

"To make things easy for you, I'd have to be dead." She struggled to her feet, the room spinning. "And dead works for me."

"Oh now, don't be so dramatic. Dead doesn't work for me at all. I've been searching for you, far and wide, and yet here you are. At my home, waiting for me."

"Come on, Titus. Treat her like a person." The other man seemed far too familiar with the prince. He was lucky he wasn't also on the chopping block.

"A fight to the death, then? Give me my daggers." Sen asked. The room had stopped spinning. Maybe the dizziness and pain would pass for a few minutes. Would give her a chance for one last fight. Even without her powers, she would be able to cause a lot of damage.

"I see no reason to go through all that." Titus snapped his fingers and the huge double doors at the end of the hall opened. "I was afraid you'd get all crazy on me, so I brought a little backup plan."

A soldier pulled a young woman with a sack over her head into the room. Sen's heart dropped. No. How?

"We found this one in the woods. I assume it's the one who was with you at the inn?" He walked over and squatted in front of Meri, tipping her face up with the point of his knife. "I'm surprised she's made it this long. Traveling with you doesn't seem to be very safe. I hear that she's an initiate. How wonderful of you to find me another Orcus."

Meri struggled a bit and the man holding her shoved her to the ground by Sen.

"Sen?" The bag muffled Meri's voice, but the fear could be heard anyway.

"There is so much I can offer you. I know you believe you will be treated the same way here as you were is Uthoria," Titus spat on the ground when he said the name. "But it isn't true. Pledge yourself to me and you will become one of the most respected people in the country. An Orcus here is revered, nearly worshipped. I swear that anything you want you will have, all your life."

"Anything I want," Sen said quietly. "Anything but freedom."

Titus smiled, but the smile almost made Sen's nausea come back.

"I preferred not to force things. To have you accept this is your fate on your own, to form a working partnership. But if you can't adjust to that..."

"I will never be your slave." The words burned as they came out. Everything burned.

"Oh Senara, you speak like you have a choice in the matter." He smirked and then starting chanting. Her bracelet buzzed and automatically she nearly vomited.

No. No, this couldn't happen.

He continued, but it sounded wrong. Definitely not the binding spell the Crafter had given her, and he had obviously told her the truth since his bracelet had worked. This was another language, one she didn't know.

A tear streaked down her cheek, the first she'd let fall since she was a child. Her short time of freedom, wracked by pain and illness because of the bracelet, was ending. Back to a life of slavery. And she was too weak to even do anything about it. Her body jerked in pain.

Meri groped ahead of her with her bound hands until she grabbed Sen's. Sen pulled the bag off her head. Tears streamed down Meri's face. "What is he doing to you?"

Gritting her teeth, Sen closed her eyes a second to re-focus, the bracelet heating and searing through her entire body, making it almost impossible to think.

"I will not be a slave again," Sen said.

"What can I do?" Meri asked.

Sen stared at her for a moment. A slave again. That wasn't a choice at this point. She would be a slave to someone. The only option she had was to whom.

CHAPTER ELEVEN

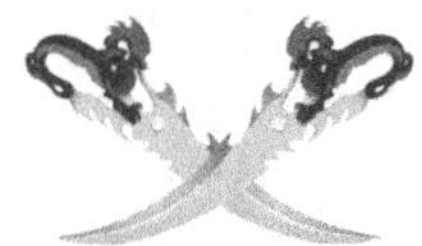

Near death didn't bother her as much anymore. Kind of sad the situations a person got accustomed to being in. The soldiers hadn't been kind after they'd grabbed her. She'd been knocked around, and at some point had slammed her head into something. With the bag over her face, she didn't even know what. The dizziness had faded a little, but still held on.

"Meri?" Sen asked from somewhere.

Dazed, Meri turned in her direction, but it took a moment to focus.

"Meri, you need to listen to me. I need you to do something."

"Okay." It came out mumbled enough that she hardly understood herself. But Sen must have understood.

"Repeat after me," Sen's voice had gone intense.

Meri barely heard her. The words didn't really register.

"This is life or death, Meri. Please."

Giving herself a mental slap, Meri concentrated on Sen's voice, her head swimming.

"Repeat after me." Sen paused for just a second, then said something in a language more guttural than she usually used.

"Is that Uthorian?"

"Focus, Meri. Repeat after me." The words she said next didn't sound any better the second time. So Sen said them a third. "Affaro, gendcsa, fleeten."

"Affaro." Meri blinked. The room started to come into focus.

"Gendcsa," Sen insisted quietly.

"Gendcsa."

"Fleeten."

Meri blinked a couple more times and looked Sen full in the face. She looked worried, nearly sick, more than she had ever since they'd met, and they'd been through some crazy stuff together. "Fleeten."

A pop and flash made Meri throw her arm up over her eyes.

"Now tell me I'm free to protect you." Sen's voice stayed calm but urgent.

"Of course you can protect me. You've been doing it since I was stupid enough to follow you through that portal."

Instantly the chains holding Sen melted. A gust of wind came up from beneath her and lifted her to her feet, while another ripped a sword from a guard's hand and it blew it into hers.

"What the heck?" Meri whispered, but there wasn't anyone to hear her.

Sen had already jumped into action, carving a swathe through the guards as she moved towards Titus.

Water blasted one guard from his feet, and another burst into flame.

Men shouted as they pulled weapons.

They ran at Sen, but there wasn't anything they could do to stop her. A whirlwind went through the room, knocking everyone from their feet, but somehow jumping right over Meri. Was this what Sen had been missing? Was this what the bracelet stopped her from doing? What had changed?

Sen stormed toward the man who had brought Meri in from the woods. Meri jumped to her feet to follow. He'd been rude, nearly cruel. "Sen, be careful with that one."

"Trust me. I know what to expect from Titus."

He smiled at her from the ground, but it wasn't quite as cocky as it had been so far.

"Time for you to die for all you've done." Sen swung her sword.

"No!" Meri yelled, grabbing her arm. The man was terrible, but he didn't deserve to die like this.

"Wait!" another man yelled. He scrambled to his feet, not far from Titus. Sen glanced at him, then went back to staring down Titus, the sword at his throat. Was he speaking English? Her sluggish mind tried to process. No way he was speaking English.

"Why should I wait? What has this man ever done that should mean he receives mercy?"

The man stepped forward, hands in the air. "Nothing. He's never done anything good. But the same could be said about you."

A muscle in Sen's cheek twitched.

"Hey!" Meri said, moving in to stand closer to Sen. "That's not fair. She didn't have a choice on most things."

"He killed the young ones. In Arnath. He deserves death." Sen ignored Meri, still focusing on the men. The ignoring only lasted a moment before she jerked to look at Meri. "You can understand what we're saying?"

Meri shrugged. "I guess so." She kept it in English, so hopefully the men wouldn't understand.

The guy on the floor, Titus? He spat on Sen's boots. She started forward with the sword.

"No. No, he didn't," the other man interrupted again. "They're alive. Captive, yes, but they were before we arrived. It's just a different set of masters now. I swear."

Now Sen did look up, taking her eyes off Titus for the first time.

"They're alive?" she whispered.

"Who's alive?" Meri asked. "I'm so lost."

"He didn't kill them. He doesn't deserve to die."

"So you say." She didn't seem to believe him. "But I don't know if you're speaking the truth. And even if you are, he may not deserve death for that one thing, but he's done more than enough to prove he needs to be removed from power. And the only way to remove someone like him from power is death."

"Sen." Meri kept her voice low, soothing. She placed a hand on Sen's arm. "I don't know what he's done to you, or to people you care about. But I do know that every time I've seen you hurt someone so far, you've been defending me, or you've been defending you. This is different. You don't get to make those choices. You can't do this."

"Did you hear that, Senara?" Titus asked, voice like a snake. "Your handler says you can't do this. You can't harm me."

"Are you forbidding me from harming him?" Sen's words came across calculated, rage boiling beneath each word in a way Meri had never seen in a person before, let alone Sen, always so in control.

"You can't just go around killing people without some kind of trial. It will change who you are."

"You don't know who I am. You don't know the things I've done. This won't even register on my balance sheet."

That thought sent a shiver through Meri. She didn't know Sen well. But there were things about a person you could know without knowing specifics about their past. Sen wasn't a murderer. She was practical. And killing Titus like this would be murder. "It would be wrong, and you know it."

Sen's face turned to stone, her body stiff. "Is that the last you have to say about this?"

This moment seemed significant in a way that was lost on Meri. Sen's wording was so specific, her anger harsh. What was going on?

"Why does what I say even matter? You've never cared before."

Eyes burning, Sen turned her gaze on Meri. "My actions are now your choice. You are responsible for my actions. Handler."

Meri let go of Sen's arm, reeling back a step. Handler? No. Those words Sen had made her repeat, they'd seemed familiar, but she'd been too out of it to truly notice. They were the ones Sen had used to bind the Crafter to her.

Did that mean?

"Sen? What have you done?"

"What I had to do." It came out from between gritted teeth. "Like I always do. What do you wish now?"

"Let's just get out of here, please. We'll figure it all out later."

"As you wish." Sen backed away from Titus, but didn't take her eyes off him.

Meri touched her arm, and sparks flew from the bracelet, sending an almost electrical impulse through her, nearly knocking her to the ground. She yelped and jumped back, heart racing.

Titus laughed. "A handler can't touch an Orcus. Where did you get this girl, who knows so little of what she now controls?" He stood and stretched, then laughed again. "You shouldn't have taken the time to discuss things, girls."

"Give me my daggers."

Titus looked like he was going to protest, but the other man walked over to the guard who had taken them, grabbed them, and threw them at her feet. Sen reached down to grab them, and Titus laughed.

"You're going to need those. But they won't do you much good."

The words were hardly out of his mouth before the back hall doors burst open, and guards poured in wearing odd armor. Odd even for here.

Now Sen's attention changed direction. She went even more tense than before, if that were possible.

"What's going on?" Meri asked quietly.

"Kill the girl," Titus called to his guards.

"Titus! She's an innocent," the other man protested.

"Once she's dead, I'll be able to bind the Orcus to me. As long as she's alive, that's impossible."

Several guards rushed forward together. Sen lifted her sword, meeting the first with a blast of ice. It didn't faze him, in whatever armor he wore.

"Run!" Sen shouted.

Meri moved to obey, but didn't make it far.

Two more blasts, this time of lightning, didn't seem to affect the soldiers at all. They just kept coming.

Sen didn't wait to see if Meri followed or not. At least they'd been traveling together long enough that they had a flow for this kind of situation.

The regular guards barreled out of Sen's way long before she needed to try any type of attack, but the beefed up guards blocked the only two exits. "Trust me?" Sen asked. She still sounded kind of miffed, but it could be hard to tell with her sometimes.

"Yep," Meri answered. She didn't have time to get anything else out before a guard took a swing at Sen with a giant sword.

Slipping beneath it, Sen popped back up on the other side, threw a patch of ice behind the guard's feet, and gave him a push. He teetered for a second, before sliding enough that he lost his balance and crashed to the ground.

"Follow me closely, but don't touch me." Sen took off for a wall of massive windows covered in wooden shutters. With a flick of her wrist, they burst open, wood splintering across the room in a whirlwind, knocking back the guards trying to follow.

Without pause, Sen threw herself out of the window. Meri didn't even take the chance to look, diving right through after her.

Wind whistled in her ears, instantly drowning out the shouting she'd left behind in the chamber. But it didn't last long. A short gust of wind blew her and Sen both against the cliff wall. Sen reached out to grab her hand, then apparently thought better of it, because instead a piece of rock pulled away from the wall and wrapped around her, keeping her from falling.

At the same time she was doing that, Sen waved her other hand and a rock shelf burst into place, hiding them from above, and then pulled two large rocks off a nearby ledge, flinging them toward the ocean below with her magic.

"Hopefully they didn't get a good look and think that's us," Sen said quietly.

Meri gulped, studiously not looking down. "I'm almost convinced, and I'm right here."

"Let's give them a minute. They won't waste much time before they all head for the docks to go out and look for our bodies. We need to leave after they do, but with plenty of time to be gone before they get on the water, or they'll see us above and shoot us down."

Shoot them down? Meri closed her eyes for a second. Who in their right mind would just shoot another person off the side of a cliff? What was wrong with this world?

A wave of homesickness hit her. Things could be bad there, but people were mostly decent. It was time to go back. Her eyes snapped open and her breathing increased. Frantically she patted at her back.

"It's there. No one seemed to have any interest in your things. They probably didn't know what they can do." Sen laughed. "Of course they don't. I still don't, and you've tried to explain it to me."

"Whew. I might have died if I lost my camera." Meri looked down at the water raging below. "Okay, maybe not a great comparison right now, but I have big plans for those pictures and videos." Meri paused to look up at the castle high above. "Have you been able to do all that this whole time?"

"I would have been able to, except for the bracelet."

"No wonder you wanted it off so bad. I'd have wanted it off too, even if it wasn't because without it I could be some uber warrior."

Sen's forehead crinkled up in a mass of confusion. "I don't know this word. Uber."

"Ah. That makes sense. It basically means epic." She still looked lost. "Great fighter? Whatever, it doesn't matter right now. We should get out of here before someone figures out how to get down from the castle and come after us. They were sure prepared for you, weren't they?"

"Yes. But that didn't help them much, did it?" Sen's voice turned smug in a way Meri had never heard from her before.

Meri grinned at her. "You got that right. Now let's get out of here and figure out what comes next."

Sen tipped her head, listening. After a moment, she seemed satisfied.

The ledge they were standing on expanded out past Sen's feet, turning into stairs. Very unsafe stairs, without a railing. Ha. That was the thing to bother her, after all the times she'd nearly died in the last week?

The shelf above them also grew, hiding them from above as they picked their way up past the castle and away from the town.

Time moved by achingly slow as they made the ascent, every step making Meri take another deep breath.

"How are you not scared right now?" Meri finally asked Sen, who just kept moving forward, never slowing.

"I have my powers back."

That was it. So simple.

"Have you always been able to do that stuff?"

Sen looked over her shoulder at Meri, staring at her, like she was making a decision. "Yes. As a child I nearly killed my brother when the earth swallowed him after he pushed me down. I was the first in my family in generations to show any signs of the gift."

A far longer answer than she'd expected, with how quiet Sen normally stayed. Was it because she was trying to distract Meri because of the sudden death to their left? Or something else.

Oh no. Did she feel like she had to, because of the whole handler thing? "Nothing's changed between us, Sen. We're still friends. I'm never going to tell you what to do. Just be you."

Now Sen wouldn't look at her at all. "That's easy to say. But the bracelet disagrees. If you make a careless comment, I have to obey. If you say you need someone to get you some water, I must go. If you say you hate someone, and want them dead, I must fulfil your wishes. And now, instead of me being the prey of every hunt, it will be you. You are the weaker, and if they control you, they control me."

Screeching to a stop, Meri's head spun. Pebbles fell to the ocean below, gone from sight in a span of seconds. Watch what she said? Oh, she was not good at that. Not good at all. And wait, prey? She was now prey? "I need to get home. Fast."

"I agree. There won't be anywhere safe for you in this entire world. Not with Titus after you."

Her gut clenched at the thought. Until now, they'd been running and hiding, staying out of sight. But it had been because of Sen, not because of her. She could have left Sen at any point and no longer been a target.

But now, the bullseye was painted directly on her back.

Inching along didn't do anything to dispel the anxiety. Though new thoughts of death did make climbing along this rock wall less intimidating. Falling to her death here might be better than whatever Titus would do.

Would he make her death quick, or draw it out, just for fun? What kind of man was he? Did all of his soldiers now have a kill on sight command, or capture and drag back?

Too many questions, no answers. The portal was her only hope.

"How far is it? To the portal?" It didn't particularly matter at the moment, but it would be very nice to think about something other than death. Or slavery. Or death.

"Two days, if we could find mounts."

That didn't seem likely. "And without horses?"

"Six, at least." Sen paused. "Unless..."

"Yes?"

"If we could get ahold of a vessel, the river runs in close proximity to the temple. It may even be faster than horses."

"Faster than horses sounds wonderful. Other than the fact that we'll be stealing someone's livelihood."

Sen rolled her eyes and started forward again. "There's no one else in this entire world who would be thinking about the poor fisherman when their life is on the line. We'll leave him a note where to find it."

Meri started back up after Sen, scooting along. "Won't that let everyone know where we're headed?"

Sen grunted but didn't say anything.

Legs quivering with a fall that far just waiting for a misstep were not great. But how to stop them? She had no idea. "You're being sarcastic anyway, aren't you. You'd tell me you left a note, when you really didn't."

"I can't." Sen's tone went stiff again, angry. The slight playfulness as she tried to distract Meri was gone. "It's impossible for me to lie to my handler."

A groan worked its way out. This may be the worst day ever. Had she just lost her best friend? Sure, they hadn't known each other long, but they'd been through a lot together. "How do we get your bracelet off? I can't leave you here with that thing on."

"It doesn't need to come off if you just tell me I'm free to do as I wish. With you not around to change the rules, it will almost be like I'm free."

Her tone was wistful on the 'almost.' This groan didn't even have to try very hard. The freedom Sen had fought so hard for had been just there, waiting, and they'd lost it.

"I'm sorry, Sen. Truly. We traveled all this way, only to have you end up in exactly the same situation as you were in before."

This time when Sen stopped, her back was stiff with anger. "In the same exact situation? That just tells me you don't understand at all what my situation was before. Will you force me to fight? To kill? Will you pit me against my fellow Orcus, make me injure them, badly, to find out where I place in the fighting ranks? At least their handler would let them heal themselves at the end, but that's little solace when you crush another's bones."

Meri's stomach roiled at the thought. How had they never talked about this? How could someone do that to another person? "Of course not. I'm sorry. I should have had more information before making a blanket statement like that."

Sen grunted, but started moving again, which probably signaled forgiveness. Hopefully. Meri looked back down over the side, the fear of falling to her death now seeming like the better distraction than the ones she had just tried to make for herself.

And there it was, the best distraction. A whole fleet of ships, pouring out of the harbor, dragging nets through the water, looking for their bodies.

"Ah, Sen?"

"I see them. Just ignore it for now. They aren't going to notice us way up here."

The rest of the ascent probably only took ten minutes. It felt like at least two hours. Steps broke free of the rest of the rock wall providing them with stairs for the last bit. Meri shook her head.

"What?" Sen asked.

"You've just been able to do this. The whole time. Just you couldn't, because of the bracelet."

Sen snorted. "How many times are we going to go over this?" She confidently stepped out in a direction Meri had no idea how she chose. Maybe that was part of the magic.

Things were deteriorating fast. This was basically the old Senara, from when they first met, before they'd become friends. Maybe it would just be better to be quiet for a bit.

They marched on in silence, Sen always knowing right where to go, even though she'd probably never been here before. Was it the magic?

Maybe it was now, but she'd been cut off from it before, so probably not. Too many maybes, not enough answers.

———

The boat was still where they'd left it. Apparently Halivar hadn't found it yet. Or was pretending to not have found it. Had he truly helped them escape? Meri had no reason to lie. And yet Sen couldn't find any answer as to why he would choose to help her over helping his own daughter.

Even her own mother hadn't wanted her.

Meri had been uncharacteristically quiet as they'd moved through the forest, avoiding everything that could even possibly be a person, or a dog, or anything that could give away their position.

When no body was found, Titus would know they were still alive. The only good thought was that he may not know where they were heading. He didn't know about the portal. Didn't know about the other world.

A power-crazed man like him could only think like someone hungry for power. He would assume she was returning to Arnath, that she would try to retake her city.

He was right. But not for the reasons he thought. If there was any chance that the trainees were still alive, she had no option. She had to go back and find out. She'd lost Turner, but perhaps Harington had somehow survived.

If she'd been thinking about that more and about trying to keep this girl alive less, she would have realized that they wouldn't kill valuable Orcus, especially young ones who could be molded into following their ideology.

"So. You did come back for the boat. To return it, or to take it even further from home?"

Sen spun to face the voice, Meri squeaking and jumping behind her.

"Bruna. Don't you have anything better to do than sit here and watch this boat?"

Bruna stepped out from behind a tree, smug. "Of course I have better things to do. But the bounty on your head... It definitely gives me a reason to put those things to rest for a bit."

"So now what?" Sen asked.

"Now, we take you in. Collect the bounty. And live like kings."

Men fanned out around them, and a larger fishing vessel floated lazily around a bend in the river. Its speed at the moment meant nothing. She knew that ship. Fastest on the river, by far. There would be no escape by water.

Ha. She'd gotten into odd habits. She no longer had to come up with escape plans. Bruna was in for a rude surprise. She had no idea that Sen had come back into her powers. She touched the flow of magic ebbing around her, just for the security of it. Meri had basically freed her to do as she wished. Which meant this would be incredibly easy.

"Let us go, Bruna. I give you a warning once, for the sake of our times together as children." She didn't mention Halivar. It wouldn't do to bring any attention to him that may call for stronger scrutiny.

"Our time together as children?" Bruna snorted, moving forward, anger in each stiff step. "I despised you, even as a child. You came into our home, took all the attention of my mother and father, and had everything given to you that you wanted. Even now, my father sides with you instead of his own daughter."

Ouch. She knew. She loved Halivar enough that Sen didn't have much fear that any harm would come to him, but hopefully this didn't ruin their relationship, for his sake. As for the other part, it came as no surprise. Of course the girl had hated and resented her. There were no other emotions when it came to her relationships.

"Now be decent and give yourself over. Don't make me hurt that girl with you. I have nothing against her other than the fact that she travels with a murderer."

"Hey!" Meri said. "No reason to be cruel! Sen can't help what she was made to do."

Sen turned and squinted at her. Not only could she now understand Uthorian, but speak it, with no accent? It had to be the magic of their connection.

Meri stared back at Sen, mouth open, dumbfounded. But then she shrugged it off and restarted her glare at Bruna.

Sen almost rolled her eyes. Like Meri could do anything about her anger, even if she wanted to. But then she bit her lip. Of course she could. She wielded the power of an Orcus now. This scrawny girl may be one of the most powerful beings in this world.

Or her own, for that matter.

The men with Bruna laughed at Meri. Bruna motioned them forward, and together they jumped toward the girls.

"May I defend you?" Sen asked, trying not to offend her new master.

"Of course! That's a given. Just do it all the time!" Meri moved directly behind Sen again. Sen lifted her hands, the pulse of fire just below the skin, itching to be released. "Just don't kill anyone."

Instantly the fire died out. "What?"

Meri cocked her head. "Don't kill anyone."

The men were almost up on them. Sen sent out a spray of ice, rooting them all to the ground instantly, then pulled her daggers. They all shouted in surprise, and began to hack at the ice.

"Don't kill anyone? But then they'll just keep coming. And they could tell Titus that we left here in a boat."

While her attention had been on Meri, Bruna had taken the chance to move forward and chop at the ground near her husband's feet. She paused to speak. "It's too late for that. Don't kill us to keep us quiet. I sent a bat to Titus as soon as one of my scouts caught sight of you."

"A bat?" Meri asked.

"That's really your question? What carries messages in your world?"

"Cell phones, mostly, but it used to be birds."

"Birds? Really?"

Bruna had her husband free now, and the other two were close to breaking through the ice. Backing away, Bruna kept her hands in the air.

"Not even going to try to fight?" Sen asked, sheathing her daggers.

"What point would there be in that? We both know I'd stand as much chance as bait in the river." She took another step back. "So what are you going to do, Orcus? Is that your master?"

Sen's jaw clenched, and she shoved down an irrational wave of anger directed at Meri. "You're free to go. But keep your mouths shut."

The extra two men scrambled off without looking back. Bruna stood glaring for a moment, hate radiating off her body. She spat on the ground at Sen's feet, and then wheeled and walked away.

"Hey!" Meri yelled after her. "We didn't have to let you go! Sen could have wiped the floor with you. Or ground. Or whatever."

Sen sighed. "I think I liked it better when you only spoke Swarian."

Meri stuck her tongue out. "Now what?"

"Now we get out of here, and fast. Titus will have the quickest horses headed in our direction. And it will take them far less time to reach this point than it did for us, skulking around in the woods." Sen headed for the boat, untying it from the tree she'd lashed it to earlier.

The fishing vessel had backed off, moving out of range.

"They know we have a boat now. Should we change direction and throw them off? Come back at the temple from a different path?"

"No. He still doesn't know our destination. The shortest path is still the best path."

"Okay." Meri didn't sound very sure. Fine. Sen didn't feel extremely sure either. He would be following them, and she'd have to deal with that at some point. But for now, she just needed to get Meri to the portal. Safety for Meri, and the closest thing she could get to freedom for Sen.

CHAPTER TWELVE

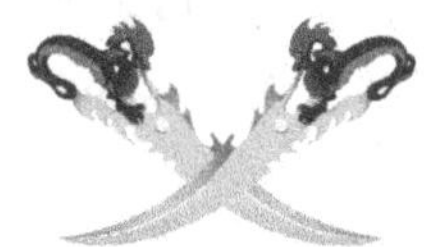

The river really did cut a lot of time off this trip. Of course, their journey to Treyor had taken a convoluted route, going up to Sen's city that she had forgotten the name of right now to find the Crafter and then back down looking for that other woman.

Wait. Had Sen found her? Obviously if she had, it hadn't gone well. She still had the bracelet on. Did she look like she was in a good enough mood that she could be asked? Eh. When was she ever really in a good mood. "Hey, Sen. What happened back in town? Did you not find who you were looking for?"

"I found her."

Well that wasn't very helpful. But she couldn't ask, could she? It seemed like everything she said made Sen blow up now. She couldn't really blame her. What would it be like, to be forced to obey every whim another person had, even when they didn't mean for whatever they said to be obeyed?

Awful. Super awful. So she wouldn't ask. But now she had so many more questions.

If it weren't so cold, and if they weren't running for their lives, this would be a pleasant trip. Well, running for her life anyway. If Sen got captured, it would be worse than just her life. No matter how many times she'd heard the phrase 'there are worse things than death,' she'd never really gotten it until now.

And now, she absolutely did. Too well.

A little whistle went through the air. Meri looked up to see Sen go ramrod straight, completely at attention. "What's that?" Meri asked.

Sen didn't get an answer out. She grabbed Meri and jerked her to the side right before a short javelin of some sort slammed into the wood, burying the tip and leaving the shaft quivering in the air.

"They found us," Sen said, and jumped for the sail.

Until now they'd been moving along at a strong but safe pace. But Sen reefed the sail enough that the wind snapped in the cloth, jerking them forward.

Sailing was something she hadn't done a lot of, but she knew what the creaking of the boat meant, the straining of the wood. "Be careful, you'll make it bust to pieces."

"It's that or be impaled. Your choice."

The whistling sound came again, but this time the javelin fell far short, thudding into the boat just above the waterline.

"They're trying to sink us," Sen said, voice grim. "Here. You're going to have to take control of the sail for a moment." She passed off the rope, and Meri nearly got pulled to the deck when she took it.

Whistles came in tandem this time, as three javelins flew through the half-light of dusk. Sen threw up her hands, and a wave of water knocked them out of the air. She hardly had time to reposition before another two came sailing into sight.

"How many of those things do they have?" Meri asked, fighting with the sail.

Sen didn't answer, just doggedly stared at the shore.

A gust of wind had Meri gritting her teeth and fighting the sail. The wind seemed to be changing direction. Or maybe the river had a slight bend to it, hard to tell. But wrestling with the sail and rudder got more and more difficult. "Sen, I'm not sure how much longer I can keep this up."

A glance apparently told Sen all she needed to know. She turned, and flicked a wrist. An extremely helpful gust of wind hit the sail this time, from the perfect direction.

"Of course you can do that. That's pretty convenient."

The side of Sen's mouth turned up in the first half-smile Meri had seen since the whole new master thing.

It didn't last long, because a dozen or so javelins all came at them at the same time and Sen had to go back to defending the boat. It was nice while it lasted.

A rider showed up along the bank, keeping up easily at a trot.

Sen blasted the sail with wind again, and then pulled a bolt of lightning out of the sky toward the horse and rider.

The horse screamed and fell over, thrashing around on the ground as the crack of thunder that accompanied lightning burst across the earth.

Okay, lightning too? No wonder everyone feared Sen. If she didn't know her so well, she'd be intimidated too. Actually, maybe intimidated did describe how she felt. But not scared. Even though she hadn't known Sen long, she did know who she was as a person.

Several other horses and riders burst from the trees. One horse jumped the fallen rider as they all tore for the next section of forest, going for cover. None stopped to check on the man. The loose horse had run off when she'd been distracted with the sail, but the rider hadn't moved.

More men poured from the trees. Sen blasted at them with lightning, and the ground smoked, Meri's ears ringing so loudly she couldn't hear the water.

She crouched down in the bottom of the boat.

Men littered the ground now. Horses too. Her stomach roiled.

Not looking would be the best plan at the moment, but somehow she couldn't look away. No matter where they went in this world, death and destruction followed them. And Sen seemed immune. How many terrible things had she seen to make her no longer feel them? Or did she feel them, but not let anyone know?

A javelin made it past Sen's latest wave, and thudded into the boat. Meri leaned over the side, and bit her lip in relief. Above the waterline.

"There have to be over a hundred riders," Sen muttered.

A hundred? Against one? Even someone like Sen would have a rough time with those odds.

The bank rose beside them, the river narrowing. It flowed faster than before, pushing the boat along at breakneck speed. Hopefully the horses would struggle to keep up with this.

There, up on the ridge. A rider appeared, his horse dripping lather in the cold, heaving his way up the slope, the ascent growing more and more treacherous.

"We aren't going to have to do anything about them if they're all stupid enough to force their horses to break a leg." The spray of the water and snap of the sails almost hid Sen's voice, and yet Meri could hear her as plain as day.

Some type of magic.

A shiver went through her. Magic was a thing. A real thing. And she was a part of that now, whether she wanted to be or not.

"Why are they risking it?" Meri yelled over the wind, but somehow, she got the feeling she didn't need to. Like somehow, the wind carried her words to Sen instead of whisking them away into nothing.

"We'll find out soon enough."

A wonderful thought. Meri lapsed back into silence, her job of attempting to keep the sail under control not a thing at the moment. While Sen could concentrate on something other than keeping Titus and his men from sinking the boat, Meri had nothing to do.

Except fret.

The river narrowed even more, the cliffs rising on either side as they barreled downstream.

"How much longer will we be on the river?" Meri asked.

"Most of the night. But once we've outrun Titus and his men, the journey will be easier."

Good. She'd never been motion sick before, but borderline needed to puke at the moment. Maybe it was the stress of the day and not the rocking of the boat. She'd definitely traveled at this speed by boat before, but back at home, where boats were made to go this speed.

A thud pulled her from her thoughts. Sen had put down the oar she'd been using to steer, and stared ahead. Meri looked to see what held her interest so strongly.

A stone arch bridged the river. Impossible to tell if it had happened naturally or if it had been built by hand, the thing had to be over sixty feet across to reach both sides.

But no hand rail.

"Is that thing actually used for crossing the river?" Meri asked.

Sen didn't get a chance to answer. Out of nowhere, a boulder slammed into the boat from above, splintering a section of the side. Meri fell, crashing to the deck. She scrambled behind the small mast, frantic.

"Sen? Senara!"

"I'm fine. See what you can do about that."

The damage mostly affected an area above the waterline, but the waves now splashed into the boat. Meri scooted over to examine it, but didn't get far before another boulder tumbled toward the river from the cliff above.

"Sen!"

Sen was already on it, of course. She threw a hand up, and a bolt of lightning blew the rock into pebbles and dirt, sand and debris raining down on them.

Ahead, men rolled a massive stone out onto the bridge, ropes tugging at it from the far side, the ones doing the pulling hidden by the trees.

"Now what?" Meri asked. Her voice didn't shake like she feared it would.

"If I bring down the bridge, it's going to make a dam. There will be too much rubble. The boat won't be able to make it through."

"Okay, let's not do that then."

"Let's?" Sen grumbled. "I wasn't going to actually do it, I'm just thinking out loud."

"So what are our options then?"

"I don't see any option other than going through."

"Going through. Great." Meri moved back over to the mast, sitting down close to it where she could grab it if she needed to. Water lapped at her cloak. The boat was too small. It couldn't take much more damage.

She shivered, the water barely on the fluid side of ice.

Two simultaneous bursts of lightning spurted from Sen's hands.

Five men fell to the water below, one screaming. But instantly five men replaced them.

The body count rose, but it didn't seem to shake the determination of the soldiers. They must have someone they truly feared giving the orders.

They were nearly under the rock, very close to within range. "You have a plan yet?" Meri called, this time her voice a little shaky.

"A plan, yes. A good plan? That remains to be seen."

"I'd take anything at this point."

"Then hold on." Sen closed her eyes for a second, then snapped them back open, face pure determination. She didn't do anything visually, but Meri could practically see the strain on her body.

The water on both sides of the boat began to rise around them, going forward toward the bridge.

One of the men shouted as he saw what was happening, but none of them seemed to understand what Sen was attempting any more than Meri did.

The water moved rapidly here, hurtling closer to the bridge far faster than she would have liked. But the water in front of them rose even faster still.

Waves lapped at the bridge before Meri finished blinking, ignoring the laws of physics and staying in line with the river even though they were far above its banks.

Soldiers scattered, leaving only three brave enough to stay. Brave, or stupid.

The boat rose with the water. Meri gripped the side until her knuckles went white, her face no doubt a matching shade, as she looked over the edge and down at the ground.

Sen's face had gone white too. Not from fear, but with the strain this much magic put on her. They barreled toward the bridge at breakneck speed. Even the three bravest realized at this point that they were powerless against the might of the water, and started to run.

Reaching its peak, a blast of water took out the three remaining men. They were swept away without a trace. The bridge groaned at the weight of the water ramming into it.

On shore, Titus came out of the woods on horseback, shouting to his men left on the other side of the river. But the roar of the water made it so even Meri couldn't make out what he said.

The bridge gave way, tumbling into the water without an extra sound, and sinking to the bottom. Sen began to let the water free, plunging them down to the normal height of the river, like some ride at Disney.

A javelin slammed into the bottom of the boat. Meri jerked back, falling to the deck, but Sen could barely call up a sneer. She looked about ready to collapse.

Meri made her way to the front. "Sit," she ordered Sen.

Sen's glare as she slowly obeyed twisted a knife in Meri's heart.

"I'm sorry, I'm sorry, still learning. Would you please take a seat? You look like you deserve a rest." Intentionally avoiding the word need showed how much she'd learned how to handle Sen in the short time they'd been friends.

The men on the Trulathian side of the chasm the bridge once spanned argued heatedly. But they didn't seem to be getting anywhere. Titus and the men on his side of the river were gone.

At least they'd drifted far enough past that the javelins stopped raining down on them.

"How many made it across the bridge before it went down?" Sen asked. "I was busy and didn't get a count."

"I don't know. I was a little distracted."

Sen snorted. "Don't let your getting distracted get us killed. If it's the soldiers Titus specifically trained to fight Orcus, they took out my whole company. Me by myself? It wouldn't probably turn out well."

"Today turned out pretty well for us."

"But we can't always stay on the river, can we? We're going to have to cut across land at some point, if you want to go home."

"I'm very ready to go home." She leaned back to relax for just a second. With everything that had happened today, she was either going to sleep like an exhausted baby, or have nightmares and not get a wink. Meri bolted upright. "Oh shoot, I hope they didn't get my camera wet!" Meri jerked her bag over and quickly unzipped it, pulling out her camera with shaking hands. If she lost this, she would have no proof of what she'd seen here.

Water had seeped into the bag. The lens dripped.

Meri dropped her head to her knees, letting her hand with the camera fall to her side.

"What's wrong?" Sen asked from the front.

"There's water inside my camera. It will ruin everything if it makes it all the way to the interior, and I have no way of knowing how far the water has seeped in."

Sen moved over and sat on the bench beside her, holding out her hand.

"What are you supposed to do? You don't know anything about Earth tech."

Sen lifted an eyebrow and kept her hand out.

Meri sighed and placed the camera in her hand.

Tipping it, Sen looked the camera over, considering for a moment. Then she held up her free hand, and droplets of water began to flow up from the camera, latching onto her hand until none were left and Sen shook her hand out over the side of the boat, releasing the water.

"Thank you!" Meri snatched the camera back. The temptation to turn it on battered at her, but she resisted. If it had been damaged, it would be better not to turn it on yet.

Without answering, Sen went back to the front of the boat, keeping watch out over the water.

"So. Did you do that because you're my friend, or because you thought you had to?"

"Because you're my handler?" Sen looked down at the water churning under the bow for a long pause. "Because you're my friend. I think. But that's one of the things I hate about this. Now I'll always question my motives. For everything."

Meri stood and made her way to stand by Sen. "I won't."

The side of Sen's mouth tipped up. "At least that will be one of us." She wobbled a bit, and Meri jumped forward to grab her and help her to the deck.

"Are you okay?"

"Yes. Just exhausted."

"I would think so! You just took on, like, a whole army by yourself!

You're epic!" Meri crashed to the deck beside Sen, suddenly very tired herself. "I'm exhausted too, and I didn't even do anything."

"Your first skirmish. The adrenaline rush itself is enough to make you sleep for the rest of the night." Sen leaned back against a bench, not even seeming to notice how damaged it was. "I think I'll sleep now. Wake me when we reach the heated water. That's when we're getting close." And then she passed out.

Meri leaned in close. "Sen? Sen?"

No answer.

"Now what?" Meri asked herself under her breath. "She obviously needs the rest, Meri. You can at least watch the boat while it drifts downstream. What could happen?" She shivered and looked back at the chaos and destruction they'd just somehow survived. They weren't the only ones to make it through. And Titus had made it obvious, he would never give up on owning Senara.

CHAPTER THIRTEEN

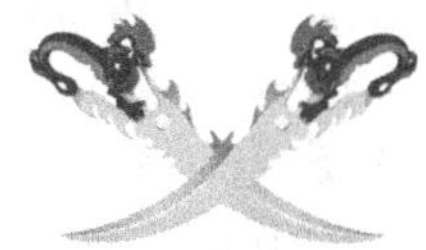

Ugh. Sen blinked several times, but it didn't help much. The stars lit up the sky, but the moons were hiding tonight.

Better that way anyway. Titus would still be looking for them. And he would have the help of every person within a hundred miles. There were very few who would shed a tear if the Orcus were exterminated with her.

But she might not actually be the last. Titus had lied to her before. Somewhere out there, the children were still alive, being trained.

Being forced to fight by handlers who didn't care a whit about their well-being.

Not for long.

Now she had a purpose. A fight that was actually hers.

The healing touch of magic washed through her body, poking and prodding, looking for anything that needed repaired. But, for once, there wasn't anything wrong with her.

At least nothing that a week of sleep couldn't fix.

That would come after. Right now, Harington might be waiting for her. Her second was the closest thing she had to family. He either waited for her, or believed her to be dead, as she had thought him until today. Or yesterday. Things had begun to run together.

"How far have we come?" Sen asked the darkness, her voice rough with sleep.

"You were asleep forever." Meri's groggy voice came from the back of the boat. She must have figured out how to steer, or they would have been stuck on an outcropping by now. Sen almost smiled. The girl had stayed awake. That wouldn't have happened when they'd first met. She might make something of herself yet.

"Have we hit the heated waters yet? Any sign of Titus?"

"I've been sticking my hand in the water once in a while, and it's freezing. I'm not even sure how it's still flowing. And no sign of Titus or his men. Maybe he went back for reinforcements."

Meri didn't say maybe he'd given up. She knew just as well as Senara did that Titus wouldn't be giving up.

It didn't matter. Soon she'd have an army of young Orcus with her. They'd go into the mountains, start their own colony. Somehow.

A slight sizzling sound caught Sen's attention. "Do you hear that?"

"What?"

"When's the last time you tested the water?"

"I don't know. Fifteen, twenty minutes ago?"

Sen looked over the side of the boat. Though they still moved along at a good clip because of the nice breeze, the water over the side almost looked like glass, with little ice, the constellations burning brightly back at her. She peeled off her glove, and held her hand down close to the water.

"Check the water now. But don't quite touch it."

"I'm not going to touch it," Meri grumbled. Apparently she got grumpy when she was tired. A funny thought, a grumpy Meri. But she obeyed, holding her hand down close to the water.

Steam rose, evaporating into the air and leaving behind a sweet smell and light fog.

"It's hot!"

"That's why it's called the heated water." Did all Swarians have the same logic flaw?

Meri muttered something that Sen couldn't make out. "Does that mean we're close?"

"As close as we can get by boat. If we drift too much further the pitch will begin to melt, the boat will fill with water, and we'll be boiled. Not a pleasant way to die, or so I would imagine."

"Does anyone die pleasantly here?" Meri asked. "You know, old and surrounded by family and what not?"

What a strange question. "Maybe a king?" Sen paused. "No, that was foolish of me. Kings don't live long enough to grow old." She paused again, and Meri raised an eyebrow. "No one that I know of."

"Well that's awful. I never thought I'd be glad to get back to regular ol' Florida, but here we are."

A longing in Meri's voice sparked something in Sen's chest. To want to go home. To have a place you ached to return to... It was something she couldn't imagine with any clarity. "What's it like? Living in this, 'Florida?'" The whole time they'd been in Arnath, Sen had been teaching Meri about life here. She'd never really thought to ask her about her normal life.

"There isn't much to tell. I get up in the morning, go eat breakfast, go to class. Study. Sometimes go out with a friend or two, but I don't have many of those. Everyone's too busy with their own stuff, and I don't like most of what they do. Someday I'm going to be an explorer, an archeologist, or something along those lines. I'm going to find something no one else has ever found before, and everyone is going to know who I am."

Half of what Meri said went straight over Sen's head. But she sounded happy.

"This is the discovery of a lifetime, coming here. If I can prove that I visited another world, I'll be more famous than anyone has ever been. Everyone in the world will know my name. And I'll be able to buy my mom anything she could ever want. Who knows what kinds of scholarships I could start!"

Sen sighed. She'd asked for this. She moved to the back and took the oar they used for steering from Meri, while the girl prattled on and on. If Sen waited until Meri finished speaking, they'd be at the bottom of the very large river.

The oar in place, she gave the sail a little shot of wind, directing them toward the bank of the river. Nearly inaudible at first, the water began to hiss. Here was the point they truly needed to leave the river. Where the lukewarm and hot met, causing the air to fog.

But then she did see something. A horse and rider, on shore, waiting for them. "Meri, hush."

Meri stopped speaking instantly. At least that much she'd picked up on.

One horse and one rider were no threat to them. Even as exhausted as Sen was.

But it wasn't one horse and rider. The mist peeled away as they got closer to the shore. Horses spanned the length of the river. The huge grey Titus rode squealed and kicked at the horse beside it, as bad-tempered as its master.

The riverbank on the opposite side looked normal, but she knew from previous experience, it wasn't. A stinking bog filled with sand that dropped straight into boiling pools of water. No one made it through there alive, not even an Orcus.

Especially not an Orcus with a somewhat inept Swarian following behind her.

Ouch. That thought almost hurt. When had she added the 'somewhat' onto the inept?

Though, in the bog she would lose her. She knew she would. And then, she wouldn't have a handler again...

That thought turned her stomach. Had she really become so callous that she would lead the only person in the entire world she could call friend to her death? When she hadn't even forced her to do the simplest of things, other than by accident?

No. She hadn't fallen that far. And she wouldn't ever let herself.

"Don't you think?" Meri's voice snapped her back to the present. It wasn't often Sen got caught off guard.

"What?"

Meri looked at her oddly. "Weren't you listening? Whatever. I was saying that we can probably go a bit farther in the boat before we have any problems, right?" She nodded toward Titus. "Better than having to see that man again."

Her whisper barely carried over the boat to Sen. She'd blame it for the reason she hadn't heard her earlier. "A bit farther."

They slid along the surface of the water, it hissing and gurgling beneath the wood under their feet.

Titus followed along the bank, his giant horse swirling in and out of the fog, his men only seen occasionally.

"Can you blast them with something? Or freeze them in place? Or call a tornado down on them? If you can help it, don't hurt his men. They're only here because he's making them." Meri's voice hadn't gotten any louder, but it was definitely more shrill.

"I don't have the power to do much at the moment. Today has been a bit exhausting."

Meri's face went from fear to pinched concern. "Are you okay?"

"Yes. Just very tired." A lightning bolt would take out several of the enemy, if she could get it created and aimed correctly at this distance. A difficult task even rested and well-fed at the training yard.

"What are we going to do, Sen?" Meri's voice held a note of defeat.

The girl couldn't do anything to help at the moment. She had her talents, but this wasn't one of them. She probably felt pretty useless right now.

That made two of them.

Sen dropped down to the deck, trying to get a second of rest, but jerked right back up to her feet. The wood nearly seared her skin, even through her thick layers. She leaned over the side of the boat.

Black pitch oozed down the side, dissolving when it hit the water. Sen moved to the back of the boat and stuck the oar in the water, moving the course of the ship just a bit to where a current of cooler water ran, then went back to the side.

Meri leaned over beside her to see what she was looking at and sucked in a breath. "We're going to die, aren't we. Or at least, I am."

Her voice wasn't frantic. Her tone steady. Like it was just a fact. Sen had sacrificed her friend to have a few extra hours of 'freedom,' and Meri wasn't even angry at her.

"Just say it," Sen growled.

Meri stepped back, looking confused. "Say what?"

"That this is all my fault. That I should never have made you my handler. That I should have let Titus bind me to him, and none of this would be happening."

"Look here." Now Meri's voice went sharp. She glared at Sen as she got in her face. "I can't say things I'm not thinking. You're apparently the one thinking that, and you had better stop. Because if I had known what was going on in that throne room, I'd have told you to go for it. And if I'd have known where we would end up tonight..." She paused. "Okay, I would have told you we needed to try something else, but I still would have chosen to help you. I'm not letting that man take away your freedom. I'm not letting anyone take away your freedom. It's yours. Your God-given right."

Tears stung Sen's eyes. Good that the sun wasn't up. Meri didn't need to see that. "Meri."

"Don't argue with me. Ugh!" She threw her hands in the air. "Argue with me if you want. That wasn't an order. I just don't want you to argue with me. Wait, does that count? Can you argue with me if I don't want you to, but I say you can?"

"Meri, hush, I have an idea."

Meri's mouth clamped instantly shut.

"If we can survive another twenty or so minutes, we can give it a try."

Cocking her head, Meri squinted at Sen, appraising her. "How good a chance does this plan have of working?"

"We'll find out in a few minutes."

There wasn't much to say after that. Meri anxiously watching the water, while Sen kept an eye on Titus. His men were silent, the only sounds coming across the water were of the horses snorting and the clink of armor.

The wait seemed to last forever. The girls shifted from foot to foot, giving each a moment of relief before the heat made it through the soles of their boots.

At last they reached the stretch of water that began to boil.

"Now?" Meri whispered.

"Now."

Sen took a deep breath and walked to the front of the ship. She closed her eyes, mustering what little magic she could at the moment. She swirled her hands, and the water obeyed, mixing the nearly boiling water and the cooler water of the flowing current.

Hissing and popping, fog thick enough that Sen couldn't see to the back of the boat shot up around them, rolling away from the ship in all directions.

"This was your plan?" Meri asked. "It's great they can't see us and all, but how is this going to help?"

"Shh." Sen kept at it for a full minute, until not only the blackness of a moonless night helped hide them, but also a fog so thick she couldn't see anything in front of her. A hand grabbed her arm out of the mist and she nearly punched Meri in the face before figuring out who it was. "Don't startle me! That's dangerous to your health!"

Meri started to laugh, and Sen stared her down like she had lost her mind.

"What's so funny? Quiet down! Fog makes sound travel in odd ways."

Meri quieted instantly. "You just sounded so normal. Like you could be anyone at my school. Like we aren't floating down a boiling river with our boat melting, tracked by men on horse-things trying to turn you into a fighting machine. It just felt normal. For one second. Sorry."

Sen sighed. It would be good when Meri went back to her normal life. Their worlds were so different. And their lives hardly fit into the same category.

"What's the next part of your plan?" Meri asked.

Without a verbal answer, Sen used the oar to turn the boat around, prow into the current. It still floated lazily downstream.

This had better work. Meri watched her, waiting for some kind of miracle. She didn't have one of those. But hopefully, she did have something that would work.

And hopefully she had enough left in her to see it done.

Lifting her hands, Sen closed her eyes and took in a deep breath. In through the nose, out through the mouth. In through the nose, out from the palms of her hands.

The sail fluttered, but didn't fill. Her body ached with exhaustion. She hurt, all the way down through her bones.

But this... life or death. Not for her, but for Meri. And so she'd do this even through the pain, for Meri.

She took another deep breath. This time the sail filled, and they shot forward. They made it about ten feet before the wind died down, and they floated a few feet downstream. She repeated her breath, flinging the ship forward against the current again.

Their gains were further than their losses, but not by much. It would be a long night.

Meri squeezed her arm. "We don't have to get super far before we're off their radar. You got this."

And she did.

CHAPTER FOURTEEN

How Sen kept it up for over an hour, Meri would never understand. Meri was usually ready to give up even in the kayak after about fifteen minutes of straight paddling. Even then, she usually stopped to snap a picture here or there. Someday one of those pictures would end up on the cover National Geographic.

If she didn't die in some other world no one knew about first.

Maybe it would be pictures from here, an entire issue devoted to "The Other World." Nah. That name was too lame.

Pulling herself from her intentionally distracting thoughts, Meri side-eyed Sen. She looked past the point of exhausted, on the verge of collapse.

That made two of them, and Meri hadn't even done anything but some steering. Maybe she wasn't made for the adventuring life. Maybe she would just sell her pictures, become a celebrity, and then help people and the environment after she lived through all this.

Ha. Lived through this. At every turn they had something else trying to kill them. Even the water had tried to kill them today.

But somehow Sen always seemed to know what to do.

Growing up in a world that wanted you dead must do that to a person.

Her grandpa had always said the world these days made kids too soft. When the worst thing you had to worry about was if you could afford the latest model phone, he thought there was a problem.

Now she could definitively say she disagreed. Would she come out of this a stronger person, far more grateful for what she had? Absolutely. If she came out of it in one piece, at least.

Sen shifted and the sail slipped into a slightly different position. Finally. They were headed for shore. Meri moved the oar she used as a rudder to help Sen, whose blasts of wind had been getting less and less effective. What was her breaking point?

Hopefully they didn't find out.

The bottom of the boat scraped on the rocks under the water. Meri cringed, gaze darting around the fog. The fog hid them well, but it also hid Titus and his men. No sounds. And a group that large wouldn't be able to stay completely silent.

Stepping over the side, Sen slowly lowered herself into the water, motioning for Meri to follow.

Great. Now they were going to be wet on top of exhausted and miserable.

But no other option stood out. Meri followed Sen's example and dangled over the side until she could drop in without a splash. The water covered her to her hips, lukewarm and slightly bubbling.

Wow. This actually felt great. And it was about time her clothes got some washing. They were disgusting at this point.

Sen waded for shore, then took off, not waiting to see if Meri followed. Of course she did. She wasn't an idiot. Sticking to Sen like glue had been the only thing that had kept her alive this entire trip.

And now, leaving the water did not feel so great. Her jeans began to freeze to her legs, getting more and more stiff the longer she was in the frigid air. Her cloak stayed warm though, the moisture fizzling out.

She was so taking this cloak home with her, even though she lived in Florida and would never need it. It would be irrefutable proof that magic existed, at least in another world. Did they have magic back on Earth? With Sen now able to do magic again, it would be interesting to find out.

Stay in the moment, Meri. Getting distracted right now could mean death. But her limbs barely obeyed her at this point, and her mind floated somewhere in the fog, hardly able to concentrate long enough to come up with a clear thought.

All of the things she'd been through in the last week crashed down on her hard. Physically. Active at home was completely relative to active here.

It hadn't sounded like the portal would be far from the river. But Sen had said that before they'd had to backtrack up the river to lose Titus. How far they were now would just be a guess, unless Sen knew, and Meri wasn't stupid enough to take the risk of making any extra noise.

Something trumpeted out in the dark. Sen slid to a stop, quivering as she listened. "Faster. They've found us."

"Found us?" The words weren't out of her mouth before Sen took off. Meri bit her lip to keep the fear from causing her to freeze, and followed. "What are they?"

Sen didn't answer. They reached the end of the fog, bursting out into starlight. Without giving Meri a chance to catch her bearings, Sen plowed forward, heedless of the brush ahead of them.

A creature, almost like a bear, burst from the fog. They stumbled to a stop, taking it in for a second. Much smaller than an Earth bear, and blockier. It lifted its muzzle in the air and sniffed.

"Run," Sen said. She took off, and Meri stumbled after her, staying as close to her heels as possible.

A quick glance over her shoulder showed the bear easily gaining. It threw its head up again, and bugled a call.

The call echoed up and down the fog. How many of those things were there?

Meri tripped on something, stumbling to the uneven ground. She vaguely registered stone slabs before Sen dragged her to her feet. "Can't we hide? Climb a tree? Anything but run."

"No. Their sense of smell is far stronger than any hound's. They'll find us. The temple is the only answer. We're almost there."

Sen took off, not letting go of Meri's cloak.

A building started to take shape in the dark. As they got closer and Meri took a second to look ahead instead of at their deaths chasing them, the fact that this building had been long abandoned became obvious.

The temple! Which meant the portal. They had a chance of making it.

A beast slid across the stone walkway ahead of them, scrambling for footing on the rock. Its claws scraped as it found something to gain some traction on, then stood, roaring in Sen's face.

Sen nearly crumpled. She wouldn't make it much farther. The bracelet passed information on Sen's condition to Meri so quickly she couldn't interpret it, other than the fact that Sen was on the verge of collapse.

Meri slid around Sen, between her and the tracking bear. She held up a hand. "No!"

The bear leaned forward and roared into her face, saliva splattering across her cloak.

"I said no! Get back!"

Sen looked at her like she was crazy and raised her hands, but nothing seemed to happen. She'd done far too much in the last few hours. Meri could feel unconsciousness lapping at the edges of Sen's being.

"Get out of here. You're not welcome." Her voice stayed strong.

The bear dropped onto four feet and grumbled, but then stalked off.

"What just happened?" Meri asked Sen. "I've always heard people should stand up to bears, but I didn't know it would work that well."

"I don't care at the moment. Let's just get inside. The magic of the temple will help protect us."

Meri shivered. Hopefully it still recognized Sen. Otherwise they'd be on the ground beside the man she'd gotten the cloak off of, what seemed like eons ago.

They burst through a missing section of temple wall, and instantly the air warmed. Which still didn't make any sense since this place was as far from airtight as a block of Swiss cheese sitting on a picnic table.

"Which wall?" Meri asked. The sudden need to be home hit her.

The longing for sunshine, for warm air, for the safety and security that being at home came with. Had Sandra called anyone? Were campus police looking for her? Her mom. Probably frantic.

Sen didn't answer out loud. She just headed farther into the temple.

There. The wall with the destroyed mural. The opening to the staircase was around here somewhere.

Outside something snarled. The pounding of hooves broke the stillness of the quiet winter night.

"They're here," Meri whispered.

Sen led the way farther into the dark. She bent down and grabbed something, but then kept moving forward. Meri reached forward and almost grabbed Sen's arm so she didn't lose her before remembering why that would be a bad idea.

Pulling out her phone, Meri almost turned it on to use the last of her battery to light up a pathway, but then thought better of it. Light would attract attention, and they were doing fairly well picking their way through the rubble without it.

"Senara." The voice drifted over the snow outside, the temple bending and bringing it across the distance like Titus stood right beside them.

Meri shivered. Those stupid bears, not hibernating and tracking them down. She'd have liked to see a bear in person until today. Now they could all stay underground forever for all she cared.

"Senara. Do you really wish to see your friend die? Because that's the path you're on right now."

"Can he transfer the binding from me to him?" Meri asked, keeping her voice as quiet as humanly possible.

"No. The only way ownership can be given to someone else is if the handler dies. Trust me, I've seen it."

Titus laughed somewhere out in the starlight. "You're right, of course. And I've seen it too. Perfectly good soldiers killed so that a new handler can be appointed. You learn a lot when you join the Uthorian army."

Ouch. The voice thing must work both ways. Bad temple. Bad.

"And now we're about to see just how much this old temple has left in it." His voice changed from the sing-song inflection to a comman-der's tone. "Send in the first wave."

Sen kept them moving forward, running a hand along the wall as she followed the etchings towards the door. Towards the portal. Towards safety.

Hopefully. Hopefully these men wouldn't be able to follow them through. But even if they did, they wouldn't last long against even the smallest Earth force. Not without any type of firearm.

And wouldn't that prove everything she had to say after it happened to be true.

Lightning zapped all around her. Blinded, she fell to the floor, screams making her clamp her hands over her ears.

The soldiers with the holes through them, when she'd first gotten here. That's what had happened to them. She opened her eyes, sniffing back tears as someone called for help.

Apparently they didn't all die instantaneously.

The flash had been too bright, her eyes too adjusted to the dark. She couldn't see a thing. This rivaled the time she'd looked into the sun as a kid, just because her mom had told her she couldn't.

"Sen?" Sen!"

"Here. Can you see?"

"No, not a thing." A thread of hysteria had worked its way into what was supposed to come across as a statement. To get this close to home, and die right at its door...

"Follow my voice. We can still find the door."

Obeying, Meri moved forward slowly in the direction Sen's voice had come from. She found her rough cloak and grabbed onto it, tight. Nothing happened. Apparently she could touch Sen's cloak without a problem.

The sounds from outside had died down.

"The temple is old. Eventually it will not be able to stand against us." His voice. Titus. She would hear his voice in her dreams for a long time, if she survived this. She knew she would. "Second wave. Forward."

Meri clenched her eyes closed this time, and even with them as sealed as possible, the flash of light that came through had her gripping her head. Realizing she'd lost her hold on Sen's cloak, she frantically reached for it, hand waving in the air until she found it.

A horse screamed somewhere outside the temple, wailing in pain.

"Are they sending animals in?" Meri asked. "Would the temple allow animals through?"

"I don't know." Sen's voice came across reserved, even more than normal. "I wouldn't think the temple would have any problem with animals coming through. If it can tell the difference."

As if in answer, a snuffle sounded to their right.

Meri froze.

It snuffled again.

"What's that?" Meri whispered to Sen.

"I can't see either, but I'd say it's one of the tracking bears."

Oh great.

"But hopefully it's as blind as we are."

Hopefully. Sen was trying to be encouraging. At any other point, Meri would have thought that a huge step in the right direction. But right now as they were about to die, encouraging didn't seem very helpful.

Sen stepped forward, and as soon as Meri felt the tug on her cloak, she followed. She shuffled her feet, trying not to trip, breath racing and heart pounding enough that she wouldn't be able to hear the bear about to attack even if it already stood straight in front of them.

An eternity went by as they stumbled forward.

"Wave three," Titus shouted somewhere outside. The temple didn't even need to bring his voice to them this time.

Meri dropped her hold on Sen's cloak to throw her own up over her face. It blocked some of the light, but she still blinked repeatedly, trying to get rid of the flashes going on behind her eyelids.

When she opened her eyes, she could at least tell she was in the dark. A small amount of progress.

It was only a few more steps forward before a loud click burst through the air. Meri froze. "Something else trying to kill us?"

"No." Sen sounded happy. Strange, considering they were about to die. "That was the secret entrance to the portal. We made it."

Tamping down the burst of joy and excitement proved difficult, but absolutely necessary. Getting killed right at the doorway because they'd become too comfortable would not happen. She wouldn't let it.

Maybe they'd die anyway, but not because of complacency.

The bear sniffed somewhere far too close. Much closer than the last noise it had made. "Ah, Sen?"

"You're the one that stopped it last time," Sen grumbled. "Do whatever you did then." She tugged Meri forward, headed for the hole in the wall. Hopefully she could see better than Meri could.

"I don't know what I did! I probably didn't do anything. It was just a coincidence."

"Sure. Let's go with that."

"Fourth wave!" Titus no longer sounded relaxed. Anger leaked through his voice.

Both girls covered their faces, but the flash wasn't nearly as strong as the last time.

Sen looked around. Ha! Meri could see her looking around. An improvement. "The temple is fading," Sen said.

The bear cried behind them, digging at its eyes. Poor thing. But wait. A terrible thought struck. "What does the temple losing its power mean for the portal?"

Sen's face was grim. "No way of knowing. But I don't think anything good."

"My brother gave me away." His voice snaked through the temple, smooth and in control again. "There are other Orcus who live. I wanted one fully trained and ready to go into combat. But if that isn't an option, I'll find another."

"Harington," Sen whispered. She had a far-off look of horror in her eyes.

"Harington?" Meri asked.

"Let's get down to the portal first," Sen said. She took off towards a section of wall that had moved. Behind them the bear bellowed, sniffing the air. It still didn't seem to be able to see, but must have gotten a good whiff of them.

It charged forward.

Sen grabbed Meri's cloak and pulled her down the stairs. She would have fallen all the way to the bottom if Sen hadn't kept a tight grip on her. The magic of the cloaks somehow seemed to act as a barrier to the spell that didn't allow Orcus and handlers to touch.

They were there. They'd made it. Against all odds, somehow, they had lived. A short flight of stairs, a trip through the portal, and then safety.

Never again would she complain about her life being boring. Hanging out in the swamp looking for signs of a panther sounded pretty good about now. Canoeing in the sun. Real food, how could she have forgotten that one?

The door ground shut behind them, and all sounds from above instantly stopped. As if here was, in itself, a whole other world, between Arnath and Earth.

"Let's get out of here." Meri started down the stairs, carefully feeling each step. Somehow the dark here comforted her, rather than making her nervous.

Almost home. That was the only real feeling that got through.

Sen stopped, which in turn made Meri jerk to a stop.

A small flame winked into existence in Sen's hand. She had an odd look on her face. One Meri couldn't decipher.

"I can't go with you."

"What?" She had to have heard that wrong. Anything else would be crazy. No way Sen wanted to stay here, not with half an army waiting outside to drag her away.

"I have to stay."

"See, I keep hearing variations of you saying you're staying here, but with no explanation, I'm just not believing that I'm hearing you right, so how about you use your words."

Sen did that little half smile thing, but it didn't last. "If Titus doesn't get me, he's going to go after the initiates."

"While that's horrible, what are you going to do about it? It's not like you can turn yourself over to him."

"No. But without your life to worry about, I can cause a very large amount of destruction." Sen leaned down into Meri's face from the stair above. "I know what that life is like. And I won't leave children in it."

Meri grunted and crossed her arms in front of her chest. "You know that I think helping people is amazing, but I can't just leave you here to fight alone, not with all these soldiers and Titus just outside. Come through the portal, wait a couple days until they're gone, and then we'll come back. We can go save the kids, take them to Earth, everything will be hunky-dory."

The stairs they stood on rattled, small stones raining down from above. Both girls froze, looking at the ceiling.

"A catapult. Has to be," Sen said. "And that's the reason I can't go with you. What if when Titus is done destroying the temple, the portal no longer works? The kids, Harington, would be left to fight others wars. Nothing here would change."

This was stupid. And terrible. Terrible and stupid. "That doesn't work for me. You're the best friend I've ever had. A sister. I can't leave you here, never knowing what happened to you."

"Will you force me to come there?"

"What? Of course not. It's just the safest place for you. Don't you want to come and live a normal life? One where no one is trying to kill or control you?"

"I'd like nothing more. But the young ones need me. And I can't turn my back on them."

"I'm coming with you."

"No. That's too great of a risk, to both of us. You need to go home, where no one can find you, no one can harm you. I'll be able to live life here like I'm free, even if I'm not. Titus is after you just as much as he's after me. He needs you dead. Here." Meri barely got her hands up in time to catch two spiked bracelets, just like the one Sen wore. "Your proof. What you need, to get all of the things you want back in your world. It's better than taking some dirt."

"Will we never see each other again?"

"Never." Sen's voice was odd. "Now go, quickly. I'm not sure how long it will be before they breach the temple's defenses."

Meri shifted her weight from one foot to the other. "How am I supposed to leave here, not knowing what will happen to you? Those men, they're out there, waiting."

"You'll leave knowing there was nothing you could do to help, and that I'll now be able to fight back without distraction."

"I'm not going, I can't. Never knowing if you died today or not?"

"Is something you're going to have to live with. Goodbye. And thank you. It's been nice to have a friend." Then Sen shoved her down the stairs, sparks flying everywhere, and the portal activated before she could answer.

EPILOGUE

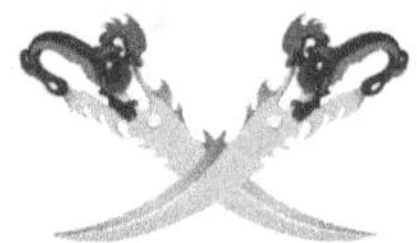

The swamp chilled Meri to her bones that morning. Ever since freezing in Arnath, everything here felt more cold than it had before. The trek to the portal had become second nature enough that she didn't even watch the path she'd started to wear in the brush.

Three weeks. It had been three weeks since she'd gotten home, and she still couldn't rest, couldn't think.

Definitely couldn't jump back into real life.

Sandra was the only one who believed her about where she'd been while she was missing. The only person she could convince was someone who'd seen it for themselves.

A cop had dropped by and returned her things to her this morning. All of her proof, discounted by them. Surprisingly the school was letting her stay after her 'psychotic break,' and hadn't made her return with her mom, who had just left the night before.

The poor school administration, dealing with her mom for the week she had been missing.

At least Professor Gredt had finally agreed to take a look at the soil, metal, and plant samples she'd brought back, now that they'd been returned. Maybe something would be different enough to snag his attention.

She hadn't shown him the bracelets. Let him look at the other stuff first. The bracelets... they had ended up somewhere else.

Dropping a blanket down near the portal entrance, she threw her backpack on top and made her way over to the element-proof storage container she'd lugged out here and chained to a tree. Still intact, still locked.

It held her cloak, and a plethora of things she would need if she ever went back. Not if. When. Sen was fine. She'd left with the temple surrounded and under attack, but Sen could get herself out of any situation. She'd proven that over and over.

Meri had to believe it had happened again.

Satisfied that her container hadn't been tampered with, she went back over and dropped down on the blanket, pulling out her lunch. She flicked on the hotspot on her fully charged phone, and booted up her tablet.

Another message from rosiegurl12. Strike the thought that Sandra was the only one she'd been able to convince. Somewhere in the world, rosiegurl believed her too. They'd met on a strange sightings messaging board shortly after Meri had gotten back, and had hit it off really well. Super weird things were going on wherever Rosie was from, and she was looking for answers, just like Meri.

A light hum in the air made Meri look up and drop her sandwich.

That was new.

In all of the times she'd come out here to check and see if Sen had come back, to wait for her, have a meal here, this had never happened.

The light hum turned into a buzzing. Meri scrambled to her feet, brushing off crumbs. Light flickered ahead of her.

Definitely the portal. Question was, who was coming through? She should hide. Should move behind a tree. But her feet were rooted in place.

A light flashed and she threw up her arm to cover her eyes for just a second, before lowering it to see Sen standing in front of her, all decked out in heavy winter clothing.

Sen smiled. "Hey Meri. I need you."

. . .

The End

Growing up, it was impossible to catch Cassie Greutman without a book in her hand, even at the most inappropriate times. Since then with the rise of ebooks, it's only gotten worse. With her full-time job of caring for over thirty horses, some of that has changed to audiobooks, but you can bet there is always some type of story rattling around in her brain. She has always loved stories in any format, whether that is a movie, video game, or book form, and hopes to tell stories that catch a person's imagination and interest like so many have done for her.

A finalist in the Cinematic Book Competition with Screencraft out of over 1200 entries, and five star ratings with Reader's Favorite, and a win with The Indie Author Project, Cassie has been throwing all of the extra time she has into building worlds for everyone to enjoy. When she isn't stuck in a book, of course.

Follow me on Facebook and TikTok for updates on new stories!

https://www.facebook.com/cassiegreutman/

https://www.tiktok.com/@cassiegreutman

Or join my newsletter for free short stories:

https://dl.bookfunnel.com/pq98nn1jof

If you'd like early access to stories as I write them and behind the scenes posts, check out. https://reamstories.com/page/lh4u19l5l3

www.ingramcontent.com/pod-product-compliance
Lightning Source LLC
Chambersburg PA
CBHW070507300726
48975CB00007B/2356